DOUGH YOU LOVE ME?

A DONNER BAKERY NOVEL

STACY TRAVIS

WWW.SMARTYPANTSROMANCE.COM

COPYRIGHT

DEDICATION

In memory of Jay, inspiration for all my cinnamon roll heroes.

CHAPTER 1

JULIA

*I*f moods came in the form of desserts, mine was an overcooked pineapple upside down cake with whipped cream on the side. It looked pleasant enough on the outside but hid a dry, unappealing middle. The topping was an afterthought, and it couldn't possibly salvage the mess of inedible cake.

It was the only fitting mood for a last-minute trip to my hometown, which guaranteed a certain amount of family drama, confusing emotions, and enough bluegrass music to soothe a troubled soul.

From my window seat on a Boeing 747 which had yet to take off, I planned to watch the sun dip beneath the California horizon where the blue Pacific kissed a fading daytime sky. By midnight, I'd land in Tennessee and drive the highways and winding roads to our family home in Green Valley.

It had been four years since I visited. Four long years. I knew this because it had been four years since I'd gone anywhere that didn't involve work. No vacations, not even a day at the beach, even though I could see it through the plate glass windows of my condo. I'd barely had time to go to the bathroom, let alone see my relatives.

And now, I was going on the kind of trip no one wants to take—destination cemetery.

"Are you sure you have to go? This isn't a good time for the company, love." Trevor Hobart's British voice filtered through my cellphone while other passengers filed past me toward their seats. I could picture the strong set of Trevor's jaw, the unreal blue of his eyes, his hair mussed just *so* as he sat at his glass-topped desk and reprimanded me on speakerphone.

His good looks and sexy voice made other people jump to do his bidding, but I was immune to his charms. Especially because I'd already fallen for his charms years ago and spent a few tepid weeks dating him. We had no messy pillow-strewn passion. No burning love between us. We had a kindly simmer, too cool to kill bacteria. Then it was over. There wasn't even any drama when we went back to being business partners.

There was far more drama at moments like this when Trevor tried to use his charm to get me to do what he wanted for the business.

"Of course I have to go. It's a funeral," I fetched my small brown leather weekender from the overhead bin and took out a paperback. I should have used the plane ride to look at spreadsheets, but the regency romance novel sounded so much more appealing. I was burned out on spreadsheets.

"It just isn't a good time for the company," Trevor insisted. I could picture him sweeping a lock of hair back from his forehead and scowling out the window at the Baldwin Hills Scenic Overlook near our headquarters.

"It's never a good time. According to you," I protested, sweeping my own unruly blondish hair into a knot on top of my head and wiping off the bright lipstick I'd worn all day. Poorly-behaved tendrils of hair freed themselves and fell into my eyes.

"My work ethic didn't bother you in the past." Trevor sounded impatient. He was probably drumming his fingers on the desk, twitchy like a sugared-up hummingbird.

"In the past, I never had to go to a funeral for my favorite family member."

"Favorite? I don't recall you mentioning her."

Why is he arguing about this?

"Well, let me mention her now. Gram was simply the best human. She would've been seventy-five in August. Spunky. Healthy. She raised me and my brother after my parents left." My voice cracked on the last word. I cleared my throat.

"Your parents left?" He sounded more annoyed than sympathetic.

Oops. I hadn't ever mentioned my upbringing to him. I hadn't mentioned it to anyone in California after moving here at age eighteen, when I won a scholarship to study culinary science at a college in the Central Valley. My Gram had shared her love for baking with me, and she was the first to celebrate from afar when I took a job with a successful bread maker in Los Angeles and eventually opened my own shop.

2

My bakery, The Bread Winner—which had turned into a restaurant, which had turned into six restaurants, which had turned into loaves in half the grocery stores on the West Coast—had fully occupied most of my waking hours for the past half decade.

I never stopped thinking about bread, how to sell it, how to manufacture more of it, how to distribute it faster. Apparently, I was good at my job, so my tasks multiplied and I scrambled to do them all.

The business had grown so large that I rarely touched a sourdough starter with my bare hands anymore. I rarely got a chance to bake, and I mostly spent my days running a business with thousands of employees and dealing with men like Trevor who cared more about the bottom line than meeting the farmers who grew our wheat. So I met the farmers alone.

Trevor dangled the threat of a "board action" whenever I rhapsodized about taking the business back to its more humble roots—to hell with the bottom line—and reminded me that investors expected profits, not relationships with wheat. So I kept quiet and the business continued to grow.

I never stopped to think about whether it was normal or healthy to be consumed by work because I was busy doing all the things. Even as the business grew, I had a small-business mentality, doing as many tasks as humanly possible before looking to others to help out.

Now, I was forced to step away. Someone else would do the things. The thought of my capable staff stepping in both thrilled and terrified me.

"You know what? Never mind. The point is, I'm going to Green Valley for a…while."

"What's "a…while?" His mocking tone irritated me.

"As long as it takes. I have family matters to attend to. This wasn't something expected where the details have been put in place. It's all out of the blue. She's just . . . she's gone," Tears pricked the corners of my eyes as my own words sunk in. How could she be gone? She was so full of life. The melting butter to my fresh sourdough bread.

I already felt guilty for having gone so long without visiting her. I had to be there now for as long as it took to see to her wishes. Those included having me sell the family home.

"Why is the funeral on a Friday? Isn't that unusual?" Trevor's common-sense question pulled me from the spin cycle in my brain.

"Because Gram wants everyone to go to the jam session afterward. It was in her will." I didn't bother to consider whether my words made sense to anyone who didn't know Gram.

Her good friend Daisy Payton was the keeper of her last will and testament, which she'd written on the backs of three pink recipe cards and handed over in a reused envelope. Gram was allergic to anything too official, so the recipe cards counted as her final word.

I felt suddenly nostalgic for the house with its wraparound porch where we'd drink tea while the day turned to night. I couldn't wait to get there.

"What the dickens is a jam session?" I'd almost forgotten Trevor was still on the line.

"It's a Green Valley thing. People play bluegrass on Friday nights." I didn't have time to explain. The flight attendants were starting to walk through the cabin and I needed to wrap up this call. "I'll fill you in when I get back. Thanks for holding down the fort while I'm gone, Trevor. I'll see you soon."

I had no idea if I'd see him soon because I had no idea how long it would take to sell a house. I'd ask Cletus when I got there. If anyone would know, it was probably him.

Cletus Winston was the one person I'd kept in touch with since leaving Green Valley, where he made it his business to quietly observe things most people would gloss over. It made him reliable and a little bit sneaky.

He and I had bonded in high school when we both ditched English class on the day we were supposed to be discussing *Hamlet*. I ditched because I hadn't read it; he skipped class because he'd already read it three times and didn't see a need for discussion.

We spent the afternoon playing chess, which we both had a knack for, and he worked to convince me that *Hamlet* held the answers to life's bigger questions until I agreed to read it.

It seemed fitting that he was the one to call and tell me about Gram. "I'm sorry, Jules," was all he said. He'd lost his mother not many years earlier and his silent understanding embraced me through the phone line.

It would be good to see him. And even though it would be strange to be in Green Valley without Gram, the idea of going felt comforting.

With that thought, I closed my book, shut my eyes, and blocked out the world.

* * *

I woke up to a mood of sticky toffee, but the funeral turned out to be beautiful. I know people don't normally find funerals uplifting, but those were people who hadn't met Gram. Or her devoted friends.

The service was held in a parklike cemetery with the kind of bright green grass I rarely saw in drought-stricken Southern California. Gram's chosen plot sat atop a knoll in the sprawling cemetery, and the graveside service drew what looked like half of Green Valley's residents. I sat in the shade of a dogwood tree, watched my Gram's friends embrace my brother, and tried to put names to faces of old acquaintances.

"You're a sight for sore eyes." Wiping away the remains of tears, Daisy Payton hugged me tight. "That was a beautiful eulogy you gave."

"Thank you. I-I can't believe she's not here. She's who I associate with this place, and without her, I just . . . I feel a little lost." My words tumbled forth before I could edit them. I'd never been to a funeral before, and even though Gram wouldn't have judged me for my words, I couldn't help but feel they were inadequate for the situation. For her.

"This *place*? It's still your home," Daisy said, tilting her head to study me.

"Yes, oh, of course it is. I didn't mean—"

Daisy waved a hand. "I know. None of us is in our right mind at a funeral." She hugged me again and tipped her head toward the small crowd of Gram's friends who waited to pay their respects. "I shouldn't monopolize you."

I noticed all of them wore various shades of blue. Together they looked like a placid sea of comfort, so I embraced them one by one, absorbing everything they had to tell me about Gram and how much they loved her. Knowing she had such good friends made me feel slightly less guilty for not having been around much over the past few years.

"She was so proud of you," Gram's bridge partner Sybil said, her cherubic face upturned, dark hair swept into a tidy ponytail. She tugged at the sleeves of a marine blue sweater she wore over a long skirt of similar color. "Always talked about how you were building an empire out in California."

"Only from the baking skills she taught me." I loved that I'd made Gram proud.

"Too bad it kept you away, though. You were missed."

"I came as much as I was able." My words were rushed. They were also a lie. Now that I was here, I couldn't remember why I'd felt so wrapped up in work that I couldn't visit.

Sybil nodded. "Well, only you'd know about that."

Gram never made me feel neglectful. Granted, over the past year or so, we didn't talk as much as we used to. But she had a busy life too. If she'd wanted me to visit more, she'd have said.

And now there would be no more chances. If someone had told me the last time I left Green Valley that I'd never see Gram again, I'd have . . . well, hindsight.

Sybil patted my shoulder and moved off to join a group of women holding hands and huddled with their arms around each other.

Subsequent interactions with other guests proved to be a variation on Sybil's sentiments—that I'd been gone too long, that Gram missed me, that she knew I had a busy life. I couldn't stop a growing wedge of guilt from lodging behind my sternum.

When I looked across the lawn at where my brother stood greeting the same friends of Gram's, the gathering around him seemed different. One woman with salt and pepper hair in a bun linked arms with Daniel as the two admired how the peacock plumes on her blue skirt matched the bright tie under his navy jacket.

So many people in blue. Gram would love it, a celebration of life rather than sadness. But no one had thought to let me know, and I knew I stood out in my funeral black.

On Daniel's other side, a petite woman in a navy dress hung her arm over Daniel's shoulder protectively and grinned up at him like he hung the moon. It was how Gram used to look at us as kids, bathing us in the warmest smile, one that nearly made us forget our parents had hit the highway without us.

Was it my imagination, or did Daniel seem like a family member to everyone here? And I, standing in my crisp dark suit, full makeup, and well-styled hair, appeared more like a family lawyer—here by obligation, viewed as essential to the situation, but not really part of the inner circle.

I tried not to let those thoughts take root. What was the point? The fact was, I didn't live here anymore. I wouldn't have the same relationship my brother had with the people in town. It was normal for my interactions to feel a little awkward.

Plus, work exhaustion and travel fatigue were wearing on me, and I would just grieve my grandmother in my own private way. Glancing skyward, I noticed a stretch of clouds blunting the otherwise pale expanse of blue. It was the first time I'd looked up since I arrived in town.

Heck, it's the first time I'd looked up in years.

Wandering over to the rows of white chairs where we all sat for the service, I lowered myself onto a seat, aware of the relief to my aching body. The three-and-a-half-hour plane trip and drive from the airport was the longest I could recall sitting in one place, unless it was to crunch numbers and revise spreadsheets for work.

At age thirty-three.

Disgraceful.

Now I sat surveying the wide expanse of verdant green and the caring people who'd assembled to honor one of their own, and I felt . . . things. Emotions that had heretofore gone unexplored.

Emotions over things like a wide-open sky.

Lost in thought, I didn't notice Daniel until he dropped into a chair in my row, leaving a space between us. Talking to my brother was inevitable, and it made me ache. I hoped it wouldn't get ugly.

"That was nice," he said, not looking at me. I followed his gaze toward the women he'd been standing with. They now meandered arm in arm toward the dirt lot where they'd parked. Sybil had offered to host a reception back at her house, which was located close to the community center, so people could amble from there to the jam session.

"It really was. Beautiful."

"You sound surprised." He turned to face me.

I kept my eyes forward, not ready for confrontation. "Not surprised, just . . . I didn't know Gram had such a large family of friends."

"Hmph."

Now I had to look at him, feeling the accusatory nature of his *hmph*. "What's that mean?" He met my eyes, no accusation, no baggage. I felt my shoulders drop in relief.

Studying my brother for a moment, I took in the whole of his twenty-nine years and felt a glimmer of the proud, protective big sister I was when we were younger. He wore his dark hair close-cropped, his beard full but neat. His dark eyes peered inquisitively, clear and bright. No shadow of the glassy, half-sauced look I remembered.

The skin outside his eyes creased from smiling or time spent in the sun. It looked good on him, and I realized he'd grown into a handsome adult. I wondered if he had a girlfriend. I wondered what else I didn't know.

I was about to ask when he answered my earlier question.

"Just that I never thought of it like that. But that's exactly what those women were to her—to us. A family of friends. They were at the house almost daily to play bridge, help her bake, help with those jigsaw puzzles she loved to do." I wondered why Gram needed help doing these things.

Sadness settled over Daniel's features. "I'm sorry she's gone." As I said the words, I realized their inadequacy.

7

He nodded, stretching his legs in front of him and crossing them at the ankles. "You have that? Family of friends? Out in LA?"

The question surprised me, so I laughed. "No, not exactly. More like people I work with and other people I work with." The weight of his gaze forced me to look away. Even as I exposed myself through information I rarely shared, I wasn't ready to expose myself to his reaction.

"Like that twat-waffle Trevor? You still dating him?" He didn't try to hide his eye-roll.

I was surprised he knew about Trevor because I couldn't recall the last time we'd had a real conversation, and certainly not one about my work or my personal life. Gram must've mentioned him.

"Ha. Nope. That lasted about five minutes and even as a business partner he's kind of annoying." I met his eyes finally, ready for judgment.

I saw none.

"Sorry," he said.

"It's okay. He's good at his job."

"Guess that's important." Again, no judgment. And he wasn't wrong.

By now, most of the folks in attendance had turned tail to make their way to Sybil's. "This place sure cleared out fast," I noted.

"Yeah, well, Sybil has the booze."

I felt myself stiffen. Daniel's partying was a sore subject, and I didn't feel equipped to get into it today with him. I'd even worried a bit this morning when I didn't see him in the kitchen that he might be so hung over that he'd miss the funeral. Or show up still half-drunk from messing around with his friends the night before.

But he'd gotten to the cemetery before me.

As if reading my thoughts, Daniel reached to cover my hand with his own. "I gave up those ways, in case you were wondering."

My head whipped to the side to gauge his meaning. He was nodding.

"What ways?" I didn't want to get my hopes up. The last time I'd spent any time with him, he was still partying hard, despite sincere-sounding promises to clean up his act. For all I knew, he was telling me what he thought I wanted to hear. Again.

"I rarely drink, and I'm pretty committed to sleeping eight hours a night." He fished something out of his pocket and presented it to me in his palm. A tube of sunscreen. "I even wear this shit now, keeping myself safe from damaging rays." Daniel fixed his eyes on me. They were searching, vulnerable, looking for the same kind of approval he'd sought when we were kids. I regretted instantly whatever I'd failed to give him.

And yet, there was an unspoken distance between us. "Why didn't you call me yourself?"

"Sorry?"

"You had Cletus tell me about Gram instead of calling yourself."

A measure of pain settled in his eyes. "Jules, I couldn't." He inhaled a deep breath and let it out slowly. "I was so broken up. Didn't know how I could possibly make that call to you. Cletus reached out to me as soon as he heard. Offered to call you and I let him do it. I'm-I'm sorry if that offended you."

I extended an arm around him and pulled him toward me. "Daniel, no. I understand. I don't know if I'd have been able to call you either."

He nodded. "I'm really glad you're here."

My throat constricted so tightly that I couldn't immediately swallow or draw breath. I loved these people—my Gram, Daniel—but that love had existed in such a deep place while I'd been away.

Too deep, too far down. Nearly lost.

Needing to get out from under the weight of Daniel's gaze, I stood and went over to the water urn and poured us each a cupful. By the time I return to my seat, I'd drawn in enough air to calm my emotions.

Exhaling a shaky breath, I faced my brother. "I'm impressed, Danny. About the drinking. Good for you." The childhood nickname came unexpectedly.

He nodded. "Well, you know, that's why I did it. Gotta impress my big sis." His lips twisted into a grin.

So sweet, this boy-turned-man.

I wanted to know more.

I wanted to know him.

"Ready for the jam session?" Daniel asked, not seeming nearly as weighed down as I felt. I envied that.

"Sure." I followed him to Gram's Chevy Impala and handed him the keys.

9

CHAPTER 2

JULIA

*W*hen Daniel pulled open the door to the community center, I was smacked by the perspiration of the overwhelming crowd.

In the center of the packed room, about seven or eight men sat in a circle playing together, lots of strumming on guitars, banjos, and even a ukulele. They kept a beat going with a stomp of their feet, and some people in the crowd clapped along from where they sat at tables or stood around the unadorned space.

The guys sounded great jamming together, but their rhythm wasn't what drew me in. There was something . . . different about their sound.

I searched the group for its source. I zeroed in on Cletus playing banjo, but none of the other faces looked familiar. Even if this was my hometown, I was basically a stranger now.

My eyes traveled to one of the musicians who stood out from the others, not just because he was tall and lean with a dark shock of hair hanging over his forehead. He sat playing the French horn, a gleaming gorgeous pretzel of brass with a bell at one end.

The sound was a love language that spoke directly to my heart.

But an intricately curved, soulful symphony instrument at a country music jam session full of Tennessee local boys . . . WTF?

I didn't have to be a country music aficionado to know that one of these things was not like the others.

Every other instrument came from the string family—banjo, guitar, fiddle. An older man with a gray beard stood behind Cletus playing the bass, plucking the strings, and nodding along with the music.

The faces in the room started looking more familiar. Maybe I'd known some of them once. Maybe I wasn't such a stranger. Not that it mattered, since I had no plans of sticking around afterward to chat. I felt worn out from the funeral and the travel.

But . . . that horn . . .

My eyes remained riveted to the instrument and the man playing it. I'd been to a couple of orchestra performances with a full brass section. Those were the types of places people normally found a French horn—with musicians wearing tuxedos and following a conductor.

This man and his instrument stuck out like a glossy gemstone in a sea of wicker and cardboard. And yet, oddly, it worked. He pursed his lips and blew out notes that had no business sounding so beautiful.

Nodding and stomping one foot, he picked up the rhythm of the other instruments and made his accompaniment sound like it belonged there.

He kept one hand in the bell-shaped end of the horn and used his other hand to draw out a melodic sound. From the first note, he had me willing to follow him down whatever path he took. For the first time since I'd arrived in town—hell, for the first time in months—I felt a glimmer of happiness. Double-chocolate cupcake happiness.

I wanted to hear more, and at the same time, I knew exactly what I would hear. Something in his beautiful aching call sounded familiar, as though I'd been hearing it my whole life.

But that was impossible.

I hadn't been in town in years. Even if I'd heard this man play before, it had to have been so long ago that surely the sounds wouldn't be familiar now.

The music called, and I answered by freeing myself of the funereal black jacket I wore over a white tank top and getting comfortable leaning against the wall. As a spectator, I had license to gaze at him for as long as I wanted.

My senses scrambled and competed for which one should win out—the sight of him, the sound of his music, or the touch I felt from him halfway across a crowded room.

Taking a couple steps closer, I cautiously took in the whole of the man playing the gleaming horn. He looked about my age, early thirties, and the strong cut of his jaw and short beard made things happen to my lady parts that hadn't happened in a very long time.

He wore a dark brown corduroy sport coat over a fine-checked plaid flannel shirt and dark blue jeans. His eyes were a pale blue, like an illusion of shallow water that actually runs deep enough to be dangerous. Soulful. Like repositories of hurt or art or knowledge.

Almost as though he could feel the heat of my stare, his eyes fastened to mine and didn't let go.

So I did the only logical thing a person could do when faced with a sexy, soulful stranger's lingering gaze.

I ran from the room.

* * *

I retreated to a table spread with homemade desserts and instinctively looked for Gram's fig cake before my brain caught up and reminded me that she wasn't here to bake it.

Instead, I reached under the long peach hem of the tablecloth to where I'd seen a few of the ladies stash bottles of gin before they went in to hear the music.

Pouring myself a small plastic cup of warm gin, I took a sip and glanced around for onlookers before downing it in a single gulp. How had the gaze of one man rattled me so much that I was slamming liquor?

"Julia?" I turned around and had to tilt my head upward to connect a face to the voice. It was him—the man who turned a French horn into a tool of seduction.

He was tall, taller than he'd appeared a minute ago when he sat among the other musicians. He also made my brains scramble and my jaw go temporarily slack because he was that freaking beautiful.

Just so . . . stunningly hotter than hot.

From those mesmerizing eyes to the lift of his cheekbones. I had to stop myself from reaching out and running my hand along the sharp line of his jaw and touching what I felt certain was a very soft beard.

"Um . . . " I ineloquently intoned. I couldn't do any better. The depth of his eyes was a little unnerving. He wasn't just looking at me; he was seeing me, knowing me better than I knew myself.

That was impossible because he didn't know me at all. But for the love of English shortbread, how I wanted him to.

Still incapable of forming words in his presence, I just gaped at him, taking in the way his generous lips curved when he moved them. They looked like strawberry-flavored pillows and I wanted to bite them.

Why were his lips moving? Oh. Because he was talking to me.

"Julia?" he said again.

"Yes?" I managed. It still didn't occur to me to ask how he knew my name. He was smiling at me now, and his smile did many things to me, not the least of which was happening low in my belly.

I might have licked my lips. I wanted to lick *him*.

"I thought that was you. My condolences on your grandmother." He put his hands together and drew them into his chest. I returned the gesture, still in a daze after seeing so many faces in one day.

Is that why he looked familiar? Had he been at the funeral? The beard was throwing me off.

"Thanks," I said, still numb from grief while at the same feeling super-charged by his presence.

"How've you been?" he asked, stepping a little closer to me. Nearby, I caught the envious, gawking glances from a couple of other women who seemed to hover in his orbit like fruit flies around a ripe peach.

They weren't my biggest problem. He thought he knew me, and I felt certain he didn't. He couldn't. I'd remember this guy.

Finally, I found my vocal cords. "I've been . . . I'm sorry, I'm not sure I remember . . . "

He smiled, and I swooned a little more. It wasn't just his face and his statuesque physique. His easy smile coupled with the way he played the horn pierced me right at my core.

I felt jittery, like a groupie in his presence, and the last time that had happened to me around a man was . . . well, high school. Around a very different guy—a shy one who never looked me in the eye. My Green Valley curse, apparently.

"Sorry. I shouldn't have assumed you'd remember me," he said, extending his hand.

I reached for it and looked down at his hand at the same time. I don't know what made me glance down. But when I did, I noticed that his hand wasn't a full-sized hand with long fingers. It was smaller, with small stubs where fingers should be. Only his thumb matched the one on his other hand.

My heart fell to my feet.

Grasping his hand to shake, I was aware of the feel of its smaller size and shape. Some people might avoid hand-shaking rather than worrying about a person's reaction or feeling the need to explain, but not this man. He'd extended his hand with the confidence of a person who knew he was more than one part of his body.

But he hadn't always behaved that way.

He was right. We had met before. And I did remember him.

"Shane. Of course, I remember. It's great to see you," I said, still feeling all kinds of star-struck and several other overwhelming emotions. Memories of that shy guy who looked nothing like the confident, dazzling man in front of me now.

Shane Meadows was a part of my past in Green Valley, even though I was having a hard time matching the gorgeous, sexy guy in front of me with the bespectacled, quiet kid who I'd known all those years ago.

As my past stood before me, burrowing its way into my heart uninvited, a hand wrapped around Shane's arm. My eyes moved from the hand to a long, lithe arm, skin milky and unmarred by the sun.

When my gaze landed on her face, I saw her wide doe eyes and shy smile aimed at Shane. She shook her shoulder length brown hair so it fell across one cheek. "You promised me a dance."

Shane was still smiling at me as though it was no big deal to stand in the community center and reminisce while another woman waited for a dance. I felt my face flush with embarrassment and was aware of an urgent need to flee.

He was one of the many reasons I'd sought to escape Green Valley.

Okay, fine. He was the main reason.

He was also the worst reminder of why it hurt to be back. Looking at his pretty face, I felt my heart ache as much as it had at the end of high school when I'd run out of his life for good. If nothing else, seeing Shane now proved that men like Trevor would never inspire passion, would never evoke the wild stir of emotions I felt after five minutes in the presence of Shane.

When faced with his smile and the confusing emotions I didn't plan on having, I did the only thing that made sense. "I've gotta go," I said.

Then I turned and ran away. Again.

CHAPTER 3

SHANE

*T*he last time anyone ran away from me so quickly was after the starting gun of the four-hundred-meter race back in high school.

In case that image wasn't clear, let's just say I was a terrible runner.

I'd signed up for the track team out of a sense of confused obligation to my awkwardly growing body. And also to impress a girl. I couldn't even remember her name now.

Except that I could remember her name just fine—it was Julia. I'd overheard her talk about runners' bodies, and I knew that meant I needed to have one.

What I didn't understand back then was that joining the track team didn't equate to having a runner's body. It just meant I'd be out there on the track with no idea how to propel my long legs any faster than they wanted to go.

My body remained the same—awkward, lanky, repellant to women.

The four hundred was an awful race, meant to be a sprint, but running a full lap on a track at sprinting speed felt near impossible without exploding a lung, so I found myself left in the dust behind the rest of the pack. Nevertheless, I stayed on the team until the end of high school because I was too stubborn to quit.

And no, I never really acquired a runner's body because back while I was still growing, all that running just made me burn calories which meant my muscles couldn't keep up with my skinny, long legs.

Funny, now, that the sight of Julia dashing out of the community center, long golden blond hair whipping behind her like the tail from a kite, would make me wish I'd worked harder at track just a little bit.

Nope. Wasn't fast then, wasn't fast now.

"So, you plan on chasing her or just looking at her dust?" Clay's voice over my shoulder let me know he'd been standing there longer than I'd realized, which was never a surprise with my older brother, who'd been looking out for me since we were kids.

Not that I needed it.

Not that he cared.

"Neither." I turned and huffed out a breath. "She's too confusing to bother doing either one." I'd blocked some of my high school years from my mind, but the memory of Julia running away from me back then still burned bright.

Just like her.

He cocked an eyebrow and regarded me. "Huh."

"What's that supposed to mean?" I suspected I knew.

"Just . . . in the years I've known you—which is all of them—I've never seen that expression on your face."

I rolled my eyes. I didn't need him analyzing my expression, and I didn't care what he thought about what he saw.

Fine, I did.

"Meaning what?"

He shrugged and tilted his head as though reconsidering whether to let me in on his thought process.

"Just say it."

"You haven't been playing the jam sessions for the past few weeks, and your reasons are your own. I'm not butting in there. But I reckon you knew she'd be here tonight, today being her grandma's funeral and all."

I reached past him for a jug of water. "Didn't cross my mind."

"I call bullshit."

"That why you chased me out here, to say that?"

"I didn't chase you. We're on a five-minute break."

I refilled my cup and took a long drink, which settled my thoughts. Then I looked Clay dead in the eyes because he needed to understand that the words about to leave my mouth would serve as the final discussion on the matter.

"She's simply someone I used to know. And judging by her being here for a brief weekend or whatnot, someone I doubt I'll run into again. But there will be no dust-watching and there will be no chasing of that woman. Now, we'd best get back to the jam session. Break's about done."

Clay nodded, but the creep of the corner of his mouth told me he'd be revisiting the conversation sometime when I felt equally disinterested in having it.

"I know who she is."

"Well, great. Nothing to talk about, then."

I didn't want to talk about her if she planned on running away from me like she had when we were teenagers. Even if I'd never forgotten her golden blond hair, her deep brown eyes shaped like almonds, or her cherry rosebud lips.

I'd forget the hell out of them now.

As we headed back over toward the circle of chairs with our instruments, I was struck by how much warmer the air suddenly felt. I took off my jacket and shrugged off the flannel I wore over a T-shirt and draped it over the back of a folding chair.

The heat was definitely not due to my brief interaction with Julia. I stifled the alarming concern that it was. Impossible that one person could have that kind of effect on me.

Impossible.

The crowd had thinned during our break, but I hoped that once the music started up again, folks would filter back into the room. Some people didn't even bother to show up until the later part of the night, but I hated to think we couldn't hold the crowd. Julia's departure notwithstanding.

"You're worried about the lack of a crowd?" Clay tipped his head toward mine and flashed his cheeky grin. Sometimes I wished I was an only child.

I ran a hand over my beard. "Nah."

"Liar."

He kept right on smiling as he tuned the strings on his guitar.

"Just makes me antsy," I admitted. I didn't love that aspect of my personality, but he understood it and didn't judge. Much.

"Never made you antsy when you were playing at SOOK," he observed, referring to the Symphonic Orchestra of Knoxville, where I used to have a steady gig before I decided I liked having evenings to myself.

Tipping his head toward the door, he kept turning the key and picking his strings, listening for the sound he wanted. Clay never used a pitch pipe. Like me, he played by ear and could tune any instrument with strings merely by listening to their sounds, even over a room half-filled with people.

"It's just a jam session. Besides, maybe she'll come back if she knows she doesn't have to talk to you," he muttered, still looking down to hide his smirk. I elbowed him, annoyed with his needling.

"I don't care whether she comes or goes. But it's nice to have a full house." I lifted my French horn out of its case and sat on the folding chair next to Clay so I could balance it on my lap. Reaching into the case, I selected a fresh mouthpiece and held it between my lips while I worked the existing one free with my left hand.

My grunt got Clay's attention, but he knew better than to ask if I needed help. We'd established a long time ago that I didn't. Being naturally right-handed had always seemed like fate's particularly bad joke.

If a person was only going to get a fist with a fully-grown thumb on one hand, it seemed fair that the other hand would be equipped to do most of the work.

Instead, my left hand wasn't naturally skilled at much of anything. Learning to write was double the chore for me as for the other kids in my class when I was a kid. Learning to hold a baseball bat would have been so much easier if I'd naturally batted lefty. Along with so many other things.

But no, my stubborn physical body didn't seem to work according to logic. Presenting my smaller right hand for something as simple as a handshake made an initial greeting more fraught and complicated. If I'd been consulted when putting my parts together, I'd have suggested that my left hand be the one with symbrachydactyly.

I know, it's a mouthful, but it essentially means I have a rare condition that exists at birth in one of every thirty-two thousand or so babies. No one knows exactly what causes it, but doctors think there's some sort of disruption to development in a fetus.

In my case, it was a surprise to everyone when I was born because nothing showed up on any of the scans or ultrasounds, mainly because my tiny hand looked like it was balled into a fist.

My parents were rugged, no-nonsense people who believed that everything happens for a reason. They never looked at me like there was anything wrong with my hand and always referred to it as my special gift.

As a kid, I bought into the "special gift" business initially, figuring I could do some cool shit with a hand that looked like a fist. I was a beast with Playdough because I could push it through graters and mash it into shapes with extra strength that came from not having skinny little fingers getting in the way.

My mom basically raised me at the local park through my early years, letting me run wild and free and play with as much sand and Playdough as a three-year-old kid could ask for. I pushed dump trucks and made sand mountains. I finger painted with the fingers I had.

Then I started kindergarten, and everything changed.

For the first time, I felt judged for being different. My peers couldn't pronounce symbrachydactyly, let alone understand it. Despite my parents' efforts to stay cheerful and positive about how capable I was, I no longer saw my ratty paw as a special gift.

I saw it as something people had to get over in order to be around me.

I covered it with my other hand in every photo that was taken. Or I stuffed it in my pocket.

To me, my hand looked like a bear paw, which seemed cool when I was little. I pretended I was part grizzly. Stubby hints at fingers no bigger than a knuckle. The barest shard of a fingernail on two of the bumps. And a full thumb—the coveted opposable appendage. Only without fingers, it turned my hand into something resembling a clamp.

And yes, I'd tried to use it with a fair bit of leverage to unwedge a pesky horn mouthpiece. But with the saliva that got in between the layers of brass, it took the firm finger grip of my left hand to pull it free.

Another grunt from me.

The sucker was really stuck, and that made me all the more determined to twist it loose, which I finally did under Clay's watchful eye, while he pretended to glance someplace else.

It wasn't really necessary to switch out the mouthpieces during a casual neighborhood jam session, but neither was it necessary—or expected—that a French horn player would jam with a bunch of bluegrass musicians.

Yet there I sat amid the banjos and guitars and a bass and a violin. An outlier.

Always was.

But tonight, with the gleaming coiled instrument on my lap, I was an outlier who could play the French horn better than anyone in the county. And yes, far as I knew, I was the only French horn player in the county.

I'd been fortunate enough to stretch my wings at the SOOK and elsewhere, so I had confidence in my abilities. I'd always had confidence in music, even back when I had no confidence in myself. I knew it had the power to transform a mood or a moment with a single riff. I just didn't know what that had to do with me until the summer after my junior year of high school.

On one muggy hot night, I tagged along with Clay, who'd just turned twenty-one and was headed to Nashville for a weekend of debauchery. At age seventeen, I was too young to get into one of the honky tonk bars, which was where Clay and his friends had big plans to drink and meet "city girls."

So I got myself some Hattie B's hot chicken and found the next best musical option, where there was no age limit to get in the door—the Nashville Symphony.

I didn't much care what the orchestra had on tap to play that night. I'd loved music of all types from the time I realized that tapping a spoon against my cup sounded like a melody. Music was the backdrop of my childhood—if anyone was home, some sort of music blasted from a speaker someplace.

I'd mostly counted myself out as someone who could play an instrument, however, because I just didn't see how I could suitably play the piano with one hand and a thumb or even properly do justice to a string instrument.

It only bothered me slightly, like all the limitations I had with respect to my hand. Eventually, I stopped thinking about music and myself in the same sentence.

That is, until I saw the Nashville Symphony.

Looking to buy a single ticket, I got lucky enough to score a seat in the third row. On one side of me sat a white-haired couple, the woman next to me wrapped in an elegant burgundy velour cape and the man tapping his leg to the piped-in preview music in faded jeans and a toothpick between his teeth. On the other side of me, a woman my grandmother's age sat in wide-eyed anticipation, her salt and pepper bob tucked against the shoulder of the sleeping man next to her.

I didn't care about any of that once the orchestra started playing. The people, the crinkling of candy wrappers, the buzz from malfunctioning hearing aids—none of it could distract me from the music.

Because my seat happened to be positioned near the brass section, I had a direct view of all the various types of horns, most of which looked familiar to me. Except for one.

The French horn that sat on one man's lap immediately struck me as a thing of beauty. No other way of describing it could do justice to the complex, circular coil of brass with the large bell on one end.

And when the man played it . . . he stuffed his right hand into the bell and kept it there the entire time, using his left hand to work the valves.

Probably my imagination, but I felt like I could hear the music of his particular instrument over all the others. He played a sweet, sad melody, moving his right hand in the bell.

I never saw his right hand for the entire performance.

No one did.

And I had myself an idea.

To be clear, the idea wasn't to be the outlier in a bluegrass jam band full of guitars and a banjo, despite the current circumstances. The story of how that came to pass had little to do with me and much to do with Clay, who pestered me until I showed up on a Friday.

But I'd be the first to assert that the plucking and strumming of all the string instruments sounded a little bit nicer accompanied by the sweet song of a well-played brass instrument. If there's one thing I'd learned how to do over the years, it was play the instrument that seemed tailor-made for me.

"You got it?" Clay didn't put down his guitar or even look at me. He knew the drill—I'd never ask for his help. He was just being brotherly, and since he was older, that translated to him always letting me know he could probably accomplish something better than me, even if it wasn't actually true.

"Yup, always sticks."

"Maybe if you didn't spit so much when you played . . . "

Finally, the layers of metal gave way, and the mouthpiece slid free. "Ah, there." I cleaned it assiduously and packed it into its case before sliding the pristine one in place.

"At least when I spit, it still sounds like music," I chided my brother. "Not sure what your excuse is." He loved to sing, and when he sang, he spit. Unfortunately, since we sat in a circle, I was often the recipient of his abundant spray.

"I sound great."

"You sound like a rusty tin can rolling down a road full of potholes."

The truth was, his singing voice *was* pretty good, but when it came to carrying a tune, I got the luckier gene. Nonetheless, he had all the confidence that I was still working on when it came to singing in front of a crowd. Baby steps.

"Fine. So you take a turn and sing for once." He looked up, his eyes challenging.

"You may not have noticed, but a person can't sing and play the French horn at the same time."

He shrugged. "Pretty sure we're the only bluegrass jam on the planet with a French horn. We can spare you playing if you want to sing a bit." He wasn't ribbing me; he was encouraging me. He knew I had a form of stage fright that only hit when I got in front of a microphone. His raised eyebrows challenged me to do this for once.

"Nah, not tonight." I had no interest in discussing the issue further.

"Whatever. Chickenshit."

I couldn't help grinning at him. "Good one. I feel suitably shamed."

He smacked me on the back of the head like he'd done for our entire life and picked up his guitar. "You ready, or do you need more time to polish your horn?" He laughed at the worn-out joke and insinuation he never missed a chance to throw my way.

"You need some new material. Please tell me you're better than this when you go on a date."

"I'm the best." He'd always been the cocky one. Always confident. Good hair, broad shoulders, green eyes, and a face women couldn't seem to get enough of. Plus, he was musical, worked as a teacher, and was not a complete asshole.

That made him everybody's favorite go-to bachelor when they had a daughter or niece they were hoping to marry off. He humored them and went on plenty of dates, though I know he had no interest in getting married soon, if ever.

That was a phobia to be investigated another time, along with my dislike for singing in public.

But I knew one thing—if Julia ended up staying in town for any amount of time, it was just a matter of days before she ended up sitting opposite my brother at dinner one night.

The thought of it made me nauseous, though I had no reason to be bothered.

There was nothing between us anymore. Less than nothing.

CHAPTER 4

JULIA

$\mathcal{T}$he first place I went when I hightailed it away from Shane was the restroom, where I locked myself in a stall until I got over the feeling of wanting to cry.

Crying was not an option.

Crying was a ridiculous response to a man I hadn't laid eyes on in a decade, especially when he seemed genuinely glad to see me after all these years.

The normal, appropriate response should have been to nod and smile and tell him how nice it was to see him again. Tell him I was pleased to be back visiting Green Valley—for it would only be a temporary stop on my path toward someplace else—and tell him I'd see him around, knowing full well I wouldn't.

Instead, all the teenage feelings of love and pain and yearning and other unnamed emotions came hurtling back at me, uninvited and unstoppable.

I'd loved Shane Meadows once. With all my heart.

Then I'd run from Green Valley just like I did tonight. Planning never to set eyes on him again.

How had this happened? How had I not been prepared?

The last time I'd visited Green Valley, Shane didn't live here. That made it easy to keep all memories of him in a vault where they belonged.

Why was he here now?

I'd assumed everything about the place would be the same. I'd come to rely on it. Green Valley was the one constant in my life, and I loved the way it didn't look different when I visited. It had no right to go and change while I was up to my elbows in business challenges, seven days a week. Even if it was my fault for not staying in touch with folks from around here.

Not to mention that it shocked me that my heart reacted all over again the exact way it did when I was in high school. It flipped, dipped, and twirled. Butterflies swarmed as if unleashed from a high-pressure cocoon and allowed to fly free.

There was a storm of wings in my gut and an ache in my heart so intense I thought it easily might split me in two.

Then I took a good look at myself in the mirror. "You did not come all this way to get intimated by a man. You will not honor your Gram's memory by folding into a heap of sadness over old feelings that have no business being revisited. You will hold your head high and walk out of this restroom like a proud, confident woman."

That, or I'd make a mad dash to my car and hope I didn't run into anyone else I knew.

Plan B sounded awesome.

I didn't stop running until I reached the sturdy Impala. My heart pounded in my chest, and I could see my breath in the cool Tennessee evening air.

Digging in the front pocket of my pants for my keys, I didn't dare turn around. If anyone saw me turn tail and dash from the jam session, I didn't want to know.

As it was, I could tell by the fierce heat across my skin that I was blushing like a schoolgirl. Damn that Shane Meadows. "Dammit, dammit, dammit," I emphasized with a stamp of my foot as I clicked the locks open.

"That's a lot of time in eternal fire for something or someone," a person observed just over my shoulder.

"Cletus Winston." I spun around and didn't hesitate before throwing my arms around his neck. He'd slipped out of the cemetery earlier before I could talk to him, and I hadn't caught his eye while he strummed his banjo. "Oh, the only person here I'm happy to see."

He embraced me briefly, then patted my shoulder and took a step back. "How'd you get away with staying out of town for so long?"

I shrugged at the question people had been posing all day. When they'd asked, it felt like a combination of scolding and guilt. But coming from Cletus, it felt like a question.

"Got busy, is all. Work needed a lot of tending to, and I've kept meaning to come back . . . " My voice trailed off when I couldn't come up with a lie that I thought Cletus would believe.

He shook his head. "Naw, you haven't. But that's okay because you're here now, and Jenn's dying to get you into the bakery. I'll let her work that out with you herself."

Cletus's wife, Jennifer Sylvester, was known as the Banana Cake Queen for her eponymous cake and she ably ran the Donner Bakery in town. He went on to drop a few more not-so-subtle hints about how Jenn would love to keep me busy baking while I was here if I so desired. I couldn't tell if it was supposed to be a favor to Jenn or to me, and Cletus would never admit to either one.

"I promise, I will," I told him. His nod communicated that my promise was ironclad law.

Cletus leaned his forearm on the roof of Gram's green sedan and looked up at the periwinkle evening sky. "I hadn't planned on having a welcome home conversation out here in the parking lot when there's a perfectly good table and chairs in the community center. There a reason you're leaving in a hurry?" He eyed me suspiciously.

"Oh. I-I might've eaten something earlier that didn't agree."

"Okay, yeah." He looked at the ground and pushed himself away from the car. It seemed like he was going to take me at my word and go back to the jam session. But Cletus never did do what I expected, so it shouldn't have surprised me when he didn't do it now. He turned and faced me square on. "Noticed you and Shane remade an acquaintance."

Nothing escaped that damned man. Normally, I loved him for it. Right now, not so much.

I nodded. Then I swallowed hard. "Guess I'm gonna be running into lots of folks I haven't seen in a while. Especially at a jam session after a funeral where half the town's in attendance." Then it occurred to me. "Hey, shouldn't you be inside? How're they playing without you and your banjo?"

He shrugged. A lot of shrugging between the two of us. And because we went way back, it substituted for full sentences.

"Chasing me down suited you better. Why?"

"I just want to make sure things are going to be okay for you here. With Shane and all. I remember how it was before you moved away."

It figured that the one person I'd poured my heart out to back in high school would have a bear trap for a brain. He'd never miss an opportunity to make me think twice about something I didn't plan on thinking once about.

"That was a long time ago," I reminded him. We'd all done stupid things when we were eighteen. We'd all had crushes.

A crush at eighteen felt like the world would end if we couldn't turn it into the unrequited love story we felt certain we were destined to have.

Then I moved across the country to Fresno, a farming city that had a college where I got to study cooking. Then I moved to Los Angeles and pursued my baking dreams.

But all that lay firmly rooted in a past I'd just as soon forget. Despite the fitful assault of butterflies that staged a coup in my belly the second I laid eyes on Shane, my old feelings were just that—old, leftover sentiments that had no business clouding my current reality.

Especially since he was probably married to or happily dating that pretty woman who'd reminded him he owed her a dance.

It was fine. I was only here to tidy things up and get some closure before heading back to California.

Meanwhile, beneath his scraggly beard, Cletus's mouth had turned down into a frown. "This doesn't strike me as good, Jules. You have unfinished business, and you ought to attend to it."

"Like I said, it was a long time ago. There's no unfinished business between me and Shane Meadows."

His cool eyes rested on me, and I fought the urge to fidget with my keys. Then I did it anyway, accidentally setting off the car alarm.

Calmly, Cletus took the keys from my hand and silenced the alarm. Then he ran a hand over his scruffy beard in a way that made him look thoughtful. It teed up his next words perfectly. "A woman doesn't run from a room like her tail's on fire because of a man she's long forgotten about. Seeing him stirred up feelings, and I see you're upset."

I let out a long exhale. It was pointless to lie to one of my oldest friends, especially if I was going to be spending time with his wife. "Fine. It startled me a little to run into him. I didn't realize he'd moved back, and seeing him brought back the *memory* of old feelings. Not the feelings themselves. And like I said, it was a long time ago. Ages. I'm sure he's not the last person here who'll jolt my senses if I'm taken by surprise."

I felt myself pull in another deep inhale and exhale. The Great Smoky Mountain air felt cleaner than the coastal California climate I'd gotten used to, and maybe my lungs were merely enjoying the change.

For once, Cletus didn't seem to have any observation to make about it.

He watched me, and I did my best to meet his gaze with something I hoped would convince him that no more discussion was needed about Shane Meadows.

"Okay. Well, memories are nice." He clapped his hand on the roof of the Impala. "Your Gram's been bringing this car into my shop for years. She may have some years on her, but I can attest that she's in perfect condition to make it up any mountain road you care to take her on."

"Thanks, Cletus." I reached for the keys he still held in his hand and tried not to worry at the uncomfortable groan the driver's door made when I pulled it open. Cletus and his brothers owned the best repair shop in the county, so if he said the car was fit for mountain roads, I believed him.

Shrugging his reply, he turned and started walking back to the community center.

I could only hope he'd report to anyone who wondered that I was fine and not unnerved at the unexpected run-in with my high school crush.

Even if it wasn't true.

And people in Green Valley heard what they wanted to hear and believed what they wanted to believe anyhow.

Myself included.

CHAPTER 5

JULIA

I woke up in a buttercream frosting mood.

That isn't to say I envisioned fairies alighting on pale yellow sugar peaks and blessing my day with moonbeams. A buttercream frosting mood meant I wanted to shovel a pint of buttered sugar into my mouth and call it breakfast.

Maybe that was because I was both excited and nervous about my first day at my new job. That's right, I said yes when Jenn asked me to bake bread for her bakery.

"It works out perfectly because we have two back-to-back events at the Lodge, and we need more than double the amount of bread we normally bake. We could use the help," she'd said when I worried she was just keeping me busy because Cletus had strong-armed her into it.

I still didn't know how long it would take me to sell Gram's house and get Daniel situated living someplace else, so if I was going to be in town a while, I might as well keep busy. Plus, it would lessen the chance of running into Shane Meadows all over town if I stayed in one place.

So I said yes to my first real baking job in years and set my alarm for four in the morning. Baker's habit.

In my early days in bread kitchens, I'd always started in the wee morning hours, turning out dough after a slow overnight rise. One final knead, a short rise, and the loaves were ready for baking. They'd come out perfect and hot just as the day's first customers showed up.

Later, as my business grew and I started delivering to restaurants all over Los Angeles, I outsourced the early morning baking to my employees, but I always woke up at the same time every day, regardless of whether I was needed in the kitchen.

Today, I made myself a pot of good coffee, did five minutes of yoga stretches in Gram's kitchen while it brewed, and worked the daily crossword puzzle in the newspaper.

I added a quick pour of cream into my coffee—I was not interested in any of the nut milk alternatives—and enjoyed those first few sips like I'd never tasted coffee before.

Then I checked on the Royal Family, which required logging into my computer and reading The Sun and the Daily Mail, plus the official Royal Family web page. It gave me a sense of security to know they were doing well, and it reminded me of Gram even more because she'd been the one to start me on the ritual of checking on Queen Elizabeth's whereabouts years ago.

She'd only visited England once, sometime before I was born, but small habits and traditions had firmly rooted themselves into her daily life. She insisted on afternoon tea, often with guests, and served it in her collection of mismatched teacups collected from eBay and the occasional antiques market.

Gram learned to make scones, and she was the only one in all of Green Valley to serve crustless tea sandwiches at a backyard barbecue, but she didn't give a "rat's hindquarters" what people thought about it.

And she loved and respected Queen Elizabeth for her dutiful service to tradition. "It speaks to my country roots," she told me once. Other than that, we didn't talk much about the royals, but since I lived with her while my parents were off gallivanting around the world, her habit of checking on Elizabeth's health and whereabouts each morning seemed as normal to me as other people checking the weather.

I'd expanded the ritual to include other members of Elizabeth's family, and it was one of my favorite morning routines. Today, I saw that Kate Middleton and Sophie Wessex represented the Royal Family at a garden party, which made me wonder about the absence of King Charles, but then I reminded myself that he couldn't possibly get to every event where royals are required.

Heck, I'd missed two of my friends' weddings in the past three months due to overcommitments at work. And that was a better three months than some I've had.

The final piece of my morning ritual was also influenced by Gram, and for the first time, it struck me how much of her I carried with me when I moved away. It didn't seem coincidental that I started my days in much the same way she did.

When she awoke each morning and finished her first cup of coffee, she calmly assessed her mood as a predictor of how the rest of her day might go.

She always described her moods in terms of baked goods.

Chocolate soufflé days were the kind that surpassed expectations. Mudpie days were a slog. Yellow cake was a good solid day. Pretzel bread . . . well, you get the idea.

"I'm feeling vanilla cupcake," was a common conclusion when the sun had yet to peek from behind clouds, and nothing was set on her calendar. Those days could easily turn devil's food by noon if she got behind a slow driver on Moth Run Road.

Or even lemon curd if the mail wasn't delivered until late afternoon.

It had always seemed like the perfect way to assess one's state of mind before other people's attitudes and unexpected situations spoiled the day like weevils infesting a bag of flour.

So even when my fellow students at my Fresno college thought I was some back country weirdo for conjuring pastry references to describe my mood, I did it anyway. Every day. Eventually, my friends got used to it, and by the time we graduated, most of them also used various baked goods as a universal yardstick for feelings.

When I finally walked inside Donner Bakery, my senses took over. The sugary scent of oven-fresh baked goods made me feel more at home than I'd been since my plane landed.

The door latched shut behind me with a jingle of a bell, causing the one man in the bakery to straighten up from where he'd been gazing through the glass at the pastry displays. "Oh, she is here!" Looking proper in wire-rimmed glasses and an expertly pressed shirt, the man cast his eyes on me and smiled broadly, revealing a dimple in one cheek.

I had the initial reaction of thinking he must have been mistaken. Surely, he was expecting someone else, someone he actually knew. But he rushed right over, extending his hand toward me and looking almost starry-eyed at my presence.

"I'm Monsieur Auclair. I run the Lodge, and I must say it's a great honor to have you here baking with us."

Just then, Jenn appeared from the kitchen, wiping her hands on an apron tied over the front of a yellow shirt. My face must have betrayed my confusion because she began explaining. "Monsieur Auclair let us know you're a bit of a baking legend. He follows these things."

He was staring at me the way I'd surely gawk at Prince William if I met him. "Oh, well, thank you. I'm happy to be able to help out while I'm in town."

"You will not be merely helping. Your bread will be the highlight of our menu at our farm-to-table restaurant. Our guests will know they're getting something special. Please, no false modesty."

I smiled and tried to think of something to say until Jenn took pity on me. "Okay, okay, enough of that, Monsieur. You'll get your bread, but not if we keep Julia out here having a conversation. Now that you've had your meet and greet, I'd like to get her started in the kitchen."

"Of course, of course. Yes. There's baking to be done," he conceded, still gazing at me as though I might melt like a pat of butter in the sun and disappear at any moment. His delight seemed to overcome him so much that he leaned toward me and air-kissed me on both cheeks. "Like the French," he said.

Jenn ushered me away from him with an arm around my shoulder. "I'll look over your menu and make sure to get you what you need," Jenn called back to him. To me, she whispered, "You'll have to forgive Monsieur Auclair. He's a bit star-struck."

"That's silly. He shouldn't feel that way."

"He takes food very seriously, so to him, you're a celebrity."

The idea seemed vaguely ludicrous, given how many years I'd spent in Los Angeles, home of real celebrities. My baking success had made a name for me, and I sort of liked the idea that people in my hometown might think I'd done well for myself in my years away.

"It's sweet. And flattering. I'll take it," I remarked as we stood in the kitchen. Taking in my temporary home, I nodded at the comfortable surroundings.

Jenn showed me around the front of the bakery, which had French bistro chairs and glass cases filled with pastries. The bell over the front door jangled and Blithe Tanner arrived for work. I remembered her from growing up, and when she saw me, she waved.

"I heard you were coming to see us. Now it's a party," she said, tying on her apron.

"That's what I love about bakeries. Always a party when there are baked goods around."

"That's the truth," Jenn said, her violet eyes alight.

The bell over the door jangled again, and this time, a man strode in the door. While he removed a pair of sunglasses and let his eyes adjust to the light, I took a step back, not wanting to get in the way of a customer. I waited for Jenn to greet him with her usual friendly smile.

She did not.

"Hello, Jenn," the man said. She cleared her throat in response and nodded. Granted, I didn't know her well, but she was a sweet, friendly woman and he was a customer, so the chilly response surprised me.

"Hi, Isaac." Blithe said. But she didn't wave at him in the friendly way she'd done to me.

"Hey, Blithe. Jenn," he said again.

Jenn cleared her throat again. "Didn't know you were in town."

"Just got here," Isaac said, encouraging her with a smile.

"Oh," she said, turning to me. "I should show you the bread ovens." Then she turned on her heel and indicated that I should follow. Having no idea what just happened between her and Isaac, I followed her but didn't ask.

For the first time since I'd arrived in Green Valley, I felt some semblance of belonging. I knew industrial kitchens. I loved the smell of the fermenting sourdough starters, the heat from the ovens, the satisfying, heady scent of fresh baked goods, and melting butter.

Jenn began pointing out the bench where I'd make bread, along with containers lining one wall of salt and jars of sourdough starter. "You can use our starters or . . . I don't know if you'd like to make your own . . . "

I nodded, and she continued pointing out various areas of the kitchen—the dishwashing area, the wall of ovens, the cold drawers.

A weight lifted—the anvil that had sat on my chest from strained conversations with my brother and suspicious glances from Gram's friends. Their looks quietly communicated that I was an outsider, even at my own Gram's funeral, and I couldn't help but agree with them.

But a kitchen was a kitchen. I could make excellent use of this one and bake up the finest bread I knew how.

With the back door open, I was also catching whiffs of the bluebonnets in full bloom out back in the meadows that stretched toward the horizon in all directions. That smell brought me back to long summer days under a yellow sun, playing in the fields before the heat withered the plants to dry stalks.

Maybe it was just that I hadn't been here for so long I was feeling nostalgic for old familiar faces and places. I loved that not much had changed in ten years.

Or it could have been the easy pace of things. I didn't feel the pressure to crank out a thousand loaves per day of artisan bread. Even a big order from the Lodge didn't feel anywhere near as stressful. For as long as I was in town, I decided to let myself enjoy the break and the slower pace. I deserved it.

All of those thoughts were instantly pushed aside when the heavy metal door to the walk-in fridge swung open, and out walked Shane, arms laden with a large burlap bag of flour.

Wait, what? Shane? Here? Why?

Muscles rippling under the weight of the bag, his face showed no sign of strain. I knew from experience that flour came in fifty-kilogram sacks, which was well over a hundred pounds. He moved quickly to the counter and set the bag down as though simply moving a feather pillow from one end of a couch to the other.

Okay, so he was strong. That didn't mean I needed to fall to pieces in the glow of his pale blue eyes, even if their color beckoned like a swimming pool in hundred-degree heat. I could just . . . look away.

I could *not* look away.

The shock of seeing him here, in my baking haven from the rest of the world, made my breath catch and the back of my neck prickle with sweat. Surely he was just doing someone a favor, lugging the big sack because he happened to be in the neighborhood, and the sack needed lugging.

He'd be gone after the task. Right?

But he made no moves to go. Instead, face expressionless, he put his fists against his hips and watched us.

Jenn continued the tour of the kitchen, but I heard none of it over the whoosh of blood in my ears as my heart pounded like a bass drum. I felt certain Shane could hear it.

Across town, Mr. Jensen with the broken hearing aid could probably hear it.

I leaned against the breadboard, gripping it with both hands to steady myself. The suggestive pinpricks of heat turned into full beads of sweat, and I debated whether I'd draw more attention to my increasingly frazzled state by wiping my face down with the back of my hand or pretending everything was fine.

It's a kitchen. It's hot in here, right?

"What are you doing here?" Shane asked, puzzled. He didn't look unhappy to see me, didn't look . . . anything. Maybe not surprising since I'd run away from him mid-conversation at the jam session.

As if noticing him for the first time, Jenn stopped talking and turned toward him. "Oh, hey, Shane. I'm giving Julia the lay of the land."

I could tell his question wasn't aimed at Jenn, but I said nothing, still puzzling through what he was doing here.

"Didn't know we were giving tours now." His tone didn't betray his thoughts on the matter, but I had a bad feeling.

Jenn laughed. "I told you about the big bread order from the Lodge because of the destination wedding, right? Then, the event the following weekend? Well, it's our luck that Julia agreed to step in and bake while she's in town. Problem solved."

It was impossible to take my eyes off Shane, and not just because his face was still painfully beautiful to me. Something shifted behind his eyes as soon as Jenn uttered the words "step in." Their normally placid blue suddenly looked stormy enough to toss ships at sea and cause substantial nausea.

"But we have a bread baker." Shane pointed to himself with both thumbs.

They did? He was a baker?

His gesture drew my eye to his right hand, which brought me right back to the jam session when shaking his hand had reduced me to a puddle of white-hot lust.

Only now, I could articulate why the handshake—and now the gesture—struck me with such force. He seemed comfortable with himself. I remember him going to great lengths to hide his hand back when we were in school together, always tucking it into a pocket or sitting with one hand covering the other.

Seeing him thrust his hand into the air sent a surge of sweet affection through my heart because it used to pain me back in school when I knew he felt less-than.

And as much as I could tell I'd unwittingly caused a conflict between him and Jenn merely by being here, I couldn't help but feel a flutter of joy in my heart that he finally seemed comfortable enough in his body to gesture freely with his hand.

Silently thanking the gods of self-confidence or whoever helped him get himself there, I felt myself getting a little choked up.

My throat felt so strangled by the effort to hold back unexpected tears that I briefly turned away and inhaled a choppy, necessary breath. When I turned back, Shane's eyes studied me intently.

Pressing my lips together, I managed to tamp down the next wave of emotion so I wouldn't need to look away. The darkness that I'd noticed in his eyes moments before was starting to subside, but I still saw something in his expression I couldn't discern. Irritability? Resignation?

With my own heart swimming around in my chest looking for purchase, I couldn't bother myself much with finding the right adjective.

I'm still emotional over Gram's death, I decided.

Um, sure. A persnickety little honest streak in me cried foul. I knew exactly why I felt it hard to swallow.

Shane still had the kind of effect on me that women wrote about in letters to soldiers at war, never certain whether their feelings would die on the battlefield. In my case, they'd died on a football field senior year.

When I'd managed to swallow back the strange jumble of feelings, I tuned back into the conversation he and Jenn were having.

"More hands make light work," Jenn said, dismissing his concern with her own pragmatic need to get the required bread loaves from Donner Bakery to the lodge in the time needed.

"How big is the order?" Shane asked, apparently still not ready to relinquish full ownership of baking responsibilities to the high school flight risk here to steal his job.

"Fifty loaves a day just for the lodge. Plus our regular standing orders," Jenn said, drawing a heart shape in the dusting of flour that covered the bread board.

Shane merely nodded.

"I don't want to step on any toes. If you don't need me, I'll keep myself busy elsewhere while I'm in town," I said when I finally felt able to form words.

I still had so many questions. Why was Shane a bread baker? Why wasn't he a professional musician? Why did Jenn ask me to work here when she already had a bread maker?

"Nonsense. You two are both being ridiculous. Two bakers are better than one when we have a large order. And besides, Julia, you heard Monsieur Auclair. He wants to talk you up as our visiting celebrity baker. He's planning a social media campaign. This is good for business."

She looked from one of us to the other like a mother who's just told her warring twins to zip their lips and stay in their opposite corners. As a business owner myself, of course I understood that any disagreements between us were our problem, not hers.

Like a semi-obedient toddler, I held my tongue. For now.

Glancing at Shane, I saw his face settle into a squinty mask of acceptance that told me we'd hash out our turf war amongst ourselves.

Nodding, Jenn wiped her hands down the front of her apron, smoothing it. Then she smiled at us and strode back toward the front of the bakery, calling back at us, "Y'all can work out amongst yourselves how to divide up responsibilities. You're old friends, according to Cletus, so enjoy spending the time, getting to know each other again."

The door swung behind her, and she was gone.

I stared at the door for a moment, not sure what to say to Shane. I didn't want him to think of me as an interloper or a competitor. "Hey, like I said, I don't want to step on your toes."

"It's fine."

"Really? It doesn't seem fine." I studied him, still standing a few paces away from me but now moving to cross his arms over his chest. His biceps flexed when he did it.

"Hmph. Interesting."

"What's that supposed to mean?"

"Just that you don't really know me anymore, seeing as how you don't spend any time in Green Valley, so your idea of what's fine with me might be skewed."

The look on his face was more curious than challenging. It said I didn't know much about anything around here because I left and didn't come back. I was starting to tire of the judgment.

Maybe that was why I felt my panties suddenly twist so tightly that they strangled whatever good feelings Shane had heretofore unleashed in my lady parts. I was mad. And I took out my anger on him because he was the closest.

"It wasn't for lack of caring, you know. I care about people. So much so that I work eighteen-hour days to make sure a thousand of them continue to have jobs and healthcare for their families. I just don't happen to live locally anymore. It's not a character flaw, it's just a fact."

I could feel the heat rise in my cheeks while the words came tumbling out, but there was no stopping me once I got rolling. "And you don't know me either, so I'd appreciate it if you could look at me without bringing in a whole bathtub full of judgment that has no basis in reality."

Shane hadn't moved. Hadn't uncrossed his arms or shifted the placid expression on his face to anything that looked like irritation with my outburst or confirmation that he understood and accepted the weight of my words.

He just . . . watched me.

For an uncomfortably long time. Then, slowly, his mouth hitched up on one side, to form something I could only describe as a smirk. "Are you finished with the rant?"

"The rant?" It was hardly a rant. I was just a little wound up, speaking the way impassioned people spoke.

"Yes. You were ranting."

"I was speaking. Passionately."

"Okay. Are you finished?"

I wasn't sure I was, but I conceded, "I guess." Then, I thought about it and decided I had more to say.

Pointing at the large refrigerator, I voiced the opinion I'd kept to myself thus far. But maybe lashing out at him some more would dull the attraction I still had toward him despite his aggravating opinions of me. "You shouldn't keep the flour in there."

"I'm sorry?" His head whipped around to see where I was pointing, even though there was nothing behind him other than the large industrial fridge I'd mentioned.

"I noticed you walk out of there with a sack of flour. Do you normally refrigerate it?"

His expression remained impassive, but a twitching muscle in his cheek let me know my flour thoughts left him slightly ruffled. "It keeps it fresh. It's hot as hades here in the summer, and with the humidity, the flour takes a hit." His eyes, now the color of the Caribbean Sea, unleashed a new wave of goosebumps along my skin.

Damn him. Or rather, damned skin.

Why did I feel compelled to antagonize the person I'd be working with —that is, unless I got myself fired, which would be embarrassing? On a long inhale, I rearranged my priorities. By the time I exhaled, I felt drained. I didn't want to fight with everyone.

"You know what? You're right. I haven't lived here in a while, and I guess I've forgotten about the Tennessee summer weather. Storing it in a cold, dry place is smart." I nodded enthusiastically. "Anyhow, I really should get back to Gram's house. I have a lot to sort through before we start baking tomorrow. What time do you normally start?"

He opened his mouth momentarily, before letting his jaw snap shut.

Blinking as though I was an apparition he could make disappear, he slowly slumped sideways until his shoulder landed against the walk-in. "Four," he said, finally.

"Okay." I tried to sound bright and cheerful, even though I could feel my mood descending into poundcake territory. Working side-by-side with Shane would test my emotional fortitude, especially if he kept insisting on looking so damn delicious.

CHAPTER 6

SHANE

a swarm of gnats jockeyed for position around my face, which dripped sweat after an hour of swinging an ax at a felled tree behind Clay's house.

A beetle infestation had savaged the tree last summer, but instead of cutting it down when its leaves turned brown, Clay bought a gardening book and started mixing his own fertilizers. He'd always had a green thumb when it came to smaller plants in his garden, so moving up to tree size didn't daunt him at all.

His interest in strange combinations of fertilizers eventually led an official from the Bureau of Alcohol, Tobacco, Firearms, and Explosives to show up on his doorstep. Apparently, some of the fertilizers were on a watchlist, having been used to make bombs.

Clay talked the guy's ear off for so long about arborist lore and beetles that I think he figured my brother was a different kind of nut job from the ones he needed to monitor. Meanwhile, the tree's been sitting in a meadow behind Clay's house, and if it stays much longer, it will turn into mulch.

Hence, my time out here with the ax.

No, Clay didn't exactly invite me to come chop wood, but I considered it implied. I also figured he wouldn't stop me when I was having a day aggravating enough to necessitate a couple of hours hacking away at lumber that was still too wet to split easily.

Like I cared.

"You shouldn't keep flour in the refrigerator."

Her words bounced around in my brain with an irritating echo that grew louder over time. She didn't live here anymore. What the hell did she know about keeping flour fresh in the Tennessee climate?

So what if the people in Los Angeles were dumb enough to pay seven dollars a loaf for her bread (Yes, I did some Googling.) Didn't make it special. It was just bread.

I heard the grind of large tires on the gravel drive as the ax fell again with a satisfying smack, the log splitting neatly in two.

Even slightly wet, the wood yielded beautifully to the blade.

And even after two hours, I hadn't scratched the surface of my annoyance.

"Whoa," Clay said, hopping out of his aging blue Toyota pickup and striding over to me without shutting the driver's side door. In his hand, he held a tall paper takeout cup and sipped through a straw. From the condensation dripping down the side, I could tell it was cold, and from Clay's smile, I surmised it was probably sweet tea. But hell if I'd ask him for some while in the throes of irritation.

Combining misery with sweet tea didn't seem fair to the tea.

Besides, with half a tree still lying on the ground in front of me, I had my work cut out. Stopping didn't seem like an option when I still had loads of frustration to take out on a pile of lumber.

Clay continued to stare at me as though waiting for a response. As far as I was concerned, his "whoa" didn't require an answer. He hadn't asked a question, and if he wondered what I was doing, he only had to look around for a few minutes to see I was chopping wood.

I did, however, think he should close the door to his truck. It's not like anyone would steal it or anything, but seeing it open messed with the part of my brain that liked order.

Even worse, he'd left the keys in the ignition, so after a moment, the truck started dinging a reminder. "You should get that," I grumbled, pointing to the open door.

But he didn't get it. He stood staring at me instead, so I ignored him right back.

"What the hell, Shane?"

Okay, so that was phrased as a question, but since it lacked specificity, I chose to ignore it as well.

Finally, knowing I could out-stubborn him when I was in one of my rare irritable moods, Clay turned and walked back to his truck, where he removed the key and shut the door. Then he came right back over to where I had a nice two-foot cut of wood balanced on a stump, ready for the next swing of my ax.

Chopping wood was always something I could do easily. My dad, surmising it might be something that only required me to balance my right hand against the handle, had me chopping wood at an age that would've gotten Child Protective Services up in arms if anyone had bothered to notify them. But since half the kids in the town were using sharp tools on gardens and trees before they could ride bikes, no one was going to turn him in.

Dad had been correct. Using my left hand to grip the handle allowed me to brace it with my right hand and use the power of my right shoulder to power the blade through the wood. I'd been doing it for so long I never really needed to hit the gym for an upper body workout.

And on days like today, chopping a tree into neat logs was purely a way to release stress.

"Why are you so worked up?" Clay stood so close to me I couldn't take another swing at the stump of wood without hitting him, so I stopped.

"Were you ever going to deal with this tree?" I looked in his direction, but I had so much sweat dripping down my face, I had to squint to see him. Mopping my forehead with my shirt sleeve, I winced at the sting of salt in my eyes.

"Eventually, I would've. But you're not gonna stand here and tell me you're chopping a red oak into matchsticks just because you're worried I might not get to it."

I rolled my eyes now that I could open them. "Needed to blow off steam. You know how it is."

He nodded, crossing his arms over his chest. "'Course I do. What I don't know is why. Who yucked your yum?" His satisfied grin let me know he understood how much I hated that expression, which meant he was goading me toward next-level grumpiness.

Couldn't show him the satisfaction. I did such a good imitation of a smile it hurt.

Nudging the ax out of my hand, he gestured to a pair of Adirondack chairs in the shade of a poplar tree. Since my back ached so badly I felt like it might split in two if I swung the ax again, I relented and followed him. It was easily ten degrees cooler in the shade, and Clay produced a second to-go cup of iced tea from somewhere I hadn't noticed.

I gratefully took it from his hand, tore the top off, and slugged down half its contents in one gulp. "Thanks," I said, feeling my spirits lift with the sugar rush.

"No prob. When you said you were starting on the tree, I figured you meant to cut it into a few chunks and haul them 'round back. But seeing how you're fixing to finish the entire job in an afternoon, I'm thinking I should go inside for the scotch." He cast me a side-eye, waiting for an explanation.

"Yeah, maybe you should. 'Cause two hours of hacking at timber hasn't touched my irritation with Julia Browne."

He nodded and rubbed a hand over his dark beard. I called it his "teacher stall." Whenever he didn't immediately have the answer to a question from one of his students, he looked toward a corner of the room and stroked his beard. When a student asked, "If banana slugs have both male and female genitalia, do they still have sex?" it bought him some time to come up with an answer that would allow him to be honest with his students while not getting him in trouble with the school board.

"What are you trying not to say?" I asked, unwilling to give him time to come up with a lie.

He shook his head. "Just that it seems like you're awfully worked up about someone you profess not to care about."

"I don't care about her, but when she shows up and *professes* to do my job better than me, I have a few choice words to say about it."

"Yeah? What are the words?"

"Things to the effect of, 'why don't you go back to California and take your ordinary bread with you?'"

I saw the dawn of understanding. "She's out-baking you?"

"Not what I said."

He raised his straw to his lips and took a sip, but it didn't hide his smile. "So it's merely a competitive thing. Has nothing to do with the fact that you never got over her."

"Keep saying that and I'll disown you."

"You can't. You didn't own me in the first place."

I closed my eyes for a loaded moment, giving myself a last chance at deflecting the conversation and not getting into it with Clay. Once I opened the floodgate and started talking, he'd be involved. And that meant opinions.

Yeah, maybe I wanted his opinions. Not because he had a proven relationship track record of any sort—the past few years had revealed plenty of glitches in his radar for women. But he was my best friend and the closest thing I had to a wingman.

In other words, I didn't have a lot of options if I wanted a place to vent my frustrations over Julia. So I let loose. "It's all kinds of things. Yes, it's competitive because I've been baking here for upwards of two years, and no one's ever suggested my bread needed improvement. And suddenly hers is sought-after countywide or something? Plus, it's the way she comes in here like she invented baking. Questioning why I keep flour in the walk-in when it's hot as blazes and the humidity's near a hundred percent. Just because she names a bakery The Bread Winner doesn't make it good. She moved away, and Green Valley was doing just fine without her damn secret sauce or whatever the hell she pretends she puts in her stupid dough. It's just bread. It has three ingredients, maybe four if you count the water."

I stopped to take a breath. Man, it felt good to say it all out loud. While I was at the bakery, I'd been holding my tongue, and for the past two hours of chopping wood, I'd stewed silently and let the satisfying sound of metal hitting wood be the conversation.

But it felt good to say the words.

"It's called The Bread Winner? I kinda like it."

"Disowned."

"So . . . to sum up . . . you're still hung up on her. You have it just as bad for her now as you did at seventeen." Clay did his beard stroking thing again and looked at the sky. For some reason, it made me glance upward, and I noticed the sharp contrast between the cerulean blue patches of sky and the green leaves that punctuated it.

Leave it to that woman to get me so worked up that I forgot to look at the sky.

CHAPTER 7

SHANE

I wouldn't say I dreaded the first day of work with Julia in the bakery kitchen. More like I anticipated it with the enthusiasm of a painful dental procedure without anesthesia.

She was just so certain her bread was superior to what I'd been baking for years. Successfully. With joy.

In the years since I returned to Green Valley, not once had anyone complained about my bread. And I always refrigerated my fucking flour.

So maybe I had just a small bit of attitude when she walked in the door at five minutes past four in the morning. And maybe she deserved it. Still, I said nothing.

I did, however, make a point of looking at my watch.

Nodding, Julia took a large red purse from across her body and hung it on a hook by the door. Unable to take my eyes off the thing, I examined its brass buckles and several outer pockets. The bag was big enough to fit two sourdough loaves. What the hell does a person carry in a purse that large?

"What do you carry in that?"

"I'm sorry?" she said, tying her hair back and putting an apron on over her white T-shirt and jeans. "What do I carry in what?"

I pointed to the purse, which was now partially obscured by a long tan cardigan sweater that had maroon and white argyle shapes on the front. "Do you cart around livestock in your purse?"

She huffed a laugh and tossed a hand in the direction of the door. "Just, you know, essentials. I read."

I had no idea what reading had to do with her purse unless it was loaded with paperbacks, but with her walking in late and my bread schedule already behind, I decided to ferry her along with our baking plans for the day.

Pointing to a chalkboard where I'd listed the orders and the timetable for delivery, I explained my strategy. "We can get twenty-four loaves out of the two ovens per bake, and the lodge needs seventy for each weekend of guests, on top of the one hundred twenty we normally bake for Daisy's and our regular customers, so—"

"Wait, hang on," Julia said, walking over to the chalkboard and picking up a piece of chalk. Very protective of my chalkboard and my baking schedule, I was having none of that.

I moved to the board as well, blocking it with my body and holding her off with outstretched hands. "Put down the chalk, lady." I reached for it as though disarming a hot-headed gangster and placed it in my pocket when she relented.

"Possessive of your agenda?" She rolled her eyes and turned around to study the board again.

"Not possessive, but I don't think it needs editing, either." I folded my arms across my chest and watched as her eyes surveyed me, starting with my forearms, moving up to my shoulders, and ending on my face. I had no idea what she thought of me, but based on her expression, it wasn't good.

"Fine. Just tell me the timeline."

"Timeline?"

"I like to know what's ahead."

I huffed a laugh and resisted the temptation to roll my eyes. "Baking bread."

She shook her head and I prepared myself for some choice words, but after pressing her lips together, she said only, "Okay."

"Okay?"

"Yeah. Okay."

"Okay."

I stared at her. She stared back. No one else had come to the bakery yet, which wasn't unusual since the pastries didn't need proofing or rising time the same way the bread loaves did, but Joy had been in such a tizzy about having the "famous" bread maker in the house that I felt certain she'd show up an hour early and roll out a red carpet or some ridiculous thing.

"I know how to manage a large order," I told her, pissed at myself for sounding like a defensive toddler, but she'd gotten my dander up the second she walked in here with her big reputation and her big . . . purse.

She didn't answer. Just stared at the board, her eyes moving down the columns until she finally seemed satisfied enough to turn around.

Then she said nothing.

"What?" I asked, ready to be annoyed at whatever came out of her mouth.

"I didn't say anything."

"Doesn't mean you're not thinking it."

Rolling her eyes, she plowed past me and went over to the containers of sourdough starters. She picked one up, and I immediately felt possessive, waiting for her to tell me I'd stored it wrong. Maybe they put the jars upside down out there in California.

Gingerly unscrewing the lid, Julia tipped her nose into the jar and inhaled, her eyes closing briefly. I watched the air fill her lungs and a contented smile spread across her face. "Is there anything in the world better than that smell?"

I could think of a few things, but I held my tongue, assuming a criticism of some sort would follow.

When I didn't respond, she replaced the lid and cocked her head in my direction. "Do you not like it?" she asked.

"No, I do."

"Okay, then. So we agree on that."

"We do."

"Okay. I'm gonna leave you to it then and get to work on the French bread."

It felt like someone had smacked me hard with a frying pan like a cartoon character. There had to be tweety birds circling my head, that's how shocked I felt.

"Wait, what?" I stammered, my eyes roaming over the jars of starter, looking for something wrong with them, wanting to assist her in finding fault and thereby getting my dander up.

"I figured since you're the sourdough baker here and half the order is for French, I'd take that part. Isn't that what you're little diagram suggests?" She gestured to my chalkboard. Just when I'd been about to consider her friendly, I had reason to get annoyed.

"It's not little."

"Wow. Compensating?" She looked me up and . . . down.

I kept my eyes locked on hers until she blushed. Satisfied, I pointed to the board. "My prep table maps out the order and the timetable for delivery, along with bake times and distribution of labor. I didn't divide the jobs because I assumed you'd want to bake your 'famous' bread." I may have used air quotes.

The flush deepened and she let out a long exhale through clenched teeth. "Fine. This is your home turf, and I'm just visiting. Why don't you tell me what kind of division of labor you'd like? I'll bake whatever you tell me."

Well, that threw me for a loop. Her being agreeable made it infinitely harder to be as irritated with her as I wanted to be.

And that irritated me.

"So . . . " I stammered. "You'll bake only the French bread? You're fine with that?"

"Sure." She was so calm, wiping her hands down the front of her apron and staring at me, challenging me not to get lost in her eyes, which were the color of chocolate cake.

The moment took me back ten years to a time when I'd faced a similar challenge. Back then, I'd yielded to reason. I'd been strong, known my limits. Looking into her eyes when I was seventeen was a cautionary tale, and I'd heeded its lessons without having to endure the pain of experiencing them.

But now . . . all these years later, did I really possess the resolve and perseverance to resist her again? Did I want to?

Exhaling a long breath, I determined to push those thoughts to a later date. Easier to focus on the division of bread labor. "Okay, well, great."

"Great." Her clench relented into a sort of half smile.

Was it great? The ease with which she'd agreed to basically be my apprentice alarmed me. Almost like she was lulling me into a false sense of calm before she took over the entire operation.

"Actually, no."

"No?" Was she fluttering her eyelashes, or was I still a version of the lovestruck seventeen-year-old who thought that even a glance from a girl equaled true love?

"I was just thinking that you own all these bakeries in Los Angeles, right? You're famous for your bread, and to hear Monsieur Auclair tell it, people will be sad if you're here and they don't get to experience what you bake. He said you're the next best thing to sliced bread."

Her face grew so serious I worried for a second that something was wrong. Then she started to laugh. "Did he really say that?"

"He . . . um, no."

"I kind of wish he had. So corny, so good."

I looked at my chalkboard again and started to rethink how we should divide up the jobs. "Actually, maybe we should work together on all of it. Compare notes, figure out rising times and get the most out of the oven space."

She shrugged. "Okay, we can do that."

"Okay," I said. Maybe this would be okay.

Or maybe it would be as awful as I'd imagined.

CHAPTER 8

JULIA

J'd gone to bed with my mood hovering somewhere near burnt pastry at the way Shane's eyes raked over me disapprovingly. Like he held me responsible for Monsieur Auclair's fanboy reception.

When our shift ended, it marked the third time in as many days that being in Shane's presence again made me run, not walk, to get away from him. If we were going to be working together daily, I'd best invest in a new pair of running shoes.

As soon as he told me what time to meet him at the bakery the next morning, I grabbed my purse and hurried from the place, saying a quick goodbye to Blithe in the front as I made my way out the door.

The satisfying slap of metal when I shut my car door made me feel protected from the outside world, protected enough that I let my proud shoulders slump for the first time since arriving in town.

In LA, I felt proud of my accomplishments. I didn't question my daily routine. I thrived.

But upon my return, I was already starting to notice what I'd been missing in my life—the rhythmic chorus of cicadas in the trees, the calming breeze as it filtered across an open landscape, the simplicity of daily activities—and it hurt that I knew it was temporary.

It meant I couldn't relax into the place and get into a groove. Everywhere I turned, I seemed to bump up against resistance.

So I fell back on old habits that had served me well—when I felt the creep of unhappiness, I fled. I came by those tendencies honestly, the child of parents who bolted.

Our parents were what could kindly be described as "inquisitive wanderers," though few people around here generally felt kindly toward them after abandoning their children to see the world. But Gram didn't seem to hold their peripatetic ways against them.

"Wanderlust is an affliction like anything else. There's no curing it, only taming it until it rears up again, bigger and more virulent than the last time," Gram told us when she decided my brother and I were old enough to understand that our parents weren't just on a long vacation—they weren't coming back.

Born in the 1960s, they took inspiration from Jack Kerouac and hit the road whenever they could. Initially, they took us with them, but traveling with two small children apparently became a burden, so they moved us to Green Valley to stay with Gram while they saw the world for weeks at a time. Eventually, weeks turned to months.

Then they went a year without coming back. I was ten years old.

Gram filed for custody and took over without any hand wringing about it.

I'd always suspected my brother Daniel might take after our parents once he got old enough to leave the nest. That, or he'd be dead weight that Gram would support well into his twenties. The saving grace was that Gram loved him to pieces and taking care of him filled the void when I moved away.

Leaving uncomfortable situations behind had always felt brave to me. I wasn't scared to face the unknown, and it always had potential.

When I left the bakery at the end of my shift, I did not look back. I did not second guess my decision to drive straight home and drop into the tub in my childhood bathroom, where I stayed for an hour, literally stewing in my own juices.

I skipped dinner, my appetite having gone the way of day-old bread—not worth having when there was a promise of something better the next day. Then, I put myself to bed, just like Gram would've done had she been alive. It comforted me to think of her standing over me like an angel, telling me to rest my head and let the day go.

I slept for nine solid hours for the first time in over two years.

* * *

Morning crept in like it was trying not to wake anyone who might be hungover from whatever they did last night. The sunlight eased through the trees, filtered by leaves and a haze that would likely burn off within the hour. It was as if someone knew that too much brightness at once would make people cranky.

Not people, just my brother.

If Shane Meadows still had the ability to heat me up like I was standing over the stove, only one person on planet earth had the ability to push me right into the oven and turn up the fire.

"You don't need to make so much noise. Some of us are trying to sleep." Daniel Seth Browne padded toward me in tasseled mukluk slippers and a long orange bathrobe that had seen some years of wear. Brown hair sticking up at all angles, his face was twisted into a grimace, his eyes nearly squeezed shut.

Yet he moved through the living room toward the coffee pot on the kitchen counter as if directed by GPS. I didn't bother to defend myself or say a single word until he'd poured his coffee, lightened it with a healthy pour of cream, and taken a large sip.

Then a second.

Finally, his eyes blinked and opened a few millimeters. They were so blue that even a mere slit brightened up the room despite his surly demeanor. Not a morning person, if that wasn't obvious enough.

"The only noise I was making produced that coffee you're enjoying. So, you're welcome." He brought out the practical, parental side of me.

I sipped my own coffee, not needing to look at him to know he was scowling at me.

"I didn't say thank you."

"I'm aware."

"You're just as much fun as ever, sis."

I took a deep breath and let it out slowly, just like I always did when my brother got on my nerves. My Gram had advised me to do it back when we were kids, but more often than not, I'd haul off and punch him when he made me mad.

Then, he'd cry, and because he was the baby, my parents would come down on me for beating up on him, never believing that he was the instigator.

But Gram knew. She always knew. Back then, I never questioned how she could be cooking a chicken pot pie two rooms away and come in mid-fight, nodding her head and beckoning me over for a few pearls of wisdom.

57

STACY TRAVIS

"You're older. You're always going to look like the bad guy until he grows and he's bigger than you. And when that happens, look out because he'll whup you, and it won't matter that you're crying because those tears will sting."

It took me a few more go-rounds where I'd hit back and taken the punishment before I heeded my Gram's advice and started breathing my way to some kind of serenity.

My thoughts jumped to how proud she'd probably be that I still used the technique now, followed by sadness that I'd missed the final four years of a great woman's life by staying away for so long.

"Tell me some things," I said quietly, seating myself on one of the twin burlwood stumps-on-legs that served as seats at the breakfast bar.

"What kinds of things?" He said the words, but I couldn't be certain whether he was sleep-talking or having an actual conversation.

"The good Gram stuff. Hilarious things she said on the daily, fun things you two did together." Daniel may have been lazy, but that made for a perfect companion for a spry septuagenarian with money in her pocketbook. I had no doubt she and Daniel had gone on a few adventures and right now, I needed to feel a sense of Gram's spirit.

Daniel's eyes edged open a bit more, gracing me with more placid blue. I took another cleansing breath. A person didn't need breathing exercises if my damned brother would just open his eyes all the way. They provided the serenity of a hundred Buddhist monks.

"Um, okay. Guess I'm gonna need to think back."

Taking a giant gulp from his cup and looking at the ceiling for seconds at least, he came over and joined me on the other burlwood seat. "These are not comfortable."

"You live here and you're just figuring this out?" It didn't shock me. Daniel had never been the most observant of the bunch.

He rolled his eyes, another proficiency of his. "Do you think I sat myself here at the counter and drank coffee alone? The couch is way more comfortable." He hitched a thumb over his shoulder to where a lumpy brown leather couch half-covered by a rainbow patchwork quilt absorbed the sunlight filtering through the paned window above it.

"Oh." I knew better than to fly into town and disrupt the way he normally did things with Gram. "We can sit over there if that's where you guys usually had breakfast."

I moved to the couch and sat, closing my eyes at the familiar groan of the stiff leather when it took my weight. Memories of time I'd spent here as

58

a child flooded my brain like someone had knocked the rust off a spigot and tested it at full volume. So much that I sucked in a breath that sounded like a gasp.

Daniel didn't budge from his hardwood perch. "Who's 'you guys'? You mean, when I'd have a date spend the night?"

Now it was my turn for an eye roll. I didn't need a play-by-play of his dating escapades, though I had no doubt he'd share them if I asked. He'd never had an issue with public displays of anything, and I couldn't imagine why that would change, just because he lived with his grandmother. Poor woman probably lost a few years off her life just trying to unhear some of what went on here.

"I meant you and Gram."

"What about us?"

"I was saying, if this is where you and Gram liked to hang out, it works for me."

He stared at me for so long I started to wonder if he'd lost some brain cells from working construction. He cocked his head and stared some more, pressing his lips together and watching me. I took a sip of my coffee, then put it on the oval coffee table that had hinged sides, all four of which were propped up on their stays, making the table as large as possible.

Daniel had been silent for so long, the low timbre of his voice shocked me out of my reminiscences about long-ago days in Gram's house. "You do know how it was, don't you?"

Having no idea what he meant, I met his gaze. The stony stare softened when I squinted in confusion. "How what was?"

He ran a hand through his hair and leaned his head back, inhaling a long breath.

"Okay, I can see you're annoyed, and I don't want to start us off on the wrong foot. If we could just try to get along . . . I know Gram would want that—"

"You don't know shit." The sympathy was gone from his face.

"Excuse me?"

"You think Gram and I were having tea here in the kitchen for the last two years? Maybe playing bridge or baking cookies together?"

"I don't know—"

"That's right. You don't. Gram was sick. Really sick. We weren't sitting on those ridiculous barstools. She'd have fallen right over."

I blinked as though it would clarify what I'd just heard. Because it couldn't possibly be correct.

"Wait, what? She was healthy. She died suddenly." Maybe I could still unhear what I thought he'd said.

"She was sick," he said quietly.

I blinked a few times, speechless. If what Daniel was telling me was true, he had every right to be furious with me for not showing my face here for four years. Another reason why I really wanted to have misheard him. I was almost afraid to meet the anger and resentment in his eyes.

But when our eyes connected, I saw sadness and what looked like pity. "It's been a long time coming. Probably seemed quick to you because you didn't see her day to day, but she was deteriorating. It was a long slow decline." He didn't say it with blame or judgment, but it didn't matter. I was busy judging myself.

My hand went to my chest, and I stared at him, processing what he was saying. It seemed impossible. I'd just seen my Gram, and she'd been spry and healthy. "I don't get it. She seemed fine when I was here last."

A muscle in Daniel's jaw ticked, and I could tell he was trying to be patient, also something I never experienced in my brother before. He'd always been the first one to fly off the handle at the slightest whiff of an insult or a slight. His temper was legendary.

"That was years ago, Jules." He hadn't used that nickname since we were kids. The strain in his voice made it seem like he was frustrated and trying not to show it.

"I know. I meant to come sooner."

That elicited a bark of a laugh. "No, you didn't. If you'd wanted to come, you'd have come."

I clenched my teeth, digging in for the knock-down drag-out fight I'd been expecting to have since my plane landed. "That's not true. A person can want something and not be able to do it because of . . . reasons. I wanted to come, but I had a bakery to run. You know I've been working like a dog. I promise you that if I'd been able to get away even for a weekend, I'd have been here. Especially if I knew she wasn't doing well."

He scoffed at that, slapping a hand through the air. "I call bullshit on that, sis. I know you loved Gram and all, but every time I texted and asked if you'd be coming out, you said you couldn't find the time."

"Because I didn't know she was sick."

"Your logic is flawed." He picked up his cup and walked to the living room area and sat in a sagging green wingchair opposite me.

Incredulous, I glared at him. "I'd have come."

Daniel shrugged, apparently having no idea how annoyed a shrug from any male made me these days, thanks to the painful trail of disaffection left behind by Trevor. "Whatever lets you sleep at night."

Now I was getting angry. I felt goaded on by the absurdly calm Daniel, who could always be depended upon to fly off the handle and make me appear like the rational one. His attitude threw everything off, and I had a feeling he knew it.

"Stop being so calm." My voice pitched up, and I hated the way it made me feel unglued and hysterical.

He chuckled quietly. "No point in getting worked up."

"No?"

"No."

"Easy for you to say. You're not the one who's just hearing now that her beloved grandparent was sick for nearly two years and she never knew about it."

He crossed his arms over his chest again and did that head tilt thing again, looking at me as though I was quaint or unusual. He was playing some kind of game of chicken, waiting me out, certain I'd say something regrettable if left to my own.

I wouldn't play into it. I wouldn't say a thing. That was the beauty of being the older sibling. I had more life experience. More control over my emotions.

We stared at each other a little longer.

"What?" I finally blurted.

His lips tipped up into a smile. I knew he felt superior because I'd caved first, but I loved seeing evidence of happiness on his face. He'd always be my little brother, and I'd always wish for the best for him.

"You did know. About Gram. I texted you."

I'd also always worry that he was drinking too much whiskey to keep his brain straight. "You did not."

"I did."

There was no point in arguing with him when I could produce proof. I whipped my phone from the pocket of my denim cutoff shorts and scrolled through the text exchanges between us starting about a year ago.

Daniel: Can you make it out for a visit? It would mean a lot to Gram. It might give her a lift.

Me: Yes, of course. Let me look at my schedule and get back to you.

A month after that, another exchange between the two of us was more or less the same. It surprised me that I hadn't responded to either one, if only to explain that the bakery was crazy and I was stressed about our frozen bread operation that was losing money faster than an open faucet raining hundred dollar bills.

Daniel got a little more insistent with the more recent texts, and now that he'd told me about Gram's ailing health, I could put it into context that had eluded me three months ago.

Daniel: You should come out here. Gram would like to see you and I have no idea how long she's going to make it, so you should really get yourself on a plane.

Me: She can be pretty dramatic, can't she? Lol.

Reading the texts in hindsight, I had a whole different understanding of Daniel's words. Would it have killed him to pick up the phone when it seemed clear I wasn't understanding the gravity of the situation?

I scrolled through a few more exchanges where I basically blew off any hint from him that Gram would benefit from my presence. I could see now that he was urging me to visit her before it was too late, and in the usual fire drill that was my average day at the bakery, I took only the headline news from any message.

Finally, I landed on the most recent couple of texts between us.

Daniel: I'd fly out if I were you. Things aren't looking so hot for Gram and I'm worried you'll miss her if you don't come.

Me: I do miss her. Please tell her that. And I'll try my hardest to plan a trip this summer.

Daniel: That will definitely be too late.

In every exchange, I'd promised a reply and left him hanging.

Every. Single. Time.

That couldn't be correct. "Wait, hang on. Maybe I'm thinking of emails. I know I answered you."

Daniel leaned back in his chair and tipped his head to lean against the high back of the chair. Propping his feet on the coffee table, he shook his head. "Don't bother. You're not going to find what you're looking for."

"Why, did you selectively delete conversations?"

"Nope."

I bit my lower lip, trying to puzzle through alternate scenarios, unwilling to believe I'd dropped the ball. It was so unlike me, a crack multitasker who'd been keeping multiple balls in the air for as long as I could walk.

But . . . I'd dropped the ball.

Dropping my head into my hands, I felt an overwhelming wave of sadness take over. "Oh my God, Daniel. I'm so sorry."

I couldn't even look him in the eye. Sitting here in our childhood home with my only brother and without the woman who'd saved us by taking us in, I tried to push back the tears that welled in the corners of my eyes.

"Hey, Jules, don't be so hard on yourself. It's okay. I handled things." His voice was soft, even, forgiving. He had no reason to be patient with me, and yet he was.

"I should've come. When you first texted. Or called you at least."

"Well, sure. That would've been nice." When I looked at him, he didn't seem smug. His easy smile comforted me when I had no right to be comforted.

"How are you such a good guy?"

He shook his head like he couldn't believe I was so dumb. "I was raised by two amazing women."

My brain spun back to the years we'd spent with our mom around, barely any that I could remember. I couldn't figure out how he could recall them. "You remember Mom?"

"Not Mom. Gram," he said. "And you."

Whatever willpower still holding back my tears collapsed. As I sobbed— for Gram, for myself, for lost opportunities and time spent with people at work who didn't really know me. Daniel came closer, hesitantly at first. Then he reached out and wrapped me in his arms.

For the first time in my life, I let him.

CHAPTER 9

SHANE

*T*his was going to be awful.

I stood kneading a batch of dough before its first rise, working it hard with both hands, as Julia watched me.

"You have a nice technique," she observed.

I appreciated the compliment, but I couldn't help thinking she was observing me through bread ego-colored glasses, and that bugged me.

"Well, my pound of flesh makes for good kneading," I said, holding up my right hand. I wasn't lying. Without fingers getting in the way, I always got a better knead out of that hand. She didn't respond. At least not about my hand.

"Can we at least talk about the flour?"

I groaned and tried to drown out the request by turning on the mixer.

The day had been going well. We'd baked half the loaves we needed for the Lodge and still had plenty of time to get the rest into the ovens. I hated to admit that Jenn had been right about needing an extra pair of hands, but it was nice to have Julia's help.

Julia reached over and turned it off. She waited impatiently for me to face her, and when I did, I tried not to notice how the loose strands from her ponytail floated around her face like summer fireflies paying respect.

I tried not to set sail in her eyes which had always done crazy things to my equilibrium and were now threatening to knock me off my feet.

And I tried to listen to what she was saying without watching her lips move because when I did that, I wanted to reach out and touch them and know if they were as soft as they looked.

It had only taken one day of working together for me to remember how I felt as a shy seventeen-year-old who couldn't believe the outgoing, popular senior was giving him the time of day. And even less time to feel mortified about how things ended.

"Shane, the flour."

"Are you really going to give me shit about refrigerating the flour again?" I turned the mixer back on.

She turned it off. "You're going to ruin this batch if you keep doing that," I warned. Each time she reached for the switch, her arm brushed across my chest, sending a suggestive thrill through every part of my body, dead ending at my dick.

She moved in between me and the mixer to block my access. We were inches apart, and my body temperature ratcheted up a few degrees from the proximity. "It'll survive," she said.

It may, but will I?

I folded my arms, blocking her from getting closer. "Fine. What about the flour?"

"We should source it from local growers. Speaks to the whole farm-to-table ethic they have at the lodge."

"Oh. That's actually not a bad idea," I had to say it because it was true.

"Wow." She crossed her arms.

"What?"

"You gave me a double negative, but I think you just agreed with me."

Pressing my lips together, I regarded her. "I agreed with you."

"Great. So . . . maybe you'd even go so far as to call it a *good* idea?" Her smirk challenged me, and I accepted.

"Fine. I agree. I'll run it by Jenn."

She looked elated, and I had to take several steps away from her and go back to fussing with my sourdough starter. It was the only way to maintain composure in the face of her smile. "So . . . road trip?"

No, I couldn't have heard that correctly. I spun to face her. "I'm sorry, what?"

"We'll take a road trip on our next day off, spend some time meeting with local growers, make a decision on where to buy. If Jenn approves, that is."

It took me a moment to digest the implications of Julia's proposition.

Her. Me. In a car. All day long.

We were getting along for the moment, but that didn't mean we could handle an entire day together on the road. We'd probably want to kill each other by the end of the day, but that might be just the convincing my dick needed to turn around and back away slowly.

It would probably be awful. I'd probably come back not being able to stand the sight of her.

And that would be a goddamn relief.

* * *

"I'm worried you're in over your head," Clay said as we sanded the deck off the back of my house. I'd been meaning to do it for months. And I'd deny to anyone who asked that my sudden interest in home renovation had anything to do with wanting the place to look nice in case a certain visiting baker ever stopped by.

Deny, deny, deny.

"Getting right to the point, I see." I'd admit nothing, especially to my older brother who thought he knew everything. At only four years older than me, he couldn't possibly know much more than I did. At least, that had been the party line since the days when he enjoyed bossing me around as kids.

And who was I kidding? He'd probably boss me around now if I gave him the chance. I wouldn't.

The sander in my hand had stopped working because I'd worked the round of sandpaper until no sand remained. As I changed out the paper, I took a moment to check Clay's progress on his corner of the deck.

The cedar wood looked rosy and pristine, but I knew its color would fade unless we double-coated it with sealant. "You think we can get all this sanded today?" I asked him, not really needing his thoughts on the matter, but trying to engage him in something other than conversation about my head and how far underwater I already was with Julia.

But my stubborn brother was not easily distracted. "Yeah, if we stay on it. I've got a few hours to spare before I'm supposed to meet the guys at Genie's. You're welcome to come, you know."

He always offered; I mostly declined.

Sometimes I thought the reason he offered so readily was that he knew I'd say no, and he could look magnanimous without risk of having me tag along.

"The guys" were a few of Clay's fellow teachers at the high school, a few of their friends, and so on. It didn't much matter how one of the guys ended up one of the guys. Once he was in, he was in for life.

As Clay's brother, I had a sort of honorary "one of the guys" status, though I rarely went anywhere with them. This afternoon, however, I might be tempted, given how uneasy I felt now that Julia and I seemed to be in uncharted waters.

"You do this. It's a pattern with you," Clay said, never taking his eyes off the sander, which he had going at a low speed so we could be heard over its grinding sound. At this rate, we'd never finish the deck, and I had to weigh my interest in talking to him against my desire for progress.

"There's no pattern."

"You fixate on something—this time it's a woman—until you either figure out how to tame it to your liking or it blows up in your face. Since she appears to be of the untamable sort, I'm worried about the second option."

"No need to worry. I have it all in hand."

"Yeah?"

"Absolutely."

Since I had very little interest in having my brother dissect my life, I pushed him to turn up the speed and finish the job.

He looked at me skeptically. "It's a pattern…"

"It's not a pattern, and I'm not in over my head. We're just taking a road trip to look at some wheat. Now, let's get this thing done."

He nodded, barely able to keep the knowing grin from his face. "Sure thing, boss."

We were just taking a road trip to look at wheat.

I'd keep telling myself until I believed it.

CHAPTER 10

JULIA

"So, was Jenn just okay with sourcing local wheat or did she actually like the idea?" It may have seemed like two sides of the same coin, but as a fellow bakery owner, it mattered to me that she approved.

"She liked the farm-to-table approach for the bread, but she's going to keep on importing her cake and pastry flour from a supplier in Knoxville who sources it from Europe. Fewer pesticides, better taste, specific to cakes and pastries."

"That's smart. I like that." In fact, I loved it. Jenn was my kind of people.

"Yeah, a while back we kind of had a separation of church and state, her staying in charge of pastry—pies, cake, cream puffs—with me taking over bread, bagels, crisps, and the like. I always keep her in the loop, but she trusts me to choose which farmer to hire for the new flour."

I nodded, having anticipated his description of their division of responsibilities. Jenn had done exactly as I would have, but hearing about Shane's easy working relationship made me realize I didn't even know how he'd started baking in the first place.

"I don't even know how you started baking in the first place." I stared at his profile as he drove, enjoying the fact that I had license to stare since we were having a conversation, after all. I allowed myself to appreciate the strong line of his jaw, the nicely-manicured shape of his dark beard, and the way his generous lips quirked to the side when he thought I'd said something funny.

They were quirked as such right now.

"You never asked."

"I'm asking now."

"I have a thing for bread." The quirk edged up into a smile. I gawked at his smile like a bread groupie.

"Go on."

"My mom baked, I paid attention." He held up his right hand and dropped it back into his lap. "Seeing as how I've got my own personal power tool for kneading dough. When I was in college, I baked a lot. It was…a bit of a stress release."

His brow furrowed. I wanted to know the source of his stress. I wanted to know everything, but this was the first real conversation we'd had since high school, so I wanted to tread carefully. As if trying not to scare off a trembling rabbit.

I nodded like I understood, hoping that eventually I would.

"Anyhow. Once I came back to Green Valley and saw how Jenn had built something cool with pies and cakes, I offered my services. Been a great working relationship ever since. And I do love it."

At his admission, my head hit the seat rest. His words jabbed at me like bloodthirsty mosquitoes. After working my tail off building The Bread Winner, I should have been able to heartily second the sentiment. But I couldn't, and the niggling thought grated at me.

Why don't I love it?

Then, there were other thoughts like how I couldn't see myself leaving Green Valley anytime soon.

I probably should have predicted that the reality of breezing into town and selling a house would be much harder than the *idea* of breezing into town and selling a house.

For one thing, this wasn't just a house.

At age eleven, I'd learned to roller skate out front in the street, practicing for hours until I could do figure eights while skating backward. I'd rejected the ordinary white laces and replaced them with green ones that matched the wheels. I'd scraped both knees in a series of falls until I learned to use the toe stops to slow my pace.

And after each of those falls, Gram stood at the door, waiting with rubbing alcohol to clean my wounds and cookies to reward me for not squirming through the pain.

Back when my brother and I were an unstoppable twosome, we played hide and seek inside the house, even though I always knew he'd broken the rules and found someplace to hide outdoors, just to make it harder for me to find him. He also changed hiding spots as the game went on, perching inside cupboards where I'd already looked, slithering along on the carpet and slipping behind doors while I checked behind furniture.

My first kiss took place on the front porch. My first real hookup was in the flatbed of my boyfriend's truck under a tree and out of view of the house.

The place was a home. My home. Filled with memories and all the pieces of myself that I'd lost along the way when I moved to California and stubbornly refused to come back.

For the first few days of this trip, maybe there was a chance of keeping my emotions in a lockbox and taking care of business. But once I talked to my brother and started seeing him as the brother I remembered, all objectivity went out the window.

And in pretty short order, the idea of selling my childhood home became a whole lot more complicated.

So I took the occasion of my long drive with Shane to talk through my options while we visited three different wheat growers.

"I mean, I guess I could just keep it. The mortgage is paid off, so it's really only property taxes and upkeep, but that can get unwieldy with a place that large, especially if I'm not around to manage it," I said, immediately putting the whole issue into financial terms and thinking about the implications. I still hadn't ascertained Daniel's income, and even though I knew he was gainfully employed and sharp as a hive of wasps, that didn't mean he had the will or the interest in keeping the place up.

"What's your situation back home?" Shane kept his eyes on the road but a muscle ticked in his jaw after he said the words.

"My situation?" I wasn't being coy. "You mean my finances? Can I afford it?"

"No." The muscle jumped again as he signaled and merged the truck onto the open highway. Pale rolling hills of grass flanked the road on both sides, and the clouds painted long shadows where the sun dipped between them.

For the first time since the funeral, I felt my spirits lift with the serenity of verdant open space. It was almost as though the clear landscape ahead pried open a piece of me that hadn't been allowed to breathe before.

Immersed in my thoughts, I didn't immediately realize that Shane hadn't elaborated on his answer to my question. Instead, he'd turned his head to a midway point between me and the road ahead and was alternately glancing between me and the highway. His driving was absolutely steady, yet he somehow managed to make constant eye contact.

A skill. One of many, I was learning.

"Sorry, I think I spaced out there for a sec." Trying to lure myself back on track, I widened my eyes and focused on the roped muscles of his forearms which were partially visible under the pushed-up sleeves of his Henley.

"You apologize for things you shouldn't." His eyes went back to the road, and the blunt declaration, which normally might have taken me aback, didn't feel like criticism.

"You should know I'm fighting my every instinct not to apologize for apologizing."

When I heard a noise I didn't immediately recognize, I turned and saw him quietly laughing, his lips pulled apart to reveal a boyish, dazzling smile. I felt an alarming flip in my belly and quickly tamped down the errant feeling. "What's funny?"

He shook his head. "I realize we don't know each other well anymore, but you seem like a person who doesn't suffer fools. So why apologize for them?"

"Habit."

Waving a hand in the air, he agreed. "Thought so. Therefore, I don't accept your apology."

"Well, you can't because I rescind it."

"Good."

"Fine."

"I'm not really certain whether we're agreeing or arguing," I said, looking out the window. More rolling hills, more tall trees whipping past. And I was more intrigued by Shane Meadows than I had been when I got into his truck.

We sat silently for a few minutes, and it didn't seem strange that no music played on the radio. I almost felt equally comfortable not talking in his presence as I did talking, which was unusual for me. I generally filled gaps in conversation with mindless blather that kept anyone from being uncomfortable, least of all me.

But now, without the conversation, I realized I had no discomfort with silence at all.

Interesting.

Maybe it was because a part of me was still that spurned teenager who didn't understand why the boy she liked had rejected her. I'd been a tad overdramatic back then, prone to running away instead of staying at the table to figure things out. I feared it was genetic.

I didn't particularly want to relive that night again now, even if I remembered it like it was yesterday. But the thoughts wormed their way in anyway —how decisive Shane had been, how certain he didn't want me. I couldn't force myself to believe that anyone capable of such a frosty robotic response back then was capable of being much more human now.

And that was fine. I didn't need him to be my boyfriend or even my friend. I needed him to drive me around to look at wheat. So far, so good.

"So, you were telling me about your situation back home," he said, snapping me out of my reverie. We turned onto a larger highway headed north. I decided to trust that he knew where we were going since I didn't recognize any landmarks.

I also insisted on correcting him. "Pretty sure I wasn't telling you."

He laughed again, and despite myself, my body hummed gratefully at the sound. "We have a long time on the road. Let's talk."

"What do you want to know?"

"You dating anyone back home?"

"No!" I said it so quickly and so definitively that Shane's head whipped around. "What?" I tried to play it off with a casual shrug.

He raised an eyebrow. "Just that I don't think I've heard a person have such an emphatic answer."

"It's the only answer when a person isn't dating someone. Why not be emphatic about it?"

Finally, Shane nodded slowly, seeming to accept my one word answer. "Okay."

I volleyed back. "You?"

He paused and answered more deliberately and slowly than I had. "No."

We were silent again, and I stared out the window in awe.

I hadn't experienced the vast natural spaces like this since moving to Los Angeles, especially working as much as I did. A part of me just wanted to lose myself in the views.

"You like it there? LA?"

My lips twitched as I fought the urge to give him a pat answer. "Two weeks ago, I'd have said so. Miles of coastline, warm weather, pretty people. What's not to like?"

I could only see his profile, but it was enough to see his lips quirk into a grin. He may have even winked. "You tell me."

Exhaling the air from my lungs, I made a decision. I reached down and slid the lever to move my seat back a bit and tilted the headrest so I was reclining more comfortably. If we were going to talk about real stuff, I might as well get comfortable.

"Well, for one thing, I rarely see that coastline. I'm always at work. And our corporate offices have well-calibrated A/C, so there goes the warm weather. Most of the time, I bring an extra sweater to wear at work, even in the summer."

"Sounds like the issue isn't the location, but maybe you need to get out more."

"You think?"

He shrugged and I realized it didn't annoy me. It felt like communication when he did it, not disinterest. "It's an observation, that's all."

"Astute one."

"Life gets in the way. I get it. Used to be like that too."

"Somehow, I can't imagine that. You seem pretty free and easy with your days. Do some baking, play some music, sit in your hammock and read?"

"You been spying on me?"

"No, just made that part up. Do you have a hammock?"

This time, he definitely winked. "You'll have to come by the house sometime and see."

I turned away, pretending to be fascinated by the endless green hills, which looked just like the green hills we'd been driving past for the last hour. I didn't want him to see the blush that I knew colored my face because I wanted to come by his house sometime.

"Maybe I will."

He nodded at that, and I marveled at how easy he was to talk to and be with. It was a replay of the way I'd felt about him all those years ago, only now he seemed more willing to let me in.

"What were you like? When life got in the way?" I asked.

He smirked and squinted at a sign up ahead. "I was doing things because I thought they were the right things to do. I was confusing obligation with joy, following a path of expectations instead of thinking about what I wanted."

"Whoa. That's ten years of therapy and intense self-awareness in one sentence. I think you need to break it down a little bit for me."

He nodded. "Yeah. None of it was instantaneous or as obvious as I just made it sound."

Steering the truck to take an exit off the highway, Shane pointed to a wooden road sign in the distance. "We have lots of time to talk today. After we look at some wheat."

Despite my curiosity about the promised conversation, I felt a twinge of excitement when the sign grew larger as we neared. "Phelps Farm" was painted in blue letters across the top of a formidable white sign on twin posts. A wheelbarrow filled with sprouting flowers sat underneath the sign, and a bright red painted arrow directed us down the long dirt driveway in case there was confusion about where to go.

We passed several acres of blooming wheat before we reached the squat homestead and offices of Phelps Farm. It had been so long since I'd sourced the raw ingredients that went into our bread, but the smell of the budding wheat berries brought me right back to those days.

Shane and I exited the truck and walked up the gravel path toward the building. We both inhaled deeply, and I could tell by the way his eyes drifted closed that he appreciated the delicate scent that most people didn't even identify as the source of their daily bread.

A hint of nutty grass blew past on an easy breeze. There wasn't much to it, but there didn't need to be for it to feel like home.

"I used to do this, drive around the Central Valley meeting with growers. Been a long time."

"You stick with the same growers year after year?"

"If I can, but I also have people who do the job full time, so I rarely visit, but it was always one of my favorite parts of being a baker."

He was walking slightly ahead of me, but his "hmph" was unmistakable. Not breaking his stride, he visibly inhaled the air around us like a balm for the senses, which it was. But I was still stuck on the "hmph."

"That seemed like a judgmental exhale," I noted, eyeing him suspiciously as he pulled open the heavy oak door for us to step inside. The room was surprisingly spacious compared to how it looked from the outside. High vaulted ceilings gave off a reclaimed farmhouse vibe.

"No judgment at all. I'm just surprised that you don't get to do the things you like when you own the damn business." Extending his hands plaintively, he begged for explanation. We were alone in the room, waiting on the farm owner.

I had no explanation. But I offered what I could.

"It's a big operation. I need to outsource a lot of things I normally like to do myself. It's just the way it is."

"That's a shame." Again, he said it without judgment.

More like indisputable fact. Was it?

I didn't feel able to dispute it, despite my years of defending every decision I made as necessary.

I responded with a shrug that conveyed my inability to answer simply. "I don't really think about it." Or at least I hadn't until I showed up in Green Valley. Now every step I took felt like it was taking me on a collision course with past decisions and missed opportunities.

"But you love it, that's the important thing." He spoke a universal truth, one I used to believe.

I couldn't answer. Because I couldn't lie.

I worked around people who assumed I still loved it and never thought to ask me. So I persevered. I mistook success for love.

Shane guided us over to a bench against the window and gave me a side-eye. "Jule? Do you love it?"

I took a deep breath. "I'm good at it. And it's my job. I don't think about it like that anymore."

"Why not?"

"I just don't." It was honest, and I wanted to be honest with him.

He tapped my knee lightly with his hand.

"Just because you're good at something, it doesn't mean it brings you joy." He leaned toward a tied bundle of lavender sprigs on the table next to the bench, seemingly more interested in their scent than in the words coming out of his mouth.

But to me, they were a revelation.

And also ridiculous. I focused on the latter because I couldn't get my brain around the mind shift required to embrace the former.

"No one feels joy all the time. Even the best job that you love more than anything is going to have things about it you don't like."

He inhaled the scent of the lavender again before handing the perfect sprigs to me. "True, but you should try to love most of it, is all I'm saying." He waited until I'd inhaled the rich scent, which made it feel like he was just making conversation. Not uttering life-shattering truths with the potential to upend everything I thought I knew about my life and work.

"Of course. That's why I opened bakeries in the first place."

"Well, good."

But it had been a long time since I'd even touched a batch of dough and most days, I didn't like my job at all.

Shane had always had the effect of making me think with my heart instead of my brain. And now that I was no longer a hormonal teen, guided by emotion, I had no excuse for yielding to the whims of desire. Even if at that moment, all I wanted to do was abort the plan, abandon ship, leave my life in LA behind and hitch my wagon to Shane Meadows and follow his Zen outlook wherever it led.

Yeah, no.

It was crazy talk.

I had no reason to consider abandoning the business I'd spent twelve-hour days for years working to build. I had no reason to gamble anything on a guy who'd said no to me once and could very well do it again.

He was driving me all around to look at grain because it was his job, and just because he made good conversation that led me to reevaluate my priorities, it didn't mean he wanted to kiss me the same way I wanted to kiss him.

Oh, and I really wanted to kiss him. Sitting next to him in the truck had been tempting enough, but with almost no space between us on the bench, I was intensely aware of his tall, broad-shouldered presence.

I wanted to see how the intellectual connection that made me feel seen and understood would translate to a physical connection if I allowed my emotions to run free.

"Hi, folks." My dangerous thoughts were disrupted by Ben Sawkenny, a tall redwood of a man who emerged from a door and ushered us into a smaller office with a desk, a potted tree fern, and two high-backed wicker chairs.

Shane and I took seats opposite his old oak desk, where he sat and cleaned up a crumpled paper bag lunch. He tore a paper napkin from where it fluttered from the neck of his blue Phelps Farm T-shirt, wadded it up, and tossed it into a trashcan.

"Glad you were able to make the trip out." Mr. Sawkenny extended his hand over the desk, and I watched Shane extend his own in return, making eye contact and daring Mr. Sawkenny to react or do anything except shake the proffered hand.

Or maybe none of that was happening.

I was hovering like a nervous school mom, feeling protective of Shane, reading into a situation, and making assumptions all over the place.

But I couldn't help worrying about how Shane would feel if Mr. Sawkenny reacted badly to his symbrachydactyly.

Rationally, I knew my hovering had no place in the situation. Shane had been dealing with this his entire life, and if he felt comfortable extending his hand like it was nothing, I shouldn't throw myself down on the carpet to pave a safe passage for him.

But I wanted to do it.

Shane glanced my way, and I saw his expression cloud at whatever look I had on my face, so I did my best to blink away the wrinkles from my brow and calm down. I smiled stiffly.

I needn't have worried. Mr. Sawkenny glanced down briefly, and I saw him notice Shane's hand, but then he wrapped his beefy paw around it, and the two men shook hands vigorously.

"Good to meet you," Shane said. Introductions were made, pleasantries exchanged, and I shook Mr. Sawkenny's hand myself.

"Let's get to the good part, shall we?" Mr. Sawkenny said, tilting his head toward a glass door, through which I could see the tawny heads of wheat beckoning us with the breeze. If I thought the aroma of wheatberries was gentle on the walk up the driveway, when we got out into the fields, it reached an intoxicating intensity.

"Wow, that's glorious," Shane commented, plucking the head off a stem and inhaling it under his nose. Mr. Sawkenny did the same before popping the stem between his lips and guiding us deeper into the fields.

"It's a seventeen-year-old blend of three varieties, one of which dates back a hundred years. We know our plants," Mr. Sawkenny said, spreading his arms wide. "But honestly, so do a lot of people, not gonna lie. I don't want to sell you on a plant. I want to sell you on a process."

Shane and I walked along the rows of wheat until we'd covered nearly quarter a mile, and the property continued past where the eye could see. Mr. Sawkenny explained how his wheat could be machine harvested at three to four times the rate of his neighboring farmers because he'd invested in special equipment used in Europe.

"I know, I know, I sound like I'm selling you a pile of cow pies, but here's why this matters." He had to stop and take a breath after walking and talking, so we waited for his lungs to catch up. I had a feeling I knew what he was going to say, but I didn't want to sound like a know it all—my baking expertise seemed to be a sore spot for Shane, so I held my tongue.

"The value is that I can get the wheat from harvest to grinding to bagging within a day, which is a game changer when it comes to bread."

Shane's eyes had gone wide when he turned to me, sharing this revelation. I nodded. "That's a game changer, for sure."

"Is that what you do at your bakeries?" he asked.

"It used to be the only way we sourced flour. I needed to know the farmers, and I wanted to support them. It's how we built our reputation. Now . . . " I hated to admit that my investors were pushing me to cut corners and buy in bulk from growers who most definitely didn't harvest and grind on the same day. And we'd be lucky if they could supply us in a four-day window.

Shane nodded, by now understanding some of why I had misgivings about how my business had outgrown my ability to run it the way I'd like. "Got it. Well, while you're in town and we have all these orders, let's get back to changing the game. Might as well give folks the best thing we can, right?"

I marveled at Shane's constant ability to be chipper and optimistic. Did the man never experience bittersweet ganache settling over his emotional well-being? Was that just an LA thing? Or a *me* thing?

Meanwhile, Mr. Sawkenny continued explaining his methods, and Shane continued nodding and agreeing right along with him. While I continued to wallow in the ways my business had taken me astray, they'd made a deal to get us all the flour we needed to fill every bread order for the next three weeks.

Pulling him aside as we walked back toward the office, I wanted to make sure he'd thought this through. We hadn't even discussed price, and I knew that farm-to-table ingredients like this would cost a lot more than the bakery had paid in the past. "Do you think we should meet with the other farmers before we commit?" I asked quietly so as not to offend Mr. Sawkenny.

Shane's expression turned to a frown, and he looked behind us at the rows of wheat and then glanced skyward. When his eyes returned to me, there was resolution in them that I didn't understand. "No. I think this is it."

Clearly, he didn't understand. This option would be the most expensive. I'd done some research into the other two farms we were supposed to visit, and now I regretted that we'd seen this one first. Of course the others wouldn't measure up, but maybe if we saw them, I could convince him to at least consider their merits.

My hands were gesturing and waving of their own volition as I tried to reel him back from what I worried might be a mistake. "It feels hasty, and we have appointments. I just—"

He faced me, reached for my hands, and stilled them. Then he wrapped my fingers around his smaller hand and started us walking again. My heart surged at the contact and my eyes misted at the trust.

"It's the right decision. We can still visit the others as a courtesy since they've taken the time to meet with us, but I don't think we'll do better than this," he said quietly as we walked.

"But the price, can we afford—?"

"We can. I've already talked with Jenn about it. I know you don't know her well, but if anyone appreciates the value in personal connections and top ingredients, it's Jenn."

I immediately loved that about her, and the feeling of warmth extended right through my fingertips to Shane. Every nerve ending where our palms touched and my fingers wrapped around his hand had caught fire, begging for more. The rest of my body wanted similar treatment.

Silently, I told my body to take a chill pill. But there was no denying that the firm reassurance of his hand gave me the calm I never knew I needed.

I'd also never experienced a day like this—driving to a wheat farm with someone who shared my deep love for the provenance of ingredients, someone who loved the big expanse of nature in the way that only a native of my hometown could.

With the tiniest hint of his hand at the small of my back, I had to fight my urge to believe it meant something.

"Okay," I told Shane. "Let's do it." Walking side by side, I snuck a look at his profile. His strong jaw and the satisfied press of his lips confirmed it was the right decision, and I stared maybe a minute too long at the swell of his bottom lip and the beautiful curve of his satisfied smile.

Then I thought maybe a moment too long about what it would feel like to have those lips on mine.

Then I stopped looking because I didn't want the pain of not knowing to overtake the good feeling I had just thinking about the possibilities.

* * *

Shane and I visited the other two farms because we had appointments, but his instinct was correct in choosing Phelps Farm without even knowing what the others had to offer.

Their locations didn't quite have the grandeur and their product didn't taste as fresh. For cost reasons, they sacrificed quality, and I couldn't begrudge them. Farming, even with government subsidies, had become a difficult way to make a living.

Most farmers were forced to cut corners where they could, either by changing the seed they used, mechanizing some of their processes, or changing which crops they grew in order to save water or cope with other effects of global warming.

I'd seen the effects of drought throughout California's Central Valley, and even though Tennessee had a completely different climate, farmers had challenges here too.

DOUGH YOU LOVE ME?

By the time Shane pointed the truck in the direction of Green Valley, we both felt exhausted yet invigorated by our success. We also felt hungry.

"How long do you think 'til we'll be back?" I checked my watch when we pulled through the exit gates of the last farm on our list. We'd stayed there twice as long as we'd planned because the owner was also a chicken farmer and seventeen baby chicks had just hatched.

I spent a good hour sitting with my back against a hay bale with a lap full of chicks and loving every minute of it. Big cities had many virtues, and I'd been to a petting zoo or two, but nothing beat a real farm for the cutest animal babies on the planet.

Even Shane seemed swept away deciding whether he wanted to steal the tough-looking brown chick or the yellow one that fell asleep in his hand.

I'd done a quick visual survey of his truck when I got in, and I felt fairly confident he hadn't stolen any chicks. But I wouldn't rat him out if he had.

"We should stop somewhere, no doubt about that," Shane said, looking thoughtful and squinting in the way I'd learned meant his brain was running through other options. We stopped at a red light and he turned toward me and I felt his eyes slowly roam my face. "How about the steak place in the town where we got gas back a ways? Seems celebratory for our victorious day."

He was right, but a steak dinner also felt like a date, and I'd just spent the day learning not to feel awkward around Shane. I didn't want to test my tenuous sense of comfort out in a restaurant where I'd have to talk myself down from wishing we were there as a real couple, not just a couple of wheat peepers.

"I love the sentiment, but I'm not dressed for a celebratory place."

"Doesn't matter, does it?"

"I think takeout will do just fine, and we can save time by eating in the car. Are you okay with that?" That dialed down the romantic potential to less than zero.

The light turned green, so I was relieved of Shane's heavy gaze. His eyes flickered with what looked like disappointment, but I knew better than to read too much into their impossible depths. His looks and small touches all day had been murder on me.

If I knew anything about Shane Meadows it was that he could make people feel comfortable with sweet gestures and meaningful glances. I'd been down that road with him in the past, and I couldn't allow myself to make that mistake again.

"Sure," he said, flipping the turn signal and guiding the truck in the direction of the town with the steakhouse. There were other places we could choose from, so I wasn't too worried about the date vibe anymore. "But we're not eating in the truck. I draw the line there. As long as it's us, anyplace works for me."

Swallowing hard, I let his words wash over me and briefly imagined them to mean what I wanted them to. That had always been my problem. I'd always gazed into Shane's pretty eyes and listened to his pretty words and made up my own stories about what it all meant.

And look where it had gotten me—so far from my hometown that it took a funeral to bring me back to a place that was starting to bring me actual joy.

Breathe. Remember how it hurt when he said no all those years ago. Focus on it. Calm the flapping wings.

It was hard to remember the hurt in the presence of so much good. I wanted to believe that we were different now. I wanted to think we had potential for something real.

As I was thinking these things, I became aware of Shane parking the truck, coming around to open my door, and walking next to me, the warmth of him enveloping me and drawing me in like a magnetic field.

Over the course of dinner, we settled into something easy, which lured my heart once again into a false sense that we could be something more. Then I talked myself down. Again.

His hand brushed against mine as we walked. Once, twice. Then I felt him reach for me and squeeze my hand.

And I knew . . . my heart was stuck on this roller coaster ride.

I hated it. And I also loved it.

CHAPTER 11

SHANE

I knew why Julia didn't want to go to a steak dinner, and it had nothing to do with her clothes.

We'd had plenty of time on the drive for an explanation of why I'd said no to her all those years ago, and a part of me wanted to give it to her. But the day was going so well, and I didn't want to ruin it by bringing up the biggest mistake of my life.

And as we shared a plate of fries that went along with our club sandwiches, I didn't feel especially eager to bring it up now either.

Was there a chance we could skate along on the thin ice under our feet and hope that it froze solid? Maybe we could leave the past in the past—which would allow me to focus on the present. And how much I desperately wanted to kiss her.

And how much I knew I shouldn't.

Not when she would be leaving in a matter of weeks.

I doubted any good could come from a quick fling while she was here. Because I knew I wouldn't want it to be a quick fling.

Because it was her.

"Hey, you'd better jump in on these before I eat all of them." Julia gestured to the half-eaten plate of fries with the two sauced-dipped ones in her hand before popping them into her mouth.

I reached for a French fry and dabbed it in the ketchup. "They're pretty good, huh?"

"Very good. I didn't realize how hungry I was until these fries showed up." As if to demonstrate, she speared some barbecue sauce with another pair of fries and ate them.

Then she leaned back in the booth where she sat opposite me. I liked sitting across from her so I could look at her. We'd spent so much time in the truck sitting side by side all day, and I wanted to see her face—wanted to let my gaze trace the contours of her cheekbones and stare at her full lips unabashedly because that's what good conversationalists were allowed to do.

I didn't want to talk about the past.

I owed it to her to talk about the past.

I had no idea what to say about the past.

"I still don't know when you became a French horn player. Is that something you did back in high school and I somehow missed it?" she asked, giving up on the fries in order to take another bite of her sandwich.

So, I would gingerly revisit the past. At least, the part she was asking about. On one hand, I couldn't believe she didn't know my "story." It seemed like everyone around here did. But then, she'd moved away and rarely come back.

And I hadn't exactly given her reason to care.

I leaned back against the booth and marveled at how the diner's overhead lights made her eyes even brighter.

"It wasn't until senior year. You'd already graduated." Of course, she knew that. This already felt awkward.

"Yes, I recall." She waggled her eyebrows, mischievous.

"You're making fun of me. Awesome. This is going to go well, I can see."

She laughed and settled in, drawing her knees to her chest in the booth as though readying for a nice, entertaining story. "It's already going well. I had no idea how much you'd hate being put on the spot."

"And yet, you seem to be enjoying yourself at my expense."

"I am. But not at your expense. I'm laughing with you, not at you."

"I'm not laughing," I ground out. Exhaling, I began again. Despite how awkward I felt talking about myself, I was enjoying being with her enough that it hardly mattered.

I told her about going to Nashville with Clay, about seeing the French horn player in the orchestra, and coming back home and asking the music teacher at school about taking lessons.

"As you can probably imagine, there wasn't a French horn instructor

84

within fifty miles of Green Valley, but I got myself some music books, and with the magic of the internet, I learned the basics myself."

"You taught yourself to play the French horn?" Her eyes widened and she leaned in.

I nodded. It didn't seem so astounding. It had just been a matter of learning to read music at first, and we had my dad's old guitar in the basement, so I practiced chords on that, strumming with my thumb, until I could convince my parents to rent a French horn for me.

"Did it take a lot of convincing? They must've been impressed that you were teaching yourself to read music and learning guitar."

"They were somewhat impressed by that, but I was also a teenage guy who'd played a year of baseball here and a year of volleyball there. They'd seen me pick up hobbies and drop them like a hot frying pan, so they weren't really itching to rent me a giant brass instrument if I was going to play for a month and quit."

Thinking back, I couldn't blame my parents.

I signaled to our server and ordered us each a slice of peach pie without asking Julia if she wanted one. Everyone loved the peach pie, and she nodded along with my order and added two cups of coffee. "Good call," I told her.

As our server cleared away the remains of our dinner, Julia waited patiently until I began speaking again. "Anyhow, I finally offered to pay for the rental out of my allowance if they'd put down the deposit in case it was lost or stolen."

"Sounds like a good compromise."

I nodded. "Pretty soon, they saw how serious I was, and they took over the rental payments. I was . . . obsessed isn't even the right word. I played every waking hour of the day that I wasn't at school. Didn't go to the homecoming parade because I was practicing. Didn't go to prom because I'd gotten into a small orchestra and had a performance. I ate, slept, breathed, and lived for the French horn."

Her eyes went wide and she shook her head. "Wow. Hearing that makes me so happy."

And hearing her say it made me happy. So I told her the rest.

"Yeah. It sort of saved me. Or helped me find myself, my voice, my purpose." I held up my hand as proof. When I dropped it to the table, her hand covered it gently.

"And you never took lessons?"

"Oh, I did, eventually. As soon as I realized I could play, I was super serious about it. I drove an hour and a half across two counties to meet with a teacher three days a week. And I played in college."

"In the marching band?" she asked. Then she shook her head. "Actually, I don't even know where you went to school. Were you at the University of Tennessee? Memphis? I'm sure they had some pretty peppy marching bands."

"No. I didn't stay local. I went to school in New York."

She shook her head like she was trying to dislodge errant sounds. "Wait, what? You lived in New York? How come no one told me these things?"

I didn't want to state the obvious, which was that she disappeared after high school and never came back, at least as far as I knew. It wasn't clear how she expected news about what I was doing might be conveyed to her in California. There'd be no reason for anyone to imagine she'd even care.

But she sat there looking at me expectingly. "Um, probably because people didn't care all that much." That was a lie. People in Green Valley were suitably impressed that I earned myself a scholarship to one of the most stringent competitive music programs in the country.

But why would they tell her?

She was staring at me in rapt attention, her chin on her fist. I marveled that the dreamy expression on her face had come from listening to my story. She looked as mesmerized hearing about my crazy rapture over the French horn as I'd felt all those years ago when I'd first heard it played.

I knew she understood on a deeper level. I didn't know how she understood, but I knew she did.

Again, I had the urge to lean forward, to climb on the table if I had to, and take her face in my hand and kiss her.

But I shouldn't.

I couldn't.

So I didn't.

This was tenuous and new. And it was good. I'd be a fool to risk it or ruin it.

For now, staring back at her was enough.

"Wow, that's serious dedication."

"It was, somewhat, but I also just had something to prove. Like, I was this kid with a fucked up right paw, and I never saw my way clear to how I was supposed to feel about it, how to present myself to the world. And that instrument . . . it gave me a way."

She didn't say a word, so I admitted my last bit of truth.

"There's never going to be a day when I don't have a flicker of worry

DOUGH YOU LOVE ME?

that I'm making someone uncomfortable. Unless I'm playing the French horn, but that's only because they can't see all of me. Or so they think. The reality is they're seeing everything I've got."

I don't know what I was expecting her to do or say. Maybe just nod or tell me it made sense.

I was not expecting her to cry.

There's an important thing to understand about Julia. This girl had an inner toughness and resolve about herself that was obvious even in our teenage years when we were all young and dumb and most definitely not introspective. Back in the days of tailgate parties and shotgunning beer, none of us knew which end of our emotional spectrum was right side up and which was upside down.

Except Julia. She knew. She sailed through the eye of the teen soap opera storm with a certainty I envied. One I tried to replicate. And once I learned to play the French horn, I thought I'd succeeded. I'd finally mastered something that allowed me to step into the forefront instead of hiding in the back.

It was a good thing for me. That's what I was trying to tell Julia. "No, wait. I wasn't trying to make you sad. Don't feel sorry for me."

"I know you weren't. And I'm not . . . this isn't . . . " She inhaled a deep breath and dabbed at her eyes, but it was a useless effort. The tears continued to spill forth, and she gave up wiping them. I stood by, helpless and feeling responsible for something I didn't understand.

Finally, she cleared her throat and took in a shaky breath. Her eyes never leaving mine, she spoke as though she needed me to believe her. "Shane. I don't feel sorry for you. I've never felt sorry for you. Not ever."

It took a moment for the concept to sink in.

Because . . . of course she felt sorry for me back then. Didn't she? How could she not? Everyone did. It was why I couldn't conceive of dating her or being her prom date or anything else. I wasn't worthy of real esteem, and I didn't want to be the object of pity.

So I ran and hid.

But this—the idea that she didn't feel that way about me when I was about as pitiful as they come—I wasn't sure I could trust it. And maybe I didn't need to, not yet.

"Let's put a pin in that for a minute, okay? Because you've just blown my mind a little bit, and I need some time to process it."

She nodded, the tears starting to abate.

"First, just tell me what I did to make you cry." I spoke slowly, observing every subtle shift in her expression, wanting to record every tiny moment for posterity because I already had a feeling we were meant to be forever.

Reaching for her hand, I interlaced our fingers and clung tight. "I didn't think anything I just said was particularly sad. Tell me what just happened."

She didn't tell me anything at first, but I caught her staring down at where our hands were linked. Her thumb rubbed circles on the back of my hand.

When she finally answered, she nearly leveled me. "When I heard you play on my first night in town, I couldn't believe how beautiful it was, and I had no idea it was you playing." She steadied her voice, but another large tear rolled down her cheek. I wanted to wipe it away, but I couldn't move, mesmerized by her words.

"Shane, you took something that would have been a limitation for most people, and you turned it into the most beautiful thing. I love that so much."

I had no words after that.

I leaned back on the bench, putting as much distance between us as I could. Because I knew I was in trouble.

She'd be leaving for her real life back in LA in a matter of weeks, and I'd be here, regretting squandered opportunities once again.

CHAPTER 12

SHANE

A little rattling under my tires was normal as I drove the Tennessee backroads I knew so well, so I didn't think much about it as the truck bumped along the pitted road under the dusky sky.

The day had gone remarkably well, considering that we'd started out barely on speaking terms, and now we were laughing like old friends and . . . singing. Julia belted out the lyrics to Queen's *Bohemian Rhapsody*, complete with dramatic hand gestures and movements that matched the music video I hadn't watched in years.

We sang it as a duet, with her handling the high notes and me dropping into the base that felt much more comfortable for my deeper voice.

"I know my voice is atrocious," she giggled when she'd finished hitting every high and low note like a champ. "I don't care!"

"How can you use that word to describe your voice? You hit all the falsettos. That was awesome."

Dusk had dropped into the darker colors of night in a matter of minutes, like someone had turned out a light. Suddenly, my high beams were barely enough to guide us on the empty, poorly lit roads.

Since Julia had insisted on visiting all the farms where we'd made appointments as a courtesy, our drive had taken us almost two hundred miles from where we'd started our day. That meant a long drive back, but I didn't at all mind the time in the truck with Julia now that she didn't seem to hate me.

"Super dark out here. I don't remember it being like this. I feel like a broken record because I keep saying things like that." She peered through the windshield as though a little intimidated by the world outside.

"You afraid of the dark?" I couldn't hide my smile at the thought. Here she was, this confident, accomplished woman who'd taken the world by storm, and she'd gone doe-eyed at a dark sky.

"Nah. Not afraid." She continued to stare through the glass. "Just not used to how dark it gets here."

"Few years in a city changes a person, huh?"

She didn't even wait a beat before responding. "I don't think it changes a person on the inside, but it roughs up the outside a little bit. I feel like I'm still that girl I was growing up here, but she's a little bit buried under the layers."

"Nothing like a drive down a dark country road to shake off a few of those layers."

She laughed. "Yeah." Her expression turned serious again, and she seemed lost in thought.

"You okay?"

"Oh, yeah. Just tired, I guess. Sometimes long road trips make me introspective."

I turned up the music when a song by Madonna came up on my playlist, thinking a little more singing might lift her mood.

She didn't bite.

I tilted my head to look at her, struck as I'd been all day by how beautiful she was, not purely in the physical sense, though I could stare at her all day and never tire. She had a gentle confidence about her that didn't come from ego. It came from believing in the goodness of other people and in pushing herself to higher standards.

The result was the self-effacing woman who I'd been getting to know over the past week or so, mostly by sneaking glances at her when she wasn't looking and observing her in what I considered her natural habitat.

And despite my initial annoyance at Monsieur Auclair's fawning, I'd be the first to admit that her bread was in a class by itself.

I loved baking, and I'd learned to do it pretty damn well, but she was in another league. Not that I'd given her the satisfaction of telling her yet.

Or maybe I would.

"I have a confession to make," I said, leaning my elbow against the driver's side window and tipping my head against my hand. My other hand rested in my lap, and I lightly hooked my thumb over the wheel at the bottom.

She turned her whole body toward me and tucked her legs underneath her like a kid getting ready for story time. "Ooh, yeah? I love a good confession. Can I guess?"

Her playfulness made me laugh, and again I was struck by how different she was today, out on the open road, than she'd been for the first few days at the bakery. I wondered what had changed, but I didn't want to ruin the moment by asking.

Clay was right. I'd spent so many years of my life trying to prove to myself that I was just fine without Julia in my life.

One day with her had proven me an inveterate liar.

"Sure. Guess away."

"Um, you're going to tell me that when you're not pulverizing logs in your brother's side yard, you knit those cute little beanies you like to wear in the mornings."

"Okay, I think I take offense at the fact that you call my manly headwear cute, and how'd you know I chop logs at my brother's?"

She shrugged with an impish smile. "No secret's safe in Green Valley."

"Nah, I'm gonna need a better explanation than that. Who talked?"

"Fine. Clay came into the bakery on your day off, and we got to talking. He said you've been carving up a tree into enough kindling to last through seven winters."

"Too bad for him he'll never sit by a fire and enjoy it because I'm going to murder him."

She waved me off with a hand. "Aw, he didn't mean anything by it. He didn't say it like he was spilling family secrets. Just giving me a little insight into what Shane Meadows does when he doesn't have his hands in a pile of dough." It wasn't lost on me that she was making somewhat lewd gestures that bore no resemblance to what I actually did to knead dough.

"You look like a mad scientist."

"Maybe I am one. Mad something, I'm pretty sure."

"So what else did he tell you?" I wasn't so much concerned about what Clay might have told her—even my brother had more good sense than to walk into my place of employment and tell a woman I'd never gotten over her.

I was pretty certain of that.

What interested me more was why Julia was asking about me in the first place. "So, you asked about me?"

Turning even more squarely to face me in the bench seat next to me, she blinked her pretty eyes.

Was she . . . flirting?

Or was there dust in the truck?

Either seemed possible.

"I may have posed a question or two."

I pressed my lips together to hold back my satisfied grin. But it was impossible.

"What?" There was no mistaking the blush creeping across her cheeks, and I fucking loved the sight of it and everything it might imply.

"I like that you asked about me."

Her lips twisted into a frustrated smirk. "I didn't ask about you like that. It wasn't . . . anything. I was just making conversation because I'm a nice person, and that's what nice people do."

I held up my hands. "Okay, okay. You're right. You're nice. Forget I said anything."

"Forgotten."

It *so* wouldn't be forgotten by me.

"Anyhow, you didn't answer the part about the knitting. Is that your confession? Do you have hobbies other than manhandling dough?"

"I was going to confess that I like your bread, but I've changed my mind."

She waved a dismissive hand. "Aw, bread, shmead. I want to know about the embarrassing hobbies."

I liked her sass, and it made me want to do things to bring more of it out in her.

"What if I'm a needle pointer? Will that suit you?"

"*Are* you a needle pointer? My Gram used to do that. We had pillows all over the house with pictures the queen needle-pointed on them."

"What queen?"

She playfully smacked my shoulder. "*The* queen. Queen Elizabeth. Was there any better queen?" Then she muttered under her breath, "What queen?"

"Okay, hang on. I need a little unpacking here. I know she was England's reigning monarch, but is there something else I'm missing? Was your grandmother born in England or something?"

"Of course not. She was born outside of Nashville." I could see the delighted grin on her face at my confusion. She filled me in on her grandmother's love for Elizabeth and described a memorabilia collection worthy of Butterfield's auction house.

Turning down a darker road, if that was even possible, I pointed through the windshield. "With so much dark sky in front of us, we'll probably see shooting stars. Just watch and one will drop right in front of us in the distance."

"Seriously?"

I shot her a look. "Of course. You think I'm trying to sell you on some wide-open spaces myth just because you ran away to the city for a hundred years?"

"Kind of."

"Well, maybe I am. But the shooting star thing is real."

She turned back toward the front and studied the landscape in front of us like an assiduous student, wanting an A.

We drove in silence for a minute. I started thinking about her, stealing glances at the curve of her jaw where it met her neck, trying to stifle the urge I had to reach for her and see if her skin was as soft as it looked.

On a long exhale, I told myself to calm the heck down and stop stealing glances that only served to make me want what I couldn't have. She'd barely been able to talk to me in a civil way before today. Our shaky detente after a successful bread mission hardly meant she wanted me to kiss her.

Well, shit. I wanted to kiss *her*.

Once I'd let that thought into my head, it was impossible to corral.

One more look. I'd sneak one more look her way while she studied the sky ahead, looking for rogue stars.

I tipped my head in her direction, but mostly I followed her with my eyes, still able to shoot my vision back to the road in a heartbeat if necessary.

She was just so damn pretty, the way her eyelashes fluttered against her cheeks and the slight swell of her bottom lip that made me want to do things to it with my teeth.

So lost in my reverie, I didn't notice anything unusual picked up by the truck's high beams until we were bumping over a craggy patch of dirt so severe that the whole truck bounced up and down before riding hard on the wheels.

It didn't take long after that for the bounce to turn into the dull flap of flattening tires as the entire truck listed to the right, and I could feel our misfortune rolling along beneath us.

"What just happened?" Julia snapped out of her night sky stare and turned to me as I slowed the truck to a stop.

"Feels like we've got a flat." The next hour flashed in front of my thoughts, with the two of us needing to change the tire in the dark on the side of the road where I couldn't exactly guarantee Julia that there wouldn't be scary things lurking.

"Hang on. I'll check."

She turned her phone flashlight on, hopped out of the truck, and bent down to survey the tires. When she popped her head up, she schooled her expression to deliver the dire news. "Well, the front tire's really low, almost flat as a pancake. Just . . . pft." She demonstrated with her hands squeezing out the air until they went flat.

Then she glanced toward the back tire again to be sure. "And the back one's . . . gone."

"What do you mean, gone?"

"It's flatter than flat. Like, I'm not even sure all the rubber's still attached to the wheel. I've never seen a tire so flat."

I couldn't help but feel a little bit proud of my truck for its smooth ride under such circumstances, but that wasn't the point.

She pressed her lips together and watched me as I processed this information. The thoughts churned in my head, but I couldn't begin to formulate a plan for this. Then she burst out laughing.

It surprised me so much, I may have jumped in my seat.

Wait, was she joking? That made more sense, even though I'd yet to fully understand her sense of humor. I relaxed a little bit.

"I'm sorry, I know it's not funny. It's just . . . this is so ridiculous. Who gets two flat tires? I've never even heard of that. These tires aren't even flat, they're destroyed, but it didn't feel like we hit anything that hard."

Laughing like this, she looked free, and again I was struck by how good it looked on her. I'd yet to see it while we were at work, but this was the reward.

Still, I was confused. "You're kidding, right? We don't have two flat tires." This had to be a joke, which I was still working on finding funny. She couldn't be serious.

This was a sturdy SUV with a large, lumbering frame and big-ass tires to support it. We hadn't hit the bump that hard.

"I'm not kidding." She used her phone flashlight and walked down the road a bit behind the truck, apparently no longer afraid of the dark when ridicule was involved.

I started to get a little worried the farther away she went. I wasn't afraid of the dark, but who knew what the heck kind of animals might be lurking alongside a quiet road. The last thing I needed now was to lose her to the teeth of a coyote.

When she came back a minute later, she explained the situation in detail, as she saw it.

"There's a medium-sized hole in the road, but the thing you hit was the rock just after the hole. So I'm guessing the tires hit the pothole and then burst on their way up and over the rock."

I scrubbed a hand through my hair in disbelief at the situation. "You know I only have one spare."

My pronouncement sobered her. She nodded, the smile wiped from her face, though the traces of tears still hung in the corners of her eyes.

"I can't decide what's funnier—the fact that you think I'd be up for changing a tire in the dark in the middle of nowhere or the fact that I've never heard of a person getting two flat tires on one pothole." She covered her mouth with her hand, but it didn't hide that she was shaking with laughter.

"Yeah, this will all seem super hilarious in a second when I tell you that we're not getting a tow truck out here at this hour."

Her laughter subsided a bit. "What do you mean? Of course they'll come. It's their job to tow things."

"Not at this hour. Not when it's fifty miles from the nearest service station that may or may not have the kind of tires we need, and the place is closed until morning."

Now she looked concerned and not at all amused. "Wait, really?"

"Really."

"So, what are we going to do? What's the timeline on getting home?"

"Looks like we're spending the night in the truck. Tomorrow, first thing, I'll call and we'll either get a tow or someone will bring out two tires, and we'll change them."

Looking around at the desolate landscape, or what she could see of it in the pitch black lit only by the truck's headlights, every trace of her gorgeous smile faded. I felt more disappointed by that than I did about the two new tires I'd have to purchase. The ones for this model didn't come cheap.

"It'll be okay. Part of the adventure, right? It's a story you'll be able to tell all your friends back home. How you spent the night on a country road and survived."

Even in the dim light, when her eyes darted to mine, I could see she wasn't amused. More frightened than anything.

"I have a confession to make. And mine isn't about needlepoint."

The genuineness in her voice pierced a place in my chest that was dangerously close to my heart. "Lay it on me, sister. I can take it."

"I don't love the dark." She exhaled the sentiment, her shoulders dropping after she said it in defeat. "I'm not scared, per se, but I'm just not crazy about it. So sleeping out here . . . doesn't fill me with glee."

The hurt from her confession edged even closer to the tender organ in my chest. I reached for her hand without thinking about it.

Her eyes shifted down at where our fingers clasped, but she didn't pull away. If anything, she grasped on a little more firmly. "Listen," I told her quietly. "We'll be safe in the truck. I promise. This thing is a tank, and when the doors are closed and locked, nothing gets in. It's like a little hotel on wheels."

She bit her bottom lip and regarded our accommodations skeptically. Okay, maybe I was overestimating.

"Or a motel," I amended. "A really small motel on wheels, but you get the point. There are motels with doors and windows that are a lot flimsier than this thing." I hitched a thumb over my shoulder and gestured to my ride, which stood listing to the side like a toddler who'd just gotten scolded for throwing mud on the playground.

Truth be told, I was a little disappointed in how wimpy the tires had turned out to be, but I'd deal with that later.

Still gripping my hand, Julia took a step closer and met my eyes. "Okay," she said, nodding bravely. "Okay."

Guiding her around to the back of the truck, I popped the hatch and peered inside, thanking my organizational tendencies because the whole rear space looked pretty clean. I'd recently vacuumed the gray carpeted flatbed, and it looked pretty presentable for the inside of a truck. Fortunately, we'd turned down Mr. Sawkenny's offer to cart home sixteen bags of freshly-ground flour, or we'd be sleeping on top of the awkward sacks.

Julia seemed to share my thought. She nodded at the space. "Almost like you anticipated needing to sleep in here."

"I anticipate a lot, but I didn't see this coming," I admitted. I lifted the interior storage cover and extracted two soft blankets and a bugout bag that contained a flannel shirt and a sweatshirt, along with fresh water and a few emergency kit items.

Handing Julia a large flashlight, I could see the relief wash over her features. "Let there be light," she said, turning the round beam on and sweeping it through the interior of the trunk, where there was plenty of room for both of us to stretch out and sleep. "Not bad, Shane. Your motel on wheels is growing on me."

"Good to hear." I got to work spreading out the blankets and creating something akin to a nest in the bed of the truck. I had a few emergency granola bars in the bugout bag, so I grabbed those too, along with a small radio.

By the time I finished setting everything up, the back of my truck looked almost like a picnic spot, and Julia had visibly relaxed.

It was almost nine o'clock, and I doubted either of us was tired enough to sleep, but there wasn't much else to do out here, so we hopped into our motel on wheels. Julia toed off her shoes and scooted toward the back, so her legs extended over the blankets.

Sitting on the rear bumper, I unlaced my boots and leaned back to shove them into a corner of the trunk. Julia dimmed the flashlight and propped it on its end so the light reflected off the roof's interior.

I reached up to close the hatch and seal us inside when Julia stopped me with a hand on my arm. "Not yet." She scooted forward and joined me on the tailgate. "Can we look for some shooting stars as long as we're out here?"

I smiled at that. "Sure. Bet we'll see a bunch."

Trying not to react when she settled down right next to me, I stilled and let out a slow breath. Her head tilted to the side and rested against my shoulder as we both stared out into the night. As I inhaled her rosemary mint shampoo, I told myself to commit the smell and the scene and the woman to memory.

Because this was a damn near perfect moment.

CHAPTER 13

JULIA

*D*espite the prospect of sleeping in the truck, my mood was a light cloud of Italian meringue. I didn't think twice before leaning against Shane as we watched for shooting stars. It just felt right, and after a lifetime of doing what my rational brain told me was right all the time, I loved the idea of going by feel and instinct.

He may have flinched a tiny bit when I lay my head on his shoulder, but he either covered for his surprise, or he got over it pretty quickly. His cheek tipped against my head, and I felt the soft scratch of his stubble at my temple.

So sexy, so manly, so very . . . everything.

Stop.

There was no point in entertaining this train of thought. Considering Shane in manly, sexy terms would only make it that much harder for me to say goodbye to him again. Not to mention that we'd finally broken through the awkwardness today, and I felt like we were back on old, familiar territory.

That was it.

I'd already made the mistake once of thinking his kind gestures of friendship could mean more. If I didn't learn from my mistakes, it made me pretty dumb.

Shane's hand on my thigh jarred me from my thoughts. He squeezed and pointed just as a tiny point of light dropped through the blackness in the far distance. "Did you see it?"

I nodded against his shoulder, unwilling to move, lest he pull away. But he shifted anyway, turning his body to face me. A blaze of excitement sparkled in his eyes. "So cool, right? I knew we'd get some shooting stars tonight. We got lucky there's no cloud cover."

I thought back to my childhood here and recalled that June weather was unpredictable. "I didn't even think about that. The weather's been so perfect since I got here, but you're right."

"Different than the city, huh?"

"In many ways." I huffed a laugh. So many ways.

"Are you enjoying the break, though?" I met his eyes. He had to know I was, right? But the question sounded like something asked by a tour guide. Or a stranger.

Maybe that's what we were. Still.

I hated it, but I didn't know what to do about it.

"Shane, yes. It feels really good to be here." I kept my eyes locked on his, willing him to understand that I didn't just mean here in town. But maybe I needed to do better, be more specific, tell him what I was thinking instead of hoping he knew. "It feels good to be here with you."

I took a deep breath and shifted my gaze away. I couldn't face the heaviness of what his eyes might tell me—that I was the same silly teenager who had the wrong idea about him. Again.

It surprised me to feel Shane's fingers graze my chin as he guided my face back toward his. Feeling only slightly brave, I lifted my downcast eyes.

What I saw in his was a vast constellation of understanding and relief and curiosity and . . . contentment, which mirrored my own. "It feels really good to be here with you too," he said, his voice deep and clear.

Kiss me.

The voice in my head commanded him to obey, even if it didn't have the confidence to say the words out loud. I willed him to intuit my thoughts from the seriousness in my eyes and the electricity between us that I swear he felt too.

How could he not?

It was a forcefield that felt like it vibrated every atom of my body and made my nerves dance. It was impossible that I was the only one affected.

Right?

Maybe.

He didn't kiss me, but the weight of his stare made me believe he was considering it. The pale blue pools of his eyes drew me in like the rising tide, and we sat like that, our gazes holding each other in a weighty moment.

I didn't want to ruin it by asking what it meant, even if the moment was perfect under the dark sky that was dropping stars just for us. Maybe it only meant that I'd done the right thing by coming here with an open calendar and letting the place open my mind.

"So beautiful," he said, still staring at me.

"It's a really nice night. The sky is so pretty," I said quietly.

"Not what I meant." His words sent rivers thrilling my heart and left me with goosebumps. I couldn't help but smile.

Then, in my usual way, I sought to lighten the moment because I didn't know what else to do. "Who knew you were such a sweet talker, Shane Meadows?"

"Not sweet-talking you, Julia Browne."

But he still didn't kiss me. And even though I considered myself an empowered, can-do woman, I didn't kiss him either.

I thought about it. A lot.

I thought about the weeks I'd spent with Trevor and how I never felt the sweet, hot burn for him that I was experiencing just sitting next to Shane.

It had always been this way for me. It was the reason I had to run so fast and so far from him when I realized he didn't return my feelings in any way. Yes, I was an overly dramatic teenager prone to making dramatic entrances and exits, but none of that invalidated my feelings.

They were real then, and they were real now.

How was it possible to feel this turned on by a person without touching him at all? Every nerve ending was throwing sparks like a Fourth of July fireworks display. My body was humming with heightened feeling and a need to be touched.

When I turned to Shane, I saw a trace of the same feral desire. His eyes dilated, and he took a long deep breath and exhaled.

Our gazes stayed locked on each other—questioning, affirming. We both felt something, and neither of us knew what to do about it.

Shane pressed his lips together, and I pulled my bottom lip through my teeth. We were communicating through looks and gestures, engaging in a dance neither one of us knew, so it felt tentative.

It also felt right.

Of course, I'd think so. One hot look from Shane and I'd been transported back to high school, back to the party where I watched him from across a field, sizing him up, deciding on where and when and if I'd be bold enough to ask him to be my date.

Ten years earlier

Shane stands off to the side of the group as he often does at parties. I know this because I know him. We've had math classes together for two years because he's too smart for math at his own grade level, so the school bumped him up.

I remember the beginning of last year when he first walked into class, the only sophomore in junior math. I could tell he felt awkward, and at that point, I barely knew him. I knew he was the guy who had some issue with his hand, but we'd never crossed paths before, so I hadn't paid him much attention.

On that first day, however, he intrigued me.

Okay, fine. I also thought he was hot. No, not hot—beautiful.

To start with, he had those eyes. Placid blue and reassuring like the sea. When he looked at me, I felt like he saw more of me than most people. Because, let's face it—in high school, most people aren't really looking too far beneath the surface, especially in an honors geometry class.

But something told me those eyes could see depth because they had depth.

I barely needed to look at the rest of his face because the eyes had already sold me, but I gave it a once-over anyhow. His lips were rosy and full, his dark hair wavy and slightly messy, and I imagined him shoving his hands in it when he was thinking. Chiseled bone structure that made him look more mature than his almost-sixteen years.

He chose a seat in the back corner of the classroom, and I followed, caught in his magnetic field. I chose the seat next to him without making eye contact. I tried to seem casual because I didn't want him to see that he already had an effect on me, not before I had a plan for what to do about it.

And for over a year, I did nothing. I watched him, though.

Every day, while we studied next to each other, I was keenly aware of him—how he sat with his back straight against the chair, how he took notes in pencil but never erased anything, how he looked my way and smiled because he'd gotten used to having me there, and I no longer made him uncomfortable.

All through my junior year, we didn't talk much, other than discussing homework or math problems if we ended up partnered up for an exercise.

By my senior year, though, we graduated to an easy friendship.

I was outgoing; he was shy. With a little effort on my part, I could bring him out of his shell, and we could talk about things other than math. With a little effort on his part, he could share small details about things he found interesting, and I felt immensely gratified.

We didn't talk much about ourselves, which is to say I didn't ask him about what had happened to his hand because I didn't want to make a big deal out of it. He tried to hide or downplay it—that much was obvious—so I let him be.

Doing that for each other during the turbulent high school years was enough to form the basis for a friendship.

I didn't tell him about how my parents had gone missing in action several years earlier because I didn't want to get into it, and he never pressed, even though it was common knowledge I lived with my grandmother.

We talked about all the other things that had nothing to do with biographical details about ourselves. It was a relief to leave all the personal drama alone when we lived in a place where most people knew everyone else's business like they knew the weather.

As our friendship developed, we intentionally left that stuff out—we never overtly agreed, but we agreed.

We both found it more interesting to riff on Buddhist ethics, a nightmare Shane had about being inducted into the Iron Wraiths motorcycle gang, and the way bees build honeycomb in the most efficient hexagonal shape.

We went everywhere and we went deep.

Intellectually, we were more than friends. We connected. We understood each other.

But we'd never kissed, never even had an awkward exchange of looks that made it seem like kissing was on the table. For a long time, that seemed okay.

Until now.

It's early April, and we're at a bonfire in an empty lot back behind the Tanner twins' house, and my senior prom is one month away.

Without doing it consciously, I realize I've been ramping up to this moment for nearly two years. I've wanted something from Shane all this time. I've wanted confirmation that he feels something more for me than friendship.

I let myself believe he does because I don't think I know the difference between feeling something so intensely myself and being in love.

They seem the same.

A lot of the seniors are planning on asking people to prom tonight. It's kind of a thing. The bonfire a month before prom is when a lot of the pairing up happens. There's a buzz in the air.

My friends may have put on a little more makeup than usual tonight, spent a little more time on their hair and tweaked their outfits a couple dozen times. Even if they sort of know who's planning on asking them, there's still a superstitious feeling of needing everything to go right tonight. Lucky-bra-and-underwear kind of superstition.

I have a different feeling. I'm not waiting for someone to ask me to prom. I'm planning on doing the asking. It has to be Shane, and it has to be now.

My plans for next year aren't set in stone, but I'm pretty sure I'll go to one of the in-state colleges I got into, which means I'll be leaving, but I won't be that far away. If Shane and I . . . no, I'm getting way ahead of myself.

We're just friends as of now. Even if we go to prom and we end up dating a little bit, it doesn't mean I'll be driving home on weekends to see him. It's ridiculous to be thinking about that—but I am. Because, dammit, after spending as much time as I do with him, I'm half in love with him, and I'm pretty sure he knows it.

The second shot of Fireball goes down more easily than the first. The cinnamon candy burn in my throat gives me courage.

The bonfire in the center of the group has blazed up to nearly four feet in height. A group of popular senior guys came out early and built the bonfire, tossing on logs chopped weeks earlier so they'd be dry enough to burn quickly.

As soon as things started, people started to filter over from neighboring houses, even before sunset when the bonfire started officially. I got there early as well so I could keep an eye out for Shane. I didn't want to take a chance on coming late and end up missing him.

We'd talked earlier in the day about whether he'd be at the bonfire, and he promised he would. "But I can't guarantee I'll stay long. Those kinds of things aren't my style."

"What is your style?" I'd asked, curious. Because we talked about everything but ourselves, I didn't know what he liked to do on a Friday night.

"Maybe you'll find out." His eyebrows bounced, sending a flare of heat

through my body. I'd always worked hard to tamp down those kinds of feelings, but I let this one slip because within hours I'd know whether he felt the same way about me.

I wanted to believe he did, and I didn't allow myself to prepare for how I'd stomach it if he didn't. His comment led me down the path I wanted to race down with abandon.

When Shane arrives at the bonfire, I'm stuck in a conversation with my friend Ginny, who's heard that Cletus is rejecting the idea of going to prom altogether. Ginny can't understand it, and she's talking my ear off about it.

"That's just Cletus. You don't need to understand it," I explain.

But that isn't good enough. Ginny needs to know everything about everyone. "Why would he not want to go?" she asked again.

"Are you hoping he'll take you?"

That's the only explanation for why it matters so much to Ginny.

"No, that's not it. I just don't want him to start a trend or something, and next thing you know, all the boys decide they're not going."

"I don't think there's a big risk of all the boys following Cletus's lead on this. Don't worry."

I'm about to go look for Shane, but I get caught staring at the flames. Kids keep tossing kindling onto the fire, which is now upwards of six or seven feet in the air. No one's worried about it being a fire hazard since we're in a dirt lot, but the fact is it's an open fire blazing up into the sky, and that has me a little uneasy, just from the look of it.

"Some guys connected hoses and ran them out here. Don't worry." Shane's breath is hot on my neck as he speaks softly close to my ear. I love that he knows I'm worried about the fire when I guarantee that not another soul out here does.

The crowd around is loud, and I intentionally don't move out of the center of things, so he'll have an excuse to lean in close to be heard.

"Hey. How's your night so far?" It's not something I'd normally ask him. Normally, we'd talk about the water capacity of fire hoses or the smoke jumpers who work the fires in our area or the fact that the sky isn't dark enough to see stars tonight. Shane always likes to talk about the color of the sky.

He nods in answer to my question. "Not gonna stay long. You?"

I want him to want to stay.

I also want him to agree to be my prom date. I consider waiting until another time to ask him. Tonight feels too loaded since most of the people at this bonfire will be paired up by the end of the night.

I'm really nervous about asking him to be my date. It's the senior prom, so I need to do the asking. Juniors don't go unless they're asked by a senior.

I'm just going to do it. Just start talking. Just . . . ask him.

But I don't, and Shane stands there staring at me expectantly because I haven't answered his question. His painfully beautiful blue eyes bear down on me, lighting up the night.

All I can think is that I really wish I had one more shot of Fireball.

"Shane, would you be my prom date?" The words come flying out, not at all the way I imagined saying them the four thousand times I went through it in my head. I'm looking over his shoulder, not making eye contact. But at least it's done. I've asked. I'm finished.

When I force myself to meet his gaze, I don't like what I see.

At first, he turns a charming shade of pink that extends to the tips of his ears. With his left hand, he combs his longish hair off his forehead a few times, and when I get a good view of his eyes, I see a combination of panic and icy resolve.

Taking a step back as though he's in danger of being lassoed and dragged to the prom, he shakes his head. He blinks and exhales a breath that feels like it lasts a whole minute.

"I-I can't. It wouldn't be right. I'm sorry."

I feel the tears welling in my eyes and a lump the size of Kansas lodged in my throat, making it impossible to laugh off his response or say something casual and funny to my friend. Because that's all we are. All we were.

It wouldn't be right for him to be my date and pretend.

Realizing I can't be around him for another second before the tears fall in earnest, I turn away and start walking. I can't let him see my crestfallen expression that betrays my mortification and the fact that I hadn't accounted for him saying no. I didn't have a plan for it.

"Julia, wait," he calls after me.

But I don't wait.

I run.

I run to where my car is parked, and I drive myself straight home. Then I make myself a plan.

In full dramatic fashion, the plan includes getting out of Dodge—or in this case, Green Valley—as soon as humanly possible to avoid further mortification. The offer from a school I'd never heard of in the middle of California's Central Valley suddenly sounds like the perfect escape for the child of escape artists who taught her how to run.

Only I won't be flakey like them. I'll work hard, stay consistent, and build something stable. I won't let emotion cloud my judgment. I'll seek unflappable stability.

I don't even read the brochure or look at a map. It's California. I'll be at the beach, floating on a raft, eating my weight in cheesecake that I'll bake as part of my college education.

Done and done.

I leave the day after graduation and never look back.

CHAPTER 14

JULIA

*T*hinking about the past didn't hurt anymore. Not as much anyway.
Maybe we didn't need to talk about it. Maybe I didn't need to know what was going through his head back then. I was more interested in now.

He turned his head and looked off into the distance, across the field we couldn't see in the dark.

Sitting next to Shane, I felt my heart swell with the urge to move closer. At the brush of his shoulder against mine, I felt white-hot flames run through my veins at the prospect of touching him again. In more places.

I felt myself leaning into him, almost willing him to take advantage of the proximity and put his arm around me. My hints weren't subtle. Short of climbing into his lap, I'd given him every physical sign that I'd reciprocate the slightest affection, and he'd stayed on his side of the tailgate looking straight ahead.

He wasn't interested in me that way. I needed to get over it.

But then . . .

All the little touches, the romantic moments looking at shooting stars, the opportunities to lean in just a little bit closer until our lips connected . . .

Yeah, Shane passed on all of those.

He seemed to prefer letting the small gestures hang in the evening breeze —intimate, quiet words and tiny touches—that whispered against my skin and made me crave more.

If it was a game, he played it expertly. If he had no idea he was doing it, my body begged me to push him over the edge where he'd lose control despite himself.

And yet . . . even all these years later, even with the confidence in myself that came from conquering a new city and starting a business on my own, I still resembled the teenager I used to be who I didn't want to venture anything and be rejected. Again.

On one hand, I knew it was crazy. I was thirty-three years old, for heaven's sake. I had more self-esteem than I'd had back then. I'd walked away from a loveless relationship because it wasn't healthy for me and it no longer made me happy.

I wasn't afraid of risking my heart and not having it work out.

I was afraid of risking my heart on Shane Meadows and having it not work out.

And how could anything possibly work out, other than maybe a long-overdue, lust-fueled fling while I was in town?

Ahem . . . a long-overdue, lust-fueled fling while you're in town would be just lovely, thank you very much.

Then, there was that. Brilliant inner voice for the win.

"Shane . . . " I was going to ask for what I needed, and right now it was an explanation.

"Yeah."

"I just have to know . . . why'd you turn me down? Would it have been so awful to come with me to the prom, even as my friend?"

He froze. Then chuckled in a way that seemed like he didn't think it was funny, not with the way his brow furrowed. "Wasn't it obvious?"

"No. Definitely not to me."

He stared at me in disbelief. "Do you really not remember how I was back then? So unsure of myself, so undeserving of someone like you."

The words shocked the hell out of me. "What does that even mean—someone like me? Who did you think I was?"

"I thought you were perfect."

My heart melted like milk chocolate kisses in the oven. "I thought you were perfect too."

"But I wasn't." He held up his hand as proof.

My eyes came to rest on his "pound of flesh," as he'd referred to it the first day we baked together, a day that felt like months ago instead of weeks. When Shane started to lower his hand, I reached for it and held it in my palm. Then I scooted closer so I could take a better look.

His wide palm, slightly narrower than his other, still looked masculine and strong. His skin, weathered by work tools and everyday use, stretched over the tendons of his hand, but instead of long graceful fingers, he had the barest of nubs, barely larger than a penny.

I did it without thinking—raised his hand to my lips and kissed his palm. His thumb pinched in and grasped my hand after I did it, and the intensity of his grip sent chills down my spine.

I glanced up and found his expression serious, his eyes studying my face, searching for signs of my reaction to him. Again, following instinct, I leaned my head against his chest and enjoyed how right it felt when his arm wrapped around me.

This was the guy I used to know.

This was the guy I wanted to know better now.

"Shane . . . "

"Yeah." His hand brushed a few strands of hair out of my eyes. I didn't know how he even noticed they were there, but the gesture emboldened me to push harder for what I knew we could be together.

"After a year of friendship, I thought you knew me better than that. I know you did. I get that you didn't want me like I was hoping, but—"

He stopped me with a finger against my lips. "That's not it."

"Okay. What, then?" I felt it, that urge to sprint down the desolate road into scary darkness rather than hear the truth. I'd run off back then before some sort of explanation that might have made sense of everything, and the self-preservation instinct was equally real now.

No. Stay.

He traced the line of my jaw with his thumb and tipped my face to look at his. If it was going to be death by heartbreak, I was going down drowning in those blue eyes. Weirdly, I felt like it would be an okay way to go.

"Julia, I always have." His voice broke at the end, like it cost him something to admit it.

But I was confused, needing concrete words, modifiers for nouns, adverbs, and clauses to define verbs.

"Have what?"

His voice sounded raw when he confirmed his meaning. "Wanted you. Always."

I swallowed hard and briefly closed my eyes. It didn't matter that I'd never known or understood any of this back then. Knowing it now was everything.

"I thought you didn't even like me."

He nodded soberly. "I know. I'm sorry."

"No. No apologies."

"In this case, it's warranted. I am sorry about it, and I have been since age seventeen."

The weight of his words settled over me, hugging me like a weighted blanket, giving me a sense of security I'd never felt before. I never knew how much I wanted or needed it, but now, my body and my emotions demanded it.

I took a deep inhale of the night air and felt it trace the contours of my face. My senses felt alive and heightened, as though a part of me had been existing in a deep slumber for years and was only now sensitive to feeling.

"How-how come you pushed me away?"

"Because I hated myself back then. I know it sounds like a cop out, but I felt ugly on the outside, and that colored who I could be on the inside."

"That was never who I saw. I—"

He stopped me, holding up a hand. I wondered if he intentionally chose the right hand as if to demonstrate. "I knew that, and that made it even harder. I believed you could only want me out of pity, and that made me hate you almost as much as I hated myself. I know it was unfair to you, but like I said, I was confused and insecure and messed up."

It broke my heart to hear it. I hated that he was in that kind of pain back then and that I'd somehow made it even worse without realizing it. He reached for my hand and pulled me closer.

"Shane . . . "

"Hey. This isn't on you. You were there for me in every way that a friend could be back then, but I was only able to accept so much from you. And Jule, when I said no to you, it made me realize I had to find a way to do better. So I started looking. Because of you."

I understood. Gripping his hand, I tried to give him that reassurance. But there was still one thing I needed to get straight. "Did you think I asked you to be my date out of pity?"

Watching his face was a study in human emotion, at once thoughtful, sad, pensive, and resigned. "I-I didn't know. Probably not, but . . . maybe . . . " He shrugged—an anguished gesture that communicated his truth. "I wasn't ready for you. Not in the way you deserved. And I didn't want to break your heart or mine in the process."

I nodded. "And now?"

"I think you know."

"What if I don't?" I wasn't being coy. I needed to be sure we were on the same page. I didn't want to make the same mistake twice.

"Then let me spell it out. I still don't want to break your heart. If I'm lucky enough to have a shot now, I want to own it. And I want to deserve it."

I could have asked for more details—more specific words—but I had everything I needed. "Shane . . . " I took his face in my hands so he'd see me. I needed to make sure he understood. "You already do."

His eyes looked glassy and unfocused. I saw his internal struggle.

I wanted to push the skinny taut string of his resistance to the breaking point.

Shane exhaled a long breath but said nothing. His hands rose to wrap around mine and lower them from his face.

Then he swallowed hard and rolled to the side, rooting around in his bugout bag for something unimportant. Because unless he had a willing pair of lips in there or maybe a box of condoms, anything he found in there would prove unimportant.

Like the half-melted chocolate-covered granola bar. "Hungry?" His voice sounded like dry tinder that could ignite at the mere hint of a rogue spark.

"No."

He swallowed hard and his Adam's apple rose and fell in his throat. He chucked the granola bar off to the side and pressed his lips together, staring at the roof of the truck bed. I watched him, waiting for him to look back toward me.

He had to eventually, right?

A minute went by, maybe two. He'd been leaning back on his elbows, but he let them slide down so he was flat on his back. The rumpled blanket obscured part of his face, and I lost the battle of wills.

"Shane."

His voice sounded strained when he responded. "Yeah?"

"Are you okay?"

"I'm fine. You?" He sounded aggravated.

"Sure. Fine. Great." I wouldn't capitulate. But I also wouldn't let him weasel out of this moment. Not a second time. Not when he'd said what he'd said.

"You tired? We should probably get some sleep since you have work tomorrow."

He was nervous. Stalling.

I'd give him time.

Meanwhile, my heart was pounding so loudly in my chest after what he'd just said that half of me wanted to jump him. I was wound up like a coiled snake and ready to spring.

"I'm not tired." One more hint, one more desperate ploy of a teenager willing the cute boy to take the hint and kiss her. "Shane . . . "

"Yeah?" We could do this all night.

"Fucking kiss me already."

He stopped rooting around in the bag instantly and his eyes shot to mine. They were roaring with heat, stormy seas powerful enough to sink an ocean liner. And I felt the taut string snap and dissolve to dust.

His hands reached for my face, cupping my cheeks delicately while his mouth was anything but gentle. It was a starving kiss. Hot. Meaningful. Deep.

My body responded without thought, moving closer to press against him as he turned sideways. As he faced me more fully, he hooked a leg over my hip, holding me to him.

"You never have to ask again," he growled against my neck, still kissing me along a path from my ear to my jaw.

"Feels like I've been asking you all night." My voice sounded breathless because I was. That first kiss knocked the wind from my lungs.

Shane's hands moved gently along my jaw and pushed into my hair as he angled my face and killed me again with his lips. I felt every nerve ending in my body blaze to life, celebrating this man who'd had my heart despite a decade of efforts to talk myself out of him.

Kissing him was everything I'd ever imagined, only so much better. Every kiss made me want him more—a drug to my ailing body.

"Jule . . . " he murmured before his tongue swept against mine, searching and diving deeper. The sweet taste of him lifted me higher until I felt myself gasp for breath.

Both of us needed a moment. Shane tipped his forehead to mine, and we caught our breaths. His hand slipped down to grasp mine.

I swiped a finger across his lips and his tongue came out to lick it. Then he took it inside his mouth and sucked.

We lay on the blankets on the bed of the truck for what felt like hours, getting to know each other this way. I wanted to touch every curve of his face and discover whether his beard was as soft as it looked. I didn't want to skip an inch of his skin, starting with those incredible lips and discovering every other part of him.

He seemed to feel the same way, his hand moving slowly through the strands of my hair, brushing them aside, as our kisses turned slower, deeper, longer.

It felt so good to kiss him that my body almost gave me a pass on everything else.

Just go with it. Keep doing this. No need for more.

But I wanted more. Telling him to kiss me had worked out well, so I told him that too.

"Shane, I want everything with you."

His eyelids grew even heavier and his pupils darkened to a deeper shade. "I'll give you anything you want, Jule. You're worth the time it takes to make you believe it."

I'd noticed that he'd started shortening my name earlier today and hadn't thought much of it, except that I liked it. Now, I decided I loved it.

He rolled me onto my back and propped himself on his forearms over me. His eyes roamed my face, fixing on my lips, which he kissed. Then they moved lower and his lips followed.

Gripping his flannel shirt with both hands, I tipped my head back as his mouth devoured my neck, his teeth nipping at the skin over my collarbone. But that was all the skin he could access without stripping my shirt off, so he lifted the hem and I raised my arms to let him pull it over my head.

Gazing down at the silk and lace covering my breasts, he let out a groan. "I swear I didn't rig the truck to get those flats, but only because I wasn't smart enough to do it."

The comment made me laugh, which made him laugh. "I was going to say. Seemed a little fishy, but you've got me here, cowboy. Guess it's our lucky day."

"Our . . . "

"Yes, our."

He shook his head. "It's hard for me to fathom that I'm not the only lucky one here."

"You're not. Okay?"

He nodded and lowered his lips to suck through the silk before freeing one of my breasts from its fabric prison. I sat up and reached behind to rid us of the dumb scrap that was clearly in the way of everything good.

Each sweep of his tongue over my sensitive skin burned into my brain like memories in a photo album that I'd file away and revisit over and over again.

The scruff from his beard was rough and delicious against my skin, eliciting a new thrill of sweet pleasure every time he moved.

I reached down and lifted his shirt, pulling the T-shirt under the flannel out of his pants so I could run my fingers along the skin of his abs.

And holy hatchet-swinging hottie, he had abs honed from steel.

"Shane, this isn't fair," I said through a sigh. Which made him stop the glorious torture he was delivering to one nipple and look at me.

"What's wrong?"

"You have too much clothing on."

His expression turned to a smirk. "We both have too much clothing on, if you're going to get technical."

We'd spent too many hours locked in a car together to temper the pent-up desire. Given permission, he pushed my jeans down my ankles, and I worked on his belt buckle before freeing him of his pants.

"Shirt too," I demanded.

Shane acquiesced, pulling both shirts off and lowering the hatch on the trunk, enclosing us in the space. I let out a sigh of relief.

"I have part two of my confession to make," I said.

"What's that?" He gently arranged me on my back with my knees bent and knelt at my feet. Gazing up at the wall of muscle in front of me, I lost my train of thought. He was just so . . . damn beautiful from head to toe. His slightly rumpled hair, warm eyes, sharp jaw, and cherry lips were only the beginning. My greedy eyes traced the contours of his pecs, over his beer can abs, down to his impressive hard length, which I was dying to touch.

"Huh?" I muttered, my eyes surely glassy and unfocused.

"Your confession?"

"Oh, that. Just that I like it better with the trunk closed. Let's keep the outdoors out there if it's all the same to you."

He smiled and kissed the insides of my knees. "I'm only interested in what's inside this truck."

Then he proceeded to show me his interest in utterly fabulous ways, starting with his tongue on my inner thigh. Spreading my knees gently apart, he let his eyes roam again. I loved how he looked at me before he touched me. I saw his appreciation as his eyes, and the warmth of his gaze warmed my skin.

"So fucking beautiful, Jule. I was an idiot at seventeen. Please forgive me."

That sweet talker could make me smile even as I was about to pass out from how good his tongue felt sweeping across my skin. He delved lower, savoring every part of me until he reached my very wet center.

His thumb worked slow circles over my clit while his tongue slipped between the folds of flesh. I can't be held to more specifics than that because after a minute of that, I was seeing more shooting stars than I'd ever find in the night sky.

My orgasm rolled through me, and I may have shouted Shane's name. I may have said a prayer. I may have sung a song. Don't hold me to any of it.

But while I was still recovering from the ecstasy of that, I heard the tell-tale crinkle of a condom wrapper and somehow had the wherewithal to swipe it from Shane's hands and open the foil.

Before rolling it on, I took a long, slow stroke up and down his hard length and felt myself quiver when he gasped. "Fuck."

The man was not normally so foul-mouthed, but I loved his unrestrained expressions. "I'm a goner if you keep your hands on me like that."

So I rolled on the condom, and Shane entered me in one swift motion, burying himself inside me and bringing me to the brink of another orgasm just like that.

Shane drove into me with a steady rhythm that had me dragging my nails down his back and seeing even more stars. "Stay with me, Jule," he commanded, fixing his eyes on mine.

What I saw in them was reverence and maybe even a little bit of love—the kind that came from knowing where a person came from, appreciating the moment on a deep level. Not that he was in love with me—or that I was in love with him—but damn if this wasn't the best sex I'd ever had.

And it wasn't even close to morning.

CHAPTER 15

JULIA

I ignored the knowing glances from Daisy, whom I'd seen the day before when I picked up donuts for our drive while wearing the exact same clothes.

Nothing could destroy my light, airy chocolate soufflé mood.

Aware of her eyes on Shane and me as we sat in a corner booth, I focused on sipping my coffee and trying to force down tiny bits of food. My stomach was in knots—tentatively happy knots because I had no idea where we'd go from here—and spending half the night with him inside me had me grinning like a schoolgirl bursting with a secret.

Despite his encouragement, I barely slept at all. I was too aware of the warmth of his body so close to mine, every touch that led to a second round. And a third.

And now, sitting next to him in the booth at six in the morning, I felt the hazy combination of fatigue and the blushing smile of the cat who swallowed a canary whole.

I'd called Jenn the night before, when I knew I wouldn't make it to work at my usual early hour. She'd offered to let me have the day off, but I wasn't built that way. We'd worked it out so Joy would come in early and I'd get there by ten, which gave us time to stop for breakfast, and then some.

"People are gonna talk." I gestured to Daisy, who couldn't seem to pull her eyes from our table. "You and I showing up here together two days in a row . . ."

"Let 'em talk."

"You have to live with these people. You don't care what they say?"

He may have flinched at my implication that he lived here and I didn't, but he recovered quickly. At least, I think that was what happened. In any case, it was true. Sooner or later, I'd go back to LA, but until then, I was a hundred percent in for whatever developed between us.

"They know we work together," he said, seemingly unconcerned.

Shane looked at my mostly uneaten food and gestured at the plate. "You want to take that to go?"

I shrugged. "I guess. Maybe Daniel'll be hungry when he gets up."

Since Shane had finished his breakfast, there wasn't much reason to linger, especially since I'd noticed a few more prying eyes directed our way,

"I should get cleaned up before work," I said, relieved that Shane had today off. I didn't think I could handle the weight of his stare all day at work with other people around. And he hadn't stopped staring since he slid into the booth.

It made me blush when I caught him doing it, something about the satisfied smirk on his face that said he'd had himself some good sex. I had no doubt I looked the same way.

We made our way back to the truck, which now had two brand new tires, courtesy of Beau Winston, who had a friend at a garage thirty minutes from where we broke down. He drove over before the crack of dawn to deliver two new tires, and we'd gotten on our way within an hour.

And lucky me, I was spared from having to change the tires, even though I'd offered to help.

Neither one of us said much on the drive back to Gram's house. We'd talked so much the day before, maybe we'd run out of things to say.

Nah, that wasn't it. Somehow Shane and I never ran out of things to talk about, but neither of us had slept, and the heavy feeling of fatigue was settling in now.

"Thank you for one of the best days I've had in a long time," I said, as we pulled into my driveway. I knew my words sounded trite, but I meant them.

"Oh Jule, the pleasure was mine."

Shane insisted on walking me to my door, even though I told him he could drop me in front. His expression said I was insane, and he reminded me that he was a country boy who'd been raised to have manners.

I'd forgotten what it felt like to be with a country boy who'd been raised to have manners.

During our brief affair, Trevor held the occasional door open for me, but only when the door pulled outward. If he pushed a door open, he'd just walk in and I'd follow. His car had automatic locks, so there was no reason for him to unlock and open my door first.

It was fine. I thought of myself as modern and self-sufficient. I didn't go through life waiting for men to order for me in restaurants or help me on with my coat like I couldn't do it myself. But the chivalry that Shane showed didn't feel like that.

He did what he did without an agenda. He wasn't opening my door as a way to butter me up or make up for a shrug he knew annoyed me. It was second nature, a kindness, and I accepted it.

The gestures didn't go without notice by my body, however. They made for a new riot of wings in my belly, which were already fluttering their way to a storm.

Not wanting to make too much of the moment, I glanced at him from the corner of my eye and saw his lips pressed into the hint of a smile. I immediately wished the fifty-foot walkway between his truck and Gram's house was a mile long, but in moments, we'd reached the steps to the front porch.

I turned toward him. "Thanks for yesterday—" I barely got the words out before his lips were on mine. Gently at first, a faint brush.

Picking me up so I could wrap my legs around him, Shane turned me so my back hit the front door. I had a momentary fear that Daniel might open it and we'd tumble into the house, but then I remembered it was still early, and he probably wouldn't be awake.

Or, I thought, maybe I should open the door. Invite Shane inside and close the distance between the front porch and my bedroom without taking too much time to analyze it.

Or I could just do this. Feel the grip of his left hand on my thigh, feel the press of his right hand underneath my ass.

It. Was. So. Good.

The pace of our frantic kisses slowed into something more languid and less hurried. Our tongues melted instead of thrashing.

He kissed me reverently instead of fervently.

And I felt my heart open to him.

I felt a version of contentment that was completely foreign. I just . . . felt.

Maybe we kissed for another ten minutes. Maybe an hour.

Then Shane groaned against my lips and tipped his forehead to mine.

"I should go," he said finally, his voice gravelly and deep. If there was an atom of my being that didn't already find him to be the sexiest man I'd ever encountered, that voice split it in two like a nuclear bomb.

"You should?" I barely managed to choke out.

His words made no sense to me. He shouldn't leave, not after a kiss like that. Not ever.

But he was nodding and backing away. "Just to give us space. After last night . . . " He swallowed hard. "I wouldn't be able to stop if you invited me inside. Would. Not." His words tore at me like swords.

"I wouldn't want you to." I could barely breathe out the words because I felt short of breath.

With a hand on the rail, he backed down the stairs without taking his eyes off me. "Right. And you're only here temporarily. Need to pace ourselves, keep things casual. Easy." It felt like he was telling himself, not me. The words stung a little, even though I knew he was right.

I would only be in town a short time. We should keep things casual.

Could we?

Could I?

Did I want that?

Yes. Of course. I had a life to go back to in LA. Shane and I were living out a long-ago fantasy that had clearly been burning for us both all this time. I should just enjoy it. I would enjoy it.

"No, you're right. I'm only here temporarily. It's smart," I agreed.

"Yeah. So I'm gonna go."

I didn't have time to argue with his logic, or lack of it, before he brought a hand to his lips and sent a kiss off into the air in my direction.

"Maybe I'll swing by the bakery later."

"I hope you do."

"Or you can come by the jam session tonight."

I nodded, trying not to be bothered by the lack of a solid plan.

He was still in my sightline, and I felt the need to know when I'd see him again. How devoted did he feel to giving us space? What did it mean in his eyes?

Knowing I was tired, I decided not to wonder too much about any of it. Instead, I watched until he pulled open the creaky door to his truck. Watched him cast a final glance at me, his face so beautiful it hurt. He may have hesitated for a split second before folding his tall frame into the truck and closing the door.

When I heard the engine turn over, I exhaled a deep sigh and dropped onto the faded twill cushion of the porch swing. It barely swayed under my weight with my feet still on the ground.

Then I watched the truck move away, its engine rattle fading as Shane backed down the drive, and brought my fingers to my lips as if looking for proof they'd just received the best kiss of my life.

Under my fingertips, swollen, satisfied, they assured me they had.

And they told me they wanted more.

CHAPTER 16

JULIA

A half hour later, I'd showered and was debating an hour-long nap before going to work. When I came downstairs, I was surprised to find Daniel awake and bustling in the kitchen with a clatter of cast iron pans on the stove and cupboards opening and closing.

"You were up early," Daniel said with a smirk. "Or out late."

Without looking down, he somehow managed to pour a cup of coffee and set it on the kitchen table where I was arranging myself cross-legged into a chair next to a wall of collectible plates from Queen Elizabeth's various Jubilees.

"Yeah."

Having barely slept, I felt like a zombie, but the smell of ground coffee beans was bringing me to life.

"Out all night, if I'm not mistaken."

Two weeks earlier, a statement like that from my brother would have felt like a judgment. Today it felt like a statement of fact.

"You're not."

"Long day of looking at crops?" He regarded me carefully with a raised eyebrow and a definite smirk. Was he baiting me? Telling me he saw us? If he was, he wouldn't do it outright.

We didn't talk about our romantic lives. Never had, probably never would.

Back when we lived in the same house, each of us moved in a separate orbit. I vaguely knew who he was hooking up with, but I didn't comment. By the time he had a steady girlfriend, I'd moved away.

And I'd sure never mentioned that my drama queen departure from town had anything to do with a guy. I had more pride than that, but just barely.

Neither of us had the capacity to think of the other one as a confidante back then.

Not sure either of us had the capacity for it now.

"Something like that."

"What kinds of crops?" He was definitely baiting me.

"Lots of wheat. Made some good decisions for the bakery. It felt good to get back to basics, talking about ingredients with farmers who care about these things."

"Shane care about these things too?" I felt the blush creep across my cheeks at the mention of his name. My mind went straight to that kiss, as though it had ever been far away.

I nodded and looked away. "He was great. Super invested in the process, almost like a kid learning to ride a bike for the first time. Just . . . excited. Running around with him all day reminded me of when I was first starting out in LA, how much I loved it."

When I felt like I'd controlled my schoolgirl-with-a-crush expression, I dared glance at Daniel. He looked pleased at my discomfort.

"Good that you found someone to do that with. Look at crops. And, you know . . . " He turned away but not before I caught the smug grin on his face. He absolutely knew something. Had I given myself away simply by blushing at the mere mention of Shane's name?

Unprepared to talk about "you know" with my younger brother, I took my coffee to the fridge and poured in a healthy bit of cream. Daniel handed me a spoon, and I backed away while he continued his rummaging in the fridge. Extracting a square cardboard carton, he flipped open the top to reveal four rows of brown eggs. "Can I make you an omelet?"

I gawked at him because in my entire life, my brother had never made me a piece of pre-sliced cheese on a cracker, let alone a plate of fancy eggs. Then I began nodding enthusiastically because I loved this version of Daniel and our budding sibling relationship. "Only if I can help. Want me to shred cheese or something?"

"Yes, I was about to insist you keep your lazy ass busy with the complicated task of rubbing a block of cheese against a box grater," he deadpanned. "No freeloaders in my kitchen."

When I hopped off the stool, he stopped me with a hand. "Stop. Take a load off. Let me show you what I'm good at for once."

Not about to deprive him of cooking, I hunkered down on a stool, leaned my elbows on the counter, and watched him get to work.

"So, tell me how a day of looking at some farms didn't end before I went to sleep after midnight?"

I wagged a finger. "I didn't realize living with Gram turned you into a seventy-five-year-old woman with a love for gossip and recipe cards."

"And what if it did?" The sassy look on his face was the spitting image of how Gram's gaze would bear down on us if we ate a bite of food before saying grace, and it made me laugh.

"Then I'd say you've done well for yourself."

Leaving the eggs aside for the moment, Daniel pivoted to the oven, where he checked on a tin of cinnamon rolls. I could smell their sugary goodness the moment he opened the oven, and I didn't have to look far to see the bowl of icing he already had ready to drizzle over the tops. "I'm impressed, Danny. Really."

"I'm sure it comes as no surprise that Gram taught me everything I know." He shot me a look and waggled his eyebrows. "And then some."

I had a feeling about what he was insinuating, but I couldn't be sure.

Gram was a proud baker, and what most folks didn't realize was that the recipes on the front of the cards had less value than the choice observations written on the backs.

That's where she recorded town gossip that related to whatever recipe she made.

Gram was never one to mince words, and every time she baked something for a backyard dinner party, a town gathering or a special occasion, you can bet she kept copious notes on who was flirting with whom, who hurled the best insults, who got his boxers in a twist over something the Iron Wraiths did. She didn't make it public knowledge that the recipe cards had salacious details about nearly everyone in town, but I knew.

I'd flipped over one of the recipe cards one day when she was teaching me how to make soda bread and had eagerly read the backs of a dozen cards before she realized I was on to her. Then, we had a good long talk.

"I'm swearing you to silence, but I love that you found me out," she'd said, licking cake batter from a wooden spoon in her hand. She always baked multiple things at once. It's where she and I diverged—I like to focus on one thing, then move on to the next.

"I promise, Gram." I was all of age five, but being entrusted with my grandmother's secrets about everyone in town felt like I'd inherited a royal title.

If I knew anything all these years later, it was that I needed to find her recipe box before anyone else did. Gram would consider it more important than attending her funeral. I could hear her telling me, "You can honor me in your own time and your own way. Funerals aren't for the dead. We're dead. What do we care?"

But that recipe box—I knew she'd want me to attend to that in person.

"Do you use her recipes, the ones she kept in the—?"

He interrupted me by holding up the box. "I know all about it. And she told me the stories behind every card."

The idea of them spending time in the kitchen just like this made me happy if a little wistful for not being here to do it with them. "I just—"

Daniel interrupted me again. "Stop. I know you feel guilty, but stop. She loved you and she didn't fault you for pursuing your dream. But she did hope you'd come back someday."

Of course she did. Something told me there was an ulterior motive behind her insistence that I come and handle the house.

Daniel retrieved a box grater from a cabinet and began swiftly shredding a block of cheddar onto a plate. I leaned my chin on my fist and gave him the goggle-eyed stare of a kitchen groupie. He promptly swatted my arm away, so my chin nearly hit the counter. "Now quit changing the subject. Tell me about yesterday."

"Quit asking about my dating life."

"Aha! There we go. So you're dating him, are you?"

"No, scratch that. We aren't dating. At least not officially. We had car trouble and had to wait for a tow truck this morning. That's it." That *so* wasn't it and from Daniel's continued grin, he knew it. "Fine. Things did turn a bit date-like in the truck. And this morning."

"TMI, sis. I'm not asking for the gory details, for cripes sake."

"And I'm not volunteering any."

"Great. I don't need to hear how Mr. Phil plays you like an instrument."

"You know that's not his name, right?"

"Mr. Phil? It's a nickname. Haven't you heard people around here call him that?"

"What people?"

He laughed. "Right. I forgot you're antisocial."

The comment roused me from my stool so I could go over and flick him on the shoulder. Pure instinct. Something I'd done for so many years

DOUGH YOU LOVE ME?

as kids that apparently the habit was deeply ingrained. "I'm not antisocial."

Daniel looked down at the spot on his shoulder and up at me, barely containing his amusement. "Antisocial and immature."

"Only around you. You bring it out in me." I debated giving him one more flick for the road, but then I really wouldn't be able to deny the immaturity. Instead, I pretended I needed a little more cream in my coffee and folded myself back onto the stool.

Daniel returned to his pile of ingredients, surveying them as if devising a plan. "I s'pose I haven't heard people call him Mr. Phil as much lately. It was more a thing when he came back."

"I still don't get why people would call him by the wrong name."

"Phil? Philharmonic? People were impressed, is all. It was out of respect, I assure you."

Wait, what?

So desperate for new kernels of information about Shane, I leaned so far forward, I almost tipped out of my chair. "He played for the Philharmonic? Like, locally?"

Daniel turned and stared at me. "Wow, sis. Way to spend an entire day with a concert musician and actually talk about wheat instead of his superstar life in New York."

I replayed the conversations we'd had in the car. And over the past couple weeks. Yes, he'd told me about moving to New York.

But, superstar? Had he omitted that tiny part?

Daniel must have sensed my confusion because he began explaining without attempting to give me more grief for my ignorance.

"He's a modest guy, I'll give him that. But you heard him play at the jam session. You didn't think he got that good just from playing alongside a bunch of banjos." Daniel waited while I continued to look blankly at him. "After Julliard, he was signed by the New York Philharmonic as the Principal horn player. It was a huge deal for anyone, let alone a kid from a small town in Tennessee."

"Wait, Julliard? The music school?"

Daniel outright laughed. "Well, now I know you did stuff other than talking. TMI, again."

"Stop it. He's modest, like you said. He went to Julliard? Then he played for the Philharmonic? How? When?"

"Maybe you should ask him," Daniel deadpanned.

I shook the cobwebs from my head as though I might get some clarity on how it was possible that Shane was a concert musician—and that now he lived here and played for fun at Friday night jam sessions.

It didn't make a lot of sense.

"Why did he leave New York? Do you know?"

Daniel smirked. "You really should remove your tongue from his mouth for five minutes and talk to him."

I shook my head. "Conversation officially over." Sipping my coffee, I looked away from Daniel's accusing gaze.

The yellow morning sun streamed between Gram's red gingham curtains, which Daniel had held back with large binder clips. I wondered if that improvised solution had met with Gram's approval or if he'd clipped the curtains back only after she passed away.

I was about to ask when I noticed him start cracking eggs into a bowl—like a seasoned chef. With one hand, he cracked each egg on the countertop and split open the shells to release the egg, while whisking continually with his other hand.

The first time I'd seen anyone crack eggs so deftly was on an Anthony Bourdain travel show where he cooked with Daniel Boulud. I'd been in awe then, and I was in awe now.

"Where'd you learn to do that?" I continued staring as he picked up a small pitcher of milk and poured a bit into the eggs while continuing to whisk them to a froth.

"Do what?"

"Crack eggs with one hand? That's *Top Chef* stuff right there."

I caught his shy grin before he turned away to retrieve more ingredients from the refrigerator. "I took a class."

"What do you mean, you took a class? A cooking class?"

He rolled his eyes. "No, a Fabergé egg painting class."

"Fine, smartass. Who taught the cooking class?"

He shook his head and wagged a finger. "I took them one summer when I moved down to New Orleans with my girlfriend at the time." Then he ducked behind the refrigerator door to grab a few things.

"When was this?"

"During college. She was looking to work in the hospitality business, so she got a job at a boutique hotel there, and I tagged along and took cooking classes with Emeril."

"Emeril Lagasse?" I practically spat out my coffee and gaped at him.

"Yup. Cool guy, after you get over the whole 'bam' thing."

"You took cooking classes with Emeril Lagasse," I said again, trying to process this. "Why didn't you tell me?"

He laughed and rinsed a bunch of spinach by putting the leaves in a colander and shaking them under running water. Then he began scrubbing mushrooms with a brush. "I thought I did."

"You did not."

"Oh. Okay, well, I'm telling you now."

For the tenth—twentieth?—time in a matter of weeks, I was struck by how little I knew my brother and how wrong I'd been in my opinion of him.

And everyone around here, for that matter. I was a jerk. A certifiable, city-slicker-forgot-about-where-she-came-from jerk. And I hated it.

"Daniel, I don't know what to say. I am so sorry. I'm sorry I've been a terrible sister. I'm sorry I misjudged you. I'm sorry I haven't gotten to know you—" I felt new emotions well up, and I was stopped from letting them spill forth when Daniel put his vegetables down and wrapped his arms around me.

"Stop. You're not a terrible sister. You were busy living your best life. I don't begrudge you that."

"It wasn't even my best life. It was just me spinning my wheels because I didn't know how to get off the treadmill once I started."

He was quiet for a moment, holding me the way I needed. "I'm glad you're here," he said, finally.

I backed out of his embrace to look at him, marveling at his even demeanor. "How can you be so forgiving? I should've been here with you and Gram. I should've helped." I gripped my temples, so frustrated with myself.

"You're helping now. You're a good person, Jules. Don't be so hard on yourself."

He swirled butter in the pan a few times and poured in the beaten eggs. But he didn't understand. I needed to make him understand even if he disliked me for it.

"Do you even know why I came out here? It wasn't just to come to the funeral and check on how you were doing. I came to sell this house. I was going to kick you out and tell you to grow up. I thought you'd been sponging off Gram all these years, and I get here only to learn you'd been doing everything for her and basically keeping her alive."

He loosened his grip on me and pulled back so he could look at me. I knew my face bore the signs of the guilt I felt, but instead of pointing that out or telling me what a terrible person I was, Daniel smiled. "It's okay, Jules."

"Did you not hear me? I was going to sell this place out from under you."

"I heard you. I kind of figured as much."

"So why are you smiling? Are you okay? Do you have your wits about you?"

"I'm fine. So you think we should sell the house?" He still looked amused and a little sad, but not angry.

"I-I don't know now. It feels too special to sell. Maybe we should keep it in the family. And that way you'd always have a place to live."

"Jules, I get the impression you think I'm destitute." He went back over to his vegetables and gave the mushrooms a few more expert chops like he was powered by batteries. Then he scattered them over the eggs. "I'm not. I have a good job. And plenty of savings. Construction pays well and I'm actually good at it."

I hoped my expression didn't betray my surprise. It was time I raised my expectations and estimation of my brother. "I have no doubt you are. That's great, Danny. I'm happy for you."

"I told you I left my high school ways back in high school," he said quietly. "Why didn't you believe me?"

"Because I'm a jerk. Apparently, a few years in a city changes a person." Shane's words from the night before rattled around in my brain until they found a place to take root. I needed to tend them and figure out a way to prove them wrong. But first, I needed to begin apologizing to the people I'd underestimated. Starting with my brother.

"I'm really sorry, Daniel. I need to do better. You're not our parents, I can see that."

"Hey," he said pointedly. "Neither are you."

I looked at him. "Meaning?"

He considered me a moment before responding. "Meaning just because you left doesn't mean you can't come home." He waved a hand. "Don't be so hard on yourself. I'm just glad you came back."

He went back to his cast iron pan, giving the omelet a flip, but I was still stuck on his words. He was right. In trying to be stable and responsible, I'd also done exactly what my parents had done—I'd left my family behind.

Why hadn't I seen it before?

"I'm glad I came back too. And I meant what I said about the house. It means so much to both of us—whether or not you want to live here, maybe we should consider keeping it."

Daniel scooped a perfect omelet onto a plate and dusted it with chopped parsley. Presenting it with a flourish, he stepped back as if to admire his work.

"Fine by me, and I'll be happy to look after the place, even if we rent it out or what have you."

I really liked the sound of that until the next logical brick dropped into place in my brain. Selling the house was my main reason for staying in Green Valley, and suddenly I didn't want that to come to a hasty end. "We don't have to decide any of it today. It was just a thought."

Daniel nodded and took his eggs over to the table. I sipped my coffee and tried not to have any more thoughts.

CHAPTER 17

SHANE

I hadn't planned on kissing Julia. Or . . . any of the rest of it.

Well, let me rephrase that—I hadn't planned on kissing her initially. When I woke up yesterday morning, I dreaded the thought of driving around with her all day if she planned on grating on my nerves.

I believed it was a conscious decision on her part, one borne of frustration with me from what I did many years ago. Maybe that was behind us now.

I sure hoped so.

As soon as the frost seemed to thaw from her demeanor, which happened within the first hour of talking, all I thought about was kissing her.

And a whole lot more.

Which was why I found myself at the top of my favorite hiking trail in a full sweat after basically no sleep. My brain needed to unwind, and my body needed to move.

After my ill-fated turn on the track team, I'd continued running on my own. My body wasn't built for sprinting, but my long legs had the capacity to chew up miles of trail without much trouble. I'd run a bunch of half marathons and a few full distance ones, but now I mostly ran the trails around Green Valley.

My favorite one took me up to where I had a great view of Bandit Lake. It was still placid at this hour, with the sun having swept over the ridge to reflect the mountains on the lake. I'd always loved coming up here alone and letting my thoughts unwind as my feet hit the trail.

The view felt like a reward, and I wasn't too proud to push my fists into the air when I reached the top like Rocky Balboa on the Philly Museum of Art steps. No one was ever around to see me, and the victory after a thousand-foot climb felt real.

Not a day had gone by since I'd returned to Green Valley when I hadn't spent a good few minutes looking at the sky and feeling grateful for it.

Living in New York for half a dozen years, I'd seen the sky in strips, in the narrow areas between the tops of skyscrapers. Sure, I spent time in Central Park, but even there, the wide sky was punctuated by activity—drones flown by kids, planes headed for the airport in Newark, trees lacing the blue with leaves and branches.

I had nothing against trees, but I saw few of them in daylight. Such was my schedule of daytime indoor rehearsals and night performances, which left me struggling to find enough sleep during the day to do it all again the next night.

I hated to admit to myself that I'd left the career opportunity of a lifetime because I missed the sky, but it was true. I just didn't admit it to anyone else.

Let them think I left because I was homesick for the people. *That* they could understand.

Today, for the first time, I thought about coming up here with someone else—Julia, obviously.

She hadn't mentioned whether she enjoyed hiking or running, and I found myself harkening back to what little I knew of her when we were younger. Nope, no recollection of her hiking or running back then.

I hadn't thought to ask her during the long drive, mainly because we had so many other things to talk about. And because it didn't occur to me until now that this spot was beautiful, but it would be even more so if I could gaze at her with the view as a backdrop.

Certain things were irrefutable truths, and one of them was the welling of feelings I had for this gorgeous, accomplished woman who'd only be in town for a short time. I already felt a halo of sadness in knowing we were on borrowed time.

It was crazy to think she and I could be more than a fling. It was crazy that I was thinking beyond wanting us to be a fling.

But I was.

One kiss, and I was goddamn hooked on her.

As my heart rate returned to its resting fifty-five beats per minute, I wiped the sweat from my brow and relished the morning sun striking my skin.

I should have been talking myself down, using the run to come to my senses and realize that with her here only temporarily, I shouldn't even start something.

Instead, I started working out some lyrics in my head, and by the time I was done with my run, I had a pretty damn good song.

CHAPTER 18

JULIA

*E*ven though I knew today was Shane's day off, a part of me thought he'd show up at the bakery anyway.

He'd said he might, and I couldn't help thinking that if he wanted to, he would. Conversely, I decided, if he didn't stop by it was because he didn't want to do it. Or because he was busy. Or because he had things to do on his day off or was catching up on sleep. Or a host of other reasons that shouldn't get my panties in a bunch.

Oh, but I had it bad for him.

Couldn't stop thinking about him.

So I felt myself looking over my shoulder as Joy prepared pastries and I kneaded the dough for today's orders. I was glad to have someone else in the kitchen this afternoon to keep my thoughts about Shane from turning to blueberry muffin batter.

The guests from the first destination wedding had overlapped with those from the second, so there wasn't a moment of downtime when we had just the regular number of bakery orders to fill. I was surprised Shane had managed to wrangle a day off at all, but Jenn liked to keep everyone's schedules consistent.

Rationally, I knew there was no reason for Shane to come to the bakery on a well-deserved day off. I knew he wouldn't push me against the walk-in fridge and kiss the life back into me the way he had the night before.

Would he?

"Shane's off on a hike," Joy said, apropos of nothing. I wondered if I had tiny hearts circling above my head.

"That's nice."

"It is. He usually hikes on his days off, and today . . . well, you saw the sky this morning." It had been an especially vibrant shade of blue, almost like it had been steam-cleaned and made perfect.

"I did notice." I'd also assumed it was the impact of being kissed particularly well a few hours earlier that had me seeing new shades of color I'd never thought possible.

But then, hadn't Green Valley always yielded unexpected treasures? How had I convinced myself for so long that I didn't miss being here?

How, really, had I survived without it?

My thoughts returned to Shane, who was doing what he normally did on a day off. His world hadn't been turned on its side by our kiss. He hadn't been plunged into contemplation like I had. Or maybe he had. Hiking certainly seemed like a good place to gather one's thoughts.

"Does he hike on his own, or does he go with a group?" I asked Joy, hoping my interest didn't betray my *interest*.

"Oh, it depends. Lots of times he goes out with his brother on the early side. Sometimes he runs the trails on his own. He always says he's a mood hiker."

Despite wanting to know more, I let this dribble of information settle while I worked. It felt like a gift to learn this small thing, a faint strand I could follow later on a path to his root.

Instead of interrogating Joy further, I reached for my phone and pulled up a playlist of what I'd once termed 'baking music.' It was a combination of mellow songs that I could sing to if I wanted, but none of them required an angsty mood to compel me to belt out the lyrics.

They just felt like company.

John Mayer's voice lilted from the phone's speakers, and I refilled my water bottle before working the dough once more. I'd stay focused on the task ahead and not let my head get cluttered by all the unanswered questions about Shane.

Joy was laminating croissants, using a small machine to press the butter between layers of dough, then folding and pressing again until there were dozens of layers ready to shape and bake. I was working on the bread, feeling a slight ease in the pressure Shane and I had been under for the past week with the large order.

I also felt the renewed pleasure I used to feel in a kitchen when I was first starting out as a baker, before it turned into a business with financial demands. It had been years since I'd gotten to sink my hands into rounds of dough, and the past week had proven to me that I didn't dislike everything about my business.

But I disliked a lot.

Joy's sigh pulled me out of my reverie. It was a long, sweet exhale of breath that seemed heavy with meaning. "Everything okay?" I asked.

She looked up from the crescent shapes on the baking sheet in front of her. "Oh, yes, it's fine. I was just thinking."

"Oh? Want to share?" I still enjoyed hearing the thoughts of other people more than I liked sharing my own. Being back here hadn't changed any of that.

She twisted a few more pastries into their shapes before she answered. "I'm just curious, is all. What was Shane like back in high school? You knew him, right?"

My carefully wrought efforts to push Shane to the back of my mind exploded like a leaf in the path of a pressure washer. "I did know him. I was a year older, but you know, it was high school."

"Yeah, I figured. So . . . was he always just . . . you know, so yummy?"

That made me laugh. "I think you might need to step away from the pastries. Pretty sure Shane is not edible."

"Oh, but he so is."

I glanced at her. Was she blushing?

"Do you maybe have a crush on Shane Meadows?" I teased. I wouldn't blame her.

She waved her hands over the pastries as if shooing away the thought. "Naw. Shane is like a brother to me, but I'm seeing something else entirely."

"Yeah, what's that?"

"You."

"Me, what?"

"You're walking on clouds, and you just blushed like a sugar beet when I mentioned his name. You're smitten. It's as clear as day to anyone if they're paying attention. And I always pay attention."

I swallowed and thought about how to respond. There wasn't really anything to say. I certainly wasn't going to tell her about last night. Not until I knew whether it was a one-time burst of pent-up wondering or possibly something more.

"I don't know about that." I turned back toward my dough, which I'd now kneaded for so long, I'd pulverized it. I'd punched so much air out of the thing that it had the texture of an elastic band.

Tossing it into the trash bin, I picked up the next loaf, vowing to be more gentle. I couldn't meet Joy's eyes because I could feel my face getting even hotter.

"Well, I know," she said, carrying her tray of croissants to the oven. That gave me time to fan my face for a moment and take another sip of water.

"We go way back, you know how it is. And as to what he was like in high school . . . " What could I even say? "He was completely different. Shy. Unsure of himself. It's good to see that he's living a good life now."

Her laugh sounded like a barking seal. "That's one way to put it, I guess." She continued laughing, using a shoulder to brush a few loose strands of hair from her face as she continued to giggle. "You could also just say the man is a walking house fire."

"I'm sorry?"

"H. O. T.," she spelled out, making me laugh. It also made me blush once more, recalling his hand trailing across my cheek when he kissed me. And the pining from long ago. And the pining since I'd returned to town.

"He's nice looking. Always has been," I admitted quietly. "Back then, we were friends. He's a year younger than me, but he was super smart, so we had some classes together. When I graduated, I moved to California, and been there ever since, and that was that." I went back to over-kneading the new round of dough and had to stop myself before it too ended up in the trash.

"Nothing's ever as simple as 'and that was that,'" she observed. "Most people around here don't go all the way to California for college. You were following a dream?"

Joy Jones seemed sweet, and I didn't have many friends here. It wouldn't hurt me to open up a little bit, especially with someone who loved to bake. My Gram had taught me that anyone with a flair for baking was good people.

"I'd planned on going to college locally, but my Gram read about a school out in California that was offering scholarship money to out of town folks with a talent for baking. They were trying to expand the diversity of their student body. So I applied with some recipes she and I'd worked on together, wrote an essay, and forgot about it. Then I got in. Can you imagine?"

"Sounds dreamy. California? I've never been."

"Nor had I. The scholarship made it basically free. Too good to be true, right?"

"Well, hey, floating in the pool and hitting the beach every day sounds pretty good."

"Yeah, except that the school was in the middle of the farm belt, two hundred miles from the ocean, and I mostly learned about raising livestock. Silver lining, they were serious about their culinary program, and I did a lot of baking. And here I am."

"Somehow, I think there's more to it than that. Monsieur Auclair practically needed a fainting couch for how impressed he was with you. Did you skip a few steps?" While she spoke, Joy made two trays of almond croissants practically without looking.

I watched in awe as she spread the almond paste inside each pastry and rolled it up. When she finished the first tray of twenty-four, she painted the surfaces of each one with an egg wash. Then she sprinkled slivered almonds on the tops.

So entranced by her assembly line process, I momentarily forgot she'd asked me a question. When she stopped before starting on the second tray and stared at me, I finally answered.

"Before I graduated, I applied to apprentice at La Brea Bakery in Los Angeles, and I actually got the job. Later, I found out my favorite instructor in college knew the owner, and he pulled for me."

"Okay, and then . . . ?"

"Then I worked my tail off and learned everything I could about baking bread, eventually grew a business. And it kept growing."

I'd skipped a step here or there, but I didn't love talking about myself, so I was eager to change the subject.

"Oh, is that all?" Joy asked, her hands on her hips. Shaking her head, she wagged a finger at me. "You don't play fair, missy."

"What do you mean?"

"Why are you so modest? You should be shouting from the rooftops about what a badass you are, turning your dream into a reality, and instead, you're telling the story like it's the three bears, and you're the one who doesn't care where she sleeps."

I didn't understand her metaphor, but I got her point. I could have let it go at that, but I liked Joy and I wanted to be honest.

"Actually, it wasn't really me chasing a dream. I mean, I liked baking, but once I got going, I just stayed on the path and chased success." I pulled my hair out of the band holding it back and twirled it into a bun on top of my head before refastening the band.

Joy opened the oven and shoved her tray of almond croissants inside with such force, I feared that half of them got dislodged from the tray. I looked around the kitchen, noticing how the daylight filtered through the high windows like sunbeams casting dust shadows.

I'd always been at home in kitchens like this, from the time I started college in Fresno to the day I arrived at La Brea bakery as a wide-eyed neophyte baker with everything to learn. The smell of butter melting, bread baking, and industrial-strength dish detergents that did the heavy lifting after we finished using all the equipment. I loved it all.

And once again, it struck me that it had been far too long since I'd been in a kitchen baking bread. What had happened to me back in LA that had turned me into a zombie feeding on my success with none of the excitement that had gotten me there?

She shook her head like I'd made her dizzy. "You're saying you didn't have dreams of owning a big baking business?"

I could let her think of me as someone who ran toward opportunity, rather than running away from heartbreak, but my brother had me wanting to own my choices. "I had that dream eventually, but when I left it was because of Shane."

And now, with an ache in my heart, I realized I was wanting to stay because of Shane.

But I pushed those thoughts aside because I wasn't going back to LA anytime soon. I'd committed to helping the bakery get through the next few weeks, and Jenn needed me. There were orders to fill, guests who wanted bread. I simply couldn't leave.

Joy nodded knowingly. "Okay, sister. I understand now." She brushed her hands off on her apron and untied it. Then she pointed at me to do the same.

"What?" I asked, confused because we still had work to do.

"I told you what I saw on your face. You're here now and so is he, so let's get you over to the jam session so you can see him again." She hung her apron on a hook and yelled to Mikey at the cash register. "Can you take these out in thirty minutes to cool? I have an urgent errand."

I started to protest, but Joy was already shooing me toward the door.

144

CHAPTER 19

JULIA

*A*fter getting barely any sleep last night and working all afternoon, I was worn out. Joy dropped me off and went home to change, with the promise of picking me up in an hour.

I showered and put on a navy blue dress that fell just above my knees. Gram had always told me that I'd inherited her legs and should wear short dresses, but I'd always gone for more utilitarian clothing—comfy wide-legged pants, shapeless maxi dresses, jeans.

Until now, I didn't care that much what anyone thought about my clothes, my legs, or any other body part. But after last night and this morning, I wanted Shane to think about all of those things. I wanted him to be so persuaded that we needed to replicate the kiss that knocked me off my feet that he'd shove his awkward hesitation aside.

I wanted him to want me.

So, I put on the dress. It hugged my curves, which I'd accentuated with a pushup bra. I'd bought it with the intention of wearing it more often. Then I'd decided that running bras were more comfortable and shoved it in a drawer.

Since it was summer and I'd taken a few minutes to give myself a pedicure, I decided I ought to wear sandals. The pair I grabbed first were strappy, three-inches high, and made of tan suede.

I thought I'd done a pretty good job of looking better than usual without trying too hard. Joy disagreed.

"Oh, no, you don't," she said the moment I pulled open the car door and swung a leg inside.

"I don't?"

Shaking her head, she opened the driver's side door and began stomping over to my side before I could close myself into the car. Joy extended her hand to me. "Come with me."

I followed her back to Gram's house and unlocked the door, thinking there was an equal chance that she needed to use the restroom or wanted to lecture me about something. I waited for her to explain.

Turning to face me, she put her hands on her hips, and I watched her eyes trace over me from head to toe. "Okay, the dress is great. Love the dress." She looked down and a grin spread over her face before she pointed at my shoes. "And these, I'm dying."

"Thanks. Not too much?"

"Not at all."

Yet she still seemed oddly disappointed when her eyes came back to rest on my face. "But what's with all this?" Her finger circled around in front of my eyes and mouth. I felt my eyes go buggy following her finger.

"What?"

"No makeup? Hair in a pile? Everything's working from here down." She pointed at my collarbone. "Why'd you give up above the neck?"

"Oh. That." I'd thought about makeup, but I didn't want to put in too much effort, only to get shut down by Shane.

"Yeah, that. We're not leaving here without you fixing your eyes, dabbing some color on your lips, and taking your hair out of that rat's nest."

"For a generally kind person, you're mean when you get to the point."

"Not mean, just right."

I didn't want to argue, so I did as she told me, wondering where friends like Joy and Jenn had been in my years in Los Angeles. Sammi was my person back home, but she was also an employee. All the best people in my life were people who worked for me.

I tried not to think that I'd hired people because I liked having them around. That just sounded sad.

"And where's your liquor? You're drinking a shot of something for your nerves, and don't try to tell me you don't need it because I can see it in your eyes."

I didn't bother to dispute this opinion because she'd been right about everything else. Pointing her to the teacart in the living room that had an ample bar setup, I went upstairs and sorted through my makeup bag, which had gone unused since I'd arrived.

With a highball glass of ice and some concoction in it, Joy joined me in the bathroom and supervised my makeup application, goading me on when she thought I was going too easy on the mascara and choosing a lipstick color a few shades darker than what I usually wore.

"Drink your drink first, then we'll apply the lipstick."

"Bossy," I observed.

"Friendly," she corrected.

Fifteen minutes later, with my hair now falling in waves and Joy's seal of approval on everything, we went back to the car and drove to the community center.

Unfortunately, all the fuss made me even more nervous than I'd been initially. I felt like I was on display when I walked into the jam session and took a seat next to the wall. It was the same spot I'd chosen the first time I'd attended, after Gram's funeral.

And as though he expected to see me right there, Shane's eyes found me the moment I sat down, locking on me instantly while he sat with the horn on his lap. I watched him blink a couple times before his lips tipped up into a gorgeous smile that made my stomach flip like an Olympic diver on the high board.

Then, I relaxed and allowed my body and soul to move with the gentle plucking and strumming of all the stringed instruments. Cletus closed his eyes while he played a riff on the banjo, and the other musicians tapped their palms against their guitars or on their laps to give him a beat.

The room exploded in applause when he'd finished. Then one of the guys started singing a long note while everyone strummed away on a new song. Whoops and hollers punctuated the music as the singer shifted to a new note and held it for a long while.

Shane clapped his hands and worked the crowd up until everyone in the room was clapping too. Then he lowered his lips to the horn and played a long note that harmonized with the voice of the man singing.

The crowd had packed the room. Looking around, I saw every chair full, along with all the tables where some people had brought their own food and drinks. Spectators lined the walls of the entire perimeter of the room. Some leaned back with drinks in their hands, while others clapped and nodded to the music. There were more baseball hats than cowboy hats in the room, but the bluegrass vibe was unmistakable in the sound of the music and the collection of instruments.

Except for that horn. It stood out in its majesty, gleaming, and shined to perfection. Mostly, when Shane played, he held it in his lap, his right hand working inside the bell and three fingers on his left hand deftly playing the notes.

But sometimes, he lifted the instrument up, holding it at shoulder height and to the side like he was presenting it to the crowd. People went crazy when he did that and I didn't blame them one bit.

If Shane had a muse, it worked with a powerful hand. His eyes sometimes drifted shut while he played, his concentration so tuned to the music. Watching him sent my nerves into a fired-up frenzy. No amount of deep breathing could still them, so I gave up trying.

It didn't seem fair for a person to be able to kiss like he did and play like that if he had no intention of following through. On everything.

Head to toe, my body wanted him. And as I sat watching, I felt even more nervous about what I'd say to him later.

I also felt a little silly in my dress and makeup, like I was offering myself up to him on a platter, trying to tempt him with my physical self. Second guessing myself again, I had the urge to dart from the room.

No. Stay.

And as if he sought to reward me for that decision, Shane began to sing.

And OMG.

If I'd felt woozy before, hearing him put my senses into overdrive. When he'd sung along to the radio, I sort of noticed that he had a nice voice, but no. He had a beautiful voice.

He was singing a song by Keith Urban that I vaguely recognized, and I overheard the appreciative chatter from a few women near me. "If that man was sexy before, he just took it to a whole new level," one of them said.

"You knew he was super hot. Don't pretend you didn't," her friend said.

I pulled my gaze away from Shane long enough to glance her way. I recognized her as the woman who'd approached Shane that first night after Gram's funeral and reminded him of a promised dance.

Younger than me by a half dozen years, she had long red hair, dark eyelashes, and a pretty rosebud mouth painted pink. Was she Shane's type? I wondered how many times they'd danced. Or what else they'd done together.

Then I reeled in my jealous streak and reminded myself of this morning's kiss. A man couldn't kiss like that if he had his eye on someone else. I felt almost certain . . .

And I hated the insecure side of myself that didn't fully believe it.

Pushing the thoughts away took some effort, but I focused on Shane's soothing voice as my guiding light. Most of the musicians had quieted their strumming, and now Shane was only singing along with one acoustic guitar played by a bearded man in a cowboy hat and a flannel shirt.

This song was new. It had a more plaintive lilt, and Shane's voice tore through the room with even more earnest power than the previous song.

As I listened to the words, I tried to identify the song. It had a familiar melody, but I felt certain I'd never heard it before. I'd remember a song like that.

And yet . . . the words sounded familiar.

"I tell you you're beautiful,
    You think I'm talking about the sky.
    I tell you I'm happy,
    You look for other reasons why.
    I know you don't trust me,
    So I'll give you the time you need.
    Because you're worth all the time,
    That it takes to make you believe."

He continued singing, and I sat paralyzed in my chair. These were the words he'd spoken last night. It couldn't be a coincidence that he had a song up his sleeve that echoed our conversation perfectly.

Which meant that he wrote this song. For me. After last night.

After I'd worried about why he didn't show up at the bakery and worried he didn't want to see me, he'd written a song to convince me he wasn't just the wrong guy at the right time.

I didn't need space. And I didn't need to worry about why he didn't come to the bakery.

He was the right guy.

Always had been.

CHAPTER 20

SHANE

*I*f I'd underestimated the effect my song would have on Julia, it was only out of self-preservation.

And if I was going to sing in public for the first time in ages, I wanted it to land with an impact. I'd hoped to move her heart and soul, but I had to figure there was an equal chance of her running away. So when I saw her get up and dart from the room, I assumed the worst.

It was my own fault—my song was not subtle.

I couldn't do subtle with her. Even though I'd talked a good game this morning about keeping things light and easy, I didn't want it.

And yeah, I knew she was only here for a short time, but after spending a day and night with her, I knew I wanted to spend the rest of her time here with her, and I decided not to be a coward about letting her know it.

Some of the guys were still playing, so most of the crowd had stayed inside, but as soon as I finished the song and saw Julia move from her seat by the wall, I left my horn behind in its case, tended by Clay, who knew how to pack it up correctly.

I didn't need to explain to him what I was doing or why I needed to leave. Before I'd even opened my mouth, he was pointing and pushing me out of my seat. "Hurry up, y'all."

When I exited the room, I saw her pacing with her hand over her mouth. She had her back to me. "Jule . . . "

Not only did she not run in the opposite direction, she flew at me as soon as she saw me.

I didn't think or prepare. I caught her in my arms as she wrapped herself around me, pressing her forehead to my chest. She said nothing, so I waited until I felt her grip on me loosen.

When she tipped her head back to look at me, I saw her eyes were glassy and round, their chocolate depths burning with something more beautiful than I'd ever imagined. "You wrote that today?" she asked.

Laughing, I kissed her forehead and tipped my own head down to meet hers. "It figures the first thing you'd want to know is my timeline."

I didn't give her a chance to respond before I kissed her.

This was no replay of the slow buildup of last night. I needed to drink her in, and then I needed to take her home.

Our lips crushed against each other, searching, hungry, desperate. I didn't know what I was seeking, but I knew I'd find it in her.

The music started up again in the other room, but it faded into the distance as my other senses took over. I wanted to feel her, inhale her. The rest was just background noise. Even though music normally fed my soul, tonight was different.

Wrapping her arms around my shoulders, Julia pressed against me, and the contours of my body absorbed the softness of hers like they were carved especially for each other. Maybe they were. She was making a believer out of me.

Tracing the outline of her lips with my tongue, I reveled in her softness. Nipping at her bottom lip, I listened for signs of what she wanted. She sighed when I bit down a little harder. Sighed again when my fingers wrapped around her hip and dug into her flesh.

She opened for me and matched my tongue's desperate search stroke for stroke.

My brain couldn't decide what and where my lips and tongue wanted to be and in what order, so I went by feel, kissing her again, deeper this time.

Lifting her up, I held her while she wrapped her legs around my waist. I was aware of her short dress barely covering my hands, which meant it was barely covering her. But it was enough.

I walked us out of the center of the room and into a more isolated corner because there were kids in the other room and at this rate, we risked scandalizing them.

I turned us so I blocked any view someone might have had of her and kissed her neck, trailing a row of tiny kisses along her throat as she tipped her head back, giving me ample access to the soft sensitive skin I craved.

Her hands were everywhere, running along the length of my back and over my shoulders. She wrapped them around my neck, and her fingers danced in the hair at the nape.

I felt crazed. Frenzied. Nothing in the world made sense other than her.

And I had to tell her. Tell her what? I didn't even know.

"I was afraid you ran away." My voice sounded rough when we came up for breath. Like I'd been chewing on cement.

"I almost did," she panted, her voice equally raspy.

"Before or after I started singing?"

Her eyes went round as she stared. Then she laughed. "Figures you'd ask about the timeline."

It made me smile, but I still wanted specifics. "You didn't answer my question."

"Are you kidding? Before. There wasn't a chance in hell I was leaving once I heard that song."

That was enough talking. Cupping her jaw in my right hand, I found her lips again. Taking my time, I kissed the corners of her mouth. She tasted like tequila and lime, and I wanted to remember it forever.

She was the closest thing to heaven I could imagine, and I was not particularly religious. But this—her—it would keep me happy for an eternity and prove that I'd done something right with my life.

Anyone going in or out of the jam session could see me, and I didn't give a fat damn. I wouldn't pass up a second of this for my own propriety, and I didn't care who knew it.

Except . . . the loud clearing of someone's throat brought me back to my senses. I was still blocking Julia from view due to my height and the way I'd tucked us into a corner.

Turning my head to look over my shoulder, I saw Cletus leaning against the opposite wall, as though giving us space and invading our space at the same time.

"Go away," I growled.

"There are children present, y'all should take that into account."

"Noted. Thanks for your concern," I bit out, feeling crazed enough to punch him if he lingered. Maybe he knew as much because he nodded and turned back into the jam session.

I had no idea whether he'd left for a bathroom break and happened upon us or whether we'd somehow drowned out the music, but I doubted it.

Cletus just knew things.

It shouldn't have surprised me that he'd seen everything that went down between us when I'd sung my song, followed us out of the room with his eyes, and waited what he deemed an appropriate amount of time before coming out here, knowing what he'd find.

Once he was gone, I turned back to Julia, whose eyes looked unfocused and dazed. It was exactly how I felt, and I kissed her once more, this time softer and with more care.

Our feverish desperation turned into a slower dance that felt like caramel melting over the top of a brownie straight from the oven. I couldn't imagine a scenario where I'd ever get tired of kissing her. I didn't plan to investigate.

Pressing Julia's back against the wall, I leaned in harder, letting her feel exactly how much I wanted her. "Yes, please," she groaned, circling her hips against me.

This could get out of hand in about five seconds, and my brain had given up full control to my body. Wrenching my mouth from hers was painful, but it gave us both a second to internalize Cletus's concerns.

"Do you have a car here?" she breathed against my shoulder.

I nodded, unable to do much else.

"Let's go. It's a five-minute drive to Gram's."

Again, I said nothing, but I backed up two steps and reluctantly allowed her body to slide down mine. Then I kissed her one more time for the road.

Five minutes felt like an awfully long time.

CHAPTER 21

JULIA

*H*oly hot hunk of handsomeness.

If it hadn't been made abundantly clear to me last night, my current situation confirmed it. Shane Meadows could really kiss.

Maybe it was a good thing I never learned this back in high school because I'd never have left. Even if he'd rejected me afterward and made it clear I wasn't his type, I'd have followed him around like a puppy hoping for one more tiny treat.

And now . . . I didn't know which end was up and which was down. The drive back to Gram's felt like waiting for a winter crop of peaches to ripen on the vine. Someone must have come along and added extra roads in between the community center and Gram's house while we were busy listening to bluegrass because it took about an hour to get home.

Then it took me another hour to run around the place and make sure Daniel was nowhere to be found.

Once those items were ticked off the list, I took Shane by his hand and led him up the stairs to my old childhood bedroom, where I'd been staying for the past few weeks.

Awash in shades of pink, the room still had the hot pink throw pillows on my old gray and white flowered comforter and a corkboard on the wall. Gram had replaced some of my childhood snapshots with later ones of me graduating college and with newspaper clippings about my bakery openings.

In high school, I'd never brought Shane here—all part of our refusal, back then, to let our present day lives affect the friendship we had. Instead, we'd sat under trees and looked out at mountain views, talking about life's big things. But now, I wondered what the high school remnants of Julia Browne looked like through the eyes of her biggest crush.

Gesturing around to the One Direction posters on the walls and the piles of regency romance novels, I gave Shane a quick tour. "An ode to my high school self, who wasn't that different from my current self."

"Harry Styles fan, are you?" He smirked and regarded the two band posters as well as several framed positivity quotes that I'd tried to apply to my life. "Keep calm and carry on" had served me well.

"I'm a Shane Meadows fan," I corrected. He smiled and I pushed him gently backward until the backs of his legs hit the bed, and he dropped onto his back, pulling me with him. I sat up and straddled his legs. "That song, Shane. It was beautiful."

It was more than beautiful, but I didn't have the words to do better. So I tried to show him in other ways how it had moved me.

Reaching for his hands, I kissed each of his palms before interlacing our fingers on his left side and squeezing his right hand. "This would have been a high school fantasy," I said, "Shane Meadows in my room, laying on my bed."

His face filled with regret, and he closed his eyes for a long beat. "I was an idiot. We've established this, yes?"

"Yes, but I want to drive home the error of your ways."

"Fine. Do what you must." He pulled me forward until I was on top of him. "As long as you're naked while you're doing it."

"That can be arranged, fine sir."

For now, though, neither of us was in a rush. Over the course of twenty-four hours, our pace had slowed to something resembling the slow pour of real maple syrup instead of the wild crush of lips and hands and bodies.

Maybe it was the infernal summer heat in Tennessee. Maybe it was the fact that we both knew we were wanted. But everything slowed to a careful, patient pace.

Almost fragile. No rushing through anything at all.

"I might need to turn off the lights or something. Not sure I can do what I have in mind for you with a boy band staring down at me," Shane said, gesturing at the posters.

"What do you have in mind?" I let my lashes dust the tops of my cheeks. I'd put on the makeup—might as well let it do its thing.

It sure as heck did. Shane's eyes clouded with heat and their blue deepened.

"Kiss me, Shane," I demanded. "Close your eyes and kiss me."

As his lips brushed lightly against mine, I felt every nerve ending in my body flare to life. He made me feel like an electrical storm pulled me into its thrall each time his lips grazed mine.

And never mind how it felt when he moved across my cheek and let out a long, sexy groan near my ear. Goosebumps raced across my skin.

I may have swooned. I may have moaned.

Based on Shane's sexy chuckle, I think I did both.

He pressed into me, and I could feel him hard and thick through the thin fabric of my dress. As he circled against my core, the heat built instantly.

"I don't know how you do that," I sighed, my heart already racing.

"Do what?" He circled again harder.

"Get me so turned on in under ten seconds." I was already breathless and he'd barely touched me.

He smiled. "Next time, I'm going for nine."

Shane may have spent his early years worried about how people would perceive his symbrachydactyly, but at this stage, the man knew what to do with his hands. They moved over my shoulders and down my sides, landing at my hips, which he gripped hard before flipping me onto my back.

The way he was gazing at me made me blush. "You look like you want to eat me for dinner."

"I want to eat you for dinner and dessert. And again as a midnight snack. And I'm awfully glad you wore a dress tonight. It's so fucking sexy," he said, lifting the hem and moving down to make good on his promise of dinner and dessert.

He planted a row of kisses along my stomach and over my panties, inhaling deeply as he moved lower. "Jule, I've been thinking of this all day long."

"I love that you call me Jule. Most people add the s."

"What?"

"They call me Jules. Never mind, not important."

He stopped kissing my skin and I immediately felt bereft. But his gaze told me he had something important to say. "I'm not spelling it like that."

"Like what?"

"J-u-l-e."

"How else can you spell it?"

"When I say your name, I mean j-e-w-e-l. That's how I think of you."

"Shane . . . You're going to make me fall for you."

He flinched and I realized what I'd said. Backpedaling, I waved a hand as if to erase the words from the air. "Forget I said that. I know we're temporary. Don't freak."

"I'm not freaked." He traced a finger over my cheek and tucked a loose tendril of hair carefully behind my ear. "And I won't forget." His mouth crashed to mine, and he kissed me like he hadn't already knocked the wind from my lungs.

I struggled to keep my wits about me because I shouldn't be saying I was falling for him. And I definitely shouldn't be doing it. I knew we were temporary.

But we could still be temporarily incredible.

Hooking his thumbs in the sides of my panties, he pulled them down slowly, as though revealing a work of art. At least, that's how he made me feel.

My heart thudded in my chest. I'd never—ever—felt this way about a person. He could do things to my body and my heart that no one ever had. That no one else could.

"Shane, I want you inside me. Please."

Obeying my every wish, he unbuckled his belt so I could push his jeans and boxers down and wrap my hand around his thick length. He was already so hard and I already wanted him so badly it hurt. He quickly rolled on a condom and slowly pushed inside. I felt myself gasp as he filled me completely.

He was slow, sensual.

Furious and demanding.

Careful and sweet.

Then we were both hurling into an abyss of stars and blackness.

"Fuck," he bit out. "Fuck, Jewel."

I buried my face in his neck and lost myself in the sound of him growling out my name.

Jewel.

* * *

In the morning, I made a pot of coffee, ignored the yoga stretches because Shane had already bent me into a pretzel last night, and checked on the Royal Family.

Then I led Shane out to the back meadow where a floppy hammock made of thick white yarn hung from a centuries-old tree. I'd always envisioned a double-wide porch swing hanging from this tree, but Gram thought it was frivolous and Daniel didn't build things like double-wide porch swings.

I'd always suspected that Gram's real objection was that such a swing looked a lot like the perfect place for two people to sip a good cup of coffee together after a good night of sex. And she wasn't about to encourage that in her teenage granddaughter.

So we had the useless hammock, which could barely hold two people, though I was putting it to the test now.

I'd poured our coffee into a thermos and put two ceramic cups from the Queen's 2018 Jubilee into a canvas tote along with some donuts Daniel had bought at Daisy's the day before.

I put everything on a picnic table that sat near the tree because I knew there was no earthly way to hold coffee in a hammock.

It took a bit of balancing to get both of us onto the thing because it kept flipping over and dumping us on the ground. Which led to some hysterics and a few more failed attempts before we successfully settled.

Once we were situated and I'd managed to tuck myself under Shane's arm, we arranged ourselves into a kind of bear hug. "Okay, now, don't move," I said, breathing steadily and slowly like I was sneaking up on a sleeping viper.

"That kind of defeats the purpose of cuddling in a hammock if I need to be frozen like a statue."

"And don't talk either. We're starting to wobble."

He laughed at that, but we managed to stay upright, despite a wobble that almost dumped us out again. Shane had his arm around my shoulders, and I snuggled into him and let the leaves filter the sun as it hit my face. The moment was exactly as I'd pictured back when I tried to convince Gram to buy the swing.

I had a feeling that if she saw us here now, she'd approve.

CHAPTER 22

SHANE

"Just a hint," she begged a few days later, swinging my hand in hers as we exited my truck at the bottom of the trail.

"Nope."

"A breadcrumb. In case I get lost so I can find my way."

It was half past five in the morning, but the sun had just brightened the sky enough for us to see.

Gripping her hand a little harder, I promised, "You won't get lost. I won't let you out of my sight."

I wouldn't. Not for the foreseeable future.

Sure, I knew we had an expiration date. She didn't live in Green Valley, and as much as she seemed to be enjoying her time here, she'd go home to LA eventually. Her life was there, her thriving business was there. I had no illusions that this was permanent.

But I would enjoy the hell out of every moment I had with her until she got on the plane.

Case in point, today we were hiking to the lookout point where we could see Bandit Lake, which lay atop of an adjacent mountain.

It would take us less than an hour to reach the spot at a normal walking pace, longer if we stopped to make out every few minutes, which I anticipated because I couldn't keep my hands off her.

It was like a stopper had been pulled from a bottle of champagne. The

161

damn thing was too fat to put back in the bottle, so there was no use in trying, and the delicious elixir flowed freely until I was drunk on her.

Once we started up the trail, she took the lead, dragging me by the hand to keep up with her pace. "Come on, slowpoke. Let's get to a view or something."

Pulling her back, I folded her into my body, wrapping my arms around her and burying my face in her hair. "We have all morning, Jewel. What's the rush? You're like a firefly."

"Firefly?"

I nodded, refusing to release her. She didn't seem to mind. I felt her sigh and relax. "You're like a bright spark of magic, and you're lighting my way to better and better places."

Her sharp intake of breath was matched by her soulful round eyes as she leaned back and stared at me. "How do you do that?"

"What?"

"Make everything sound like poetry."

On a long blink, I told her the truth. "You inspire me." It was true in so many ways and for so many reasons, but I didn't think she needed to know all of them. Not when I could kiss her under the aspen trees while the leaves flickered in the slight morning breeze.

We were never going to reach the top at this rate.

Reluctantly, I drew away from her lips, leaving a trail of kisses across her cheek and whispering in her ear. "There's more of that to come. Let's keep going."

She nodded, unfolding herself from me and starting up the hill again, still gripping my hand. "I hope you're not just talking about today's hike."

I smiled. "I'm not."

We hiked and stopped and kissed and hiked, and after what felt like hours, we reached the lookout point.

The morning air still felt crisp and new. Other than the insistent chirp of birds, the air hung around us in silence. Stretching out below us, the lake looked placid, and its deep blue surface reflected an entire range of mountains in a perfect mirror.

"It still has some of the cleanest water in the whole country," I told her, proud that the locals had been able to keep it that way. The lake and the houses around it existed on former park land and could only be deeded from a relative. One of Cletus's brothers had a place up there, and so did his sister.

"Wow. You run up here every day?" she asked, her breath a pale cloud in the cool air.

Moving behind her, I wrapped my arms around her and tipped my head down. "Not every day. But on the days I'm not baking, I try to get here around this time. When it's quiet."

She tilted her head to look up at me. "Is it not always quiet? Seems pretty peaceful up here."

I pointed toward the lake, which was, in fact, peaceful at this hour. "After eight, you'll see some rowboats. They still stock it regularly with fish. Plus, a few people hiking on this trail."

It was fun being with her in Green Valley. As much as she knew the place from having grown up here, she seemed to have forgotten details and greeted all my reminders with the wonderment of learning about them for the first time.

Checking her watch, she nodded. "Guess we've got some time before all that happens." Her eyebrows bounced.

Picking up her train of thought, I swung my daypack off my shoulder and handed it to her. "Want to do the honors?"

She grabbed it and nodded, unzipping the main compartment before she'd even said yes. Inside, she found the fleece blanket I'd packed, an inflatable pillow, pecan cinnamon swirls I'd baked last night, fresh squeezed orange juice, and a wool beanie that matched my own.

"You brought me a beanie?"

I smoothed the hair back from her forehead and carefully stretched the wool over her pale blond waves, tucking the loose strands in at the temples. "There. It's perfect."

Dropping the pack, she twirled in a circle like a little girl in a party dress. "Could you tell I had beanie envy?" She patted it on the top of her hair, the rest of which hung down her back in a long ponytail. She looked adorable.

"Perfect fit." I kissed the tip of her nose, then her soft, plump lips. When I felt her shiver, I withdrew the blanket from my pack and wrapped it around her.

We stood that way for a while, enveloped in each other, kissing like we had all day to do it. I guess we did. But I had other plans, which included spreading the thick blanket on the ground and pulling out the Sunday crossword puzzle—the paper version—and having her work it with me.

It was something she'd mentioned liking to do with her Gram, so I took a chance that it would make her more nostalgic than sad.

"Oh, this is the best idea. I can't believe you thought to do this."

Removing a second puzzle from my pack, I waggled an eyebrow. "I know you like a challenge, so we can either work on it together, or we can each do our own and race to the finish."

That earned me the biggest smile I'd gotten all morning.

She shivered in the morning chill, so I wrapped an arm around her and pulled her in close. She didn't seem cold after that. Or, at least, we both forgot to think about it.

From where we sat, the view spread around us in all directions. I sighed with contentment, pulling her even closer and dropping a kiss at her temple.

"You love it here, don't you?" she asked.

I didn't need to think twice about the answer. "I do. But having you here on top of this mountain makes the view a lot better."

I could feel her smile without having to look down to see it. Then she turned sideways so she could look at me.

"So I hear people call you Mr. Phil," she said with a raised eyebrow.

Oh. That.

"You been talking to Cletus?"

"No, my brother."

Great. Even he'd picked up on it.

I extracted the thermos of coffee from my pack and went about pouring us each a cup. It was a distraction technique, but I knew I'd have to answer eventually. She waited.

"Um, some people around here have been known to call me that. But I never liked it." I kept my tone light. I didn't want to ruin what could be great mountaintop sex on a blanket with her being mad at me.

"Not the point. Why didn't you tell me?"

I shrugged.

"Shane . . . "

"Yeah."

"Did you intentionally omit or did you get sidetracked but desperately want to tell me everything about your life and yourself."

"The latter. Definitely the latter."

"Uh huh."

I hung my head. "I'm sorry. I just didn't feel like getting into why I left the best job in the world. I sound like a whiny asshole, and it's, you know, not the sexiest story."

She laughed. "I appreciate how you only think I'm here for the sexy stuff, but tell me everything, please. I want to know."

"Okay. It's not that complicated. Living in New York and playing the

French horn didn't make me happy. I won't say I hated it, but I intensely disliked it."

I explained that there was a solid reason I moved from New York after two years in the Philharmonic. It wasn't the winters. It wasn't the crowds. It wasn't even the noise.

I could accept all of those things from a city, even the biggest, most intense city crammed into the smallest impossible island space.

But I didn't like feeling lost.

When I'd first set foot in Manhattan, fresh off the Tennessee turnip truck, I had no doubt that some city slicker would knock me sideways with street smarts I knew I didn't possess. And that happened at first, as someone savvier and scrappier shoved in front of me and slipped through the closing doors of a subway car.

As I stood, waiting for the next train and wondering if I had it in me to be savvier and scrappier, I quickly realized that I did.

At only eighteen, but armed with the ability to play music, I figured out what I needed to know quickly. If the people at Julliard thought I could play music well enough to earn a scholarship to their school, I'd tackle New York City somehow.

I found my way, figured things out, had a social life, and played a lot of music.

By the time I graduated and the Phil hired me as Principal horn player, I didn't worry anymore about whether I could make it in New York. By all accounts, I'd made it.

But I didn't belong there.

The pain of walking around the city, feeling detached from the other humans who lived there, never left me. It didn't matter how successful I was at the Phil or how much money they offered when I tried to quit.

I stayed an extra two months out of guilt and indecision, but I knew I'd never be as happy in a big city as I was in Green Valley. I needed the connections to people who knew me well without me having to explain anything. I loved the shorthand that came with growing up in a place and seeing familiar faces and places every day.

Even when I was alone at the top of the hiking trail, I never felt alone in Green Valley. Community wasn't about having people around me all the time—it was just about having people around.

"It didn't make me happy, so I quit."

"I'm sorry, come again?" She looked baffled by my explanation. Like, knock her over with a feather, baffled. And that baffled me. "But you went to Julliard. You played in the Philharmonic."

I grimaced at the memories. "Those are just names, Jewel. I wasn't happy."

She shook her head. "I don't get it."

"Isn't the point of life to try and be happy?"

She had an easy answer for that and it surprised me. "No. The point is to have gainful employment and contribute to society."

"Can't a person do that and be happy?"

Again, baffled.

"Um, generally not. Work is work. That's why it's called work."

"But I love what I do now. I love baking. That's why I do it. And I get paid, see, that's the work part of it."

"You're being cute."

"No, I'm being serious. Isn't that why you bake? You built a whole empire out of it."

"Yeah, and it's a lot of work and not very much joy."

Something wasn't connecting. I couldn't figure out why she thought happiness and work were mutually exclusive.

And then I realized. The conversation that day when we were scouting wheat. It wasn't hypothetical. She'd lost the joy.

Some people need permission from others in order to give it to themselves. Maybe that was something I could give to her.

"You've gotta look up, Jewel."

"Look what up?" She seemed confused, like I was telling her to research other bakeries.

I shifted so she was leaning back on me, and I could wrap my arms around her. Then I leaned back, so she was forced to lean with me, and I pointed.

"Look up at the sky. That's perspective. That's clarity. Literally."

She did as instructed. Even though the color of the sky was paler than it would be in a few hours, every shade had a magical quality to it.

"I hate my job," she admitted, surprising me by how easily the words rolled out of her mouth. Almost like she'd never given them space to breathe before, never allowed them the possibility to thrive. But they wanted out. They needed to be said, for better or worse.

"Really?"

She nodded. "It used to be fun. I used to bake every day. Now I never do.

I used to live for the challenge, but it's been a long time since that's been enough. Now it's just a job."

"One you're killing yourself to do well."

"Yeah," she admitted.

"You deserve better."

She deserved everything.

"That's where I disagree. No one deserves anything. I made my choices." I could feel her swallow hard.

"So un-make them. Make yourself happy. Make that choice. Run that company. If you want to bake bread, bake bread. If you want to do something else, do it."

She laughed quietly but she didn't sound happy, just amused by my audacity. "You say it like it's just a choice."

"It is. An obvious one."

"Hardly obvious."

"It's obvious to me. It's just what I see."

"You're seeing something that isn't there. You're inventing me into someone you want me to be, but I'm not her. I'm not tough and certain and . . . sure of myself. Right now, I've never felt more unsure of anything in my life—I'm rudderless and lost and I hate it."

"Just because you didn't see it coming doesn't make it wrong."

She shook her head even more vehemently. "Doesn't make it right either. I don't run away from my responsibilities. I'm not like my parents. I keep my commitments."

A pair of hikers reached a lookout point a short distance down the trail and started taking photos of the view. I hoped they didn't feel like coming to our spot.

"I can see that. But walking away from something you hate doesn't make you a bad person. It doesn't put you in the same category as people who abandoned their kids."

Her eyes went wider than I'd ever seen them. She shook her head like she'd seen a ghost.

"It's a successful business. I'm responsible for it. Someday, maybe I'll feel differently, and I hope I do because I'd really like to be that person."

"You already are her."

"No. I'm not. And maybe you're projecting because you already did it. You left New York and made yourself happy here. But that's not me."

I grabbed her hand, determined to make her understand. "It could be."

Her eyes pressed shut and she inhaled deeply. When her eyelids lifted and she looked at me, I saw an inkling that maybe she believed me. Then she wrapped her arms around my waist and buried her face against my chest, so I convinced myself I was right.

CHAPTER 23

SHANE

J'd always liked coming to work at the bakery, but now I fucking loved it.

In the early hours of the morning before Blithe came into work, before customers showed up out front, before Jenn was around to cast her knowing look at us, we turned the kitchen into a playground.

That is to say, mornings at the bakery were a continuation of very late nights at my house—or sometimes at Julia's Gram's house, when she wasn't paranoid about her brother hearing us—that turned into us looking at the clock and panicking because we needed to feed the bread starters and start baking before we'd slept at all.

It was all I could do to let her escape from my arms long enough to get dressed and hurry off to the bakery with me by her side. It didn't matter that we weren't apart for more than the minutes it took for each of us to get ready for work—our nights continued when we arrived at work.

Feeding the starters turned into Julia pushed up against the walk-in fridge with her legs wrapped around me and my face buried in her neck. If Jenn knew about the shenanigans taking place in her kitchen, she'd likely fire us both, but we were careful and neat, despite our relentless desire for each other.

Afternoons were for long naps in the hammock behind her grandmother's house, drifting to sleep side by side when we were too tired to kiss anymore, and the summer breeze felt like it had a mind to wrap us up in its ways.

With her brother at work until the evenings, our lazy afternoons often led us into the house where we worked on jigsaw puzzles, attended to the myriad fix-it projects she'd listed in a notebook full of lined paper, and eventually cooked dinner, so it was ready when Daniel got home. And if he had plans and wasn't coming home until late, there was no guarantee our clothes would stay on for more than a hot minute.

After sex all night and baking all morning—with ample breaks for kissing by the bread board, the ovens, the hallway where we kept the bread baskets—we were exhausted by afternoon. I never slept better than with Julia curled up in my arms under the shade of the dogwood trees.

I worried I'd never sleep this well again once she went back to California, but I told myself not to worry too much about that and enjoy the present.

It was hard not to worry. I came from a long line of worriers, starting with my grandparents who weren't certain Green Valley was the right place to raise their kids, and continuing with my parents, who worried that having me leave for New York would mean I'd never come home.

Both of those worries proved to be unfounded, but I couldn't help suspecting that my worry trumped them all and just might bear itself out.

Julia would leave.

She'd said so when she arrived and nothing had changed, at least not to hear her say it. Since our first kiss, she hadn't uttered a single word that made me think she was reconsidering her plans.

Not that she should.

I had nothing to offer her except a chance to have some fun and remember the old days when she used to enjoy baking bread. She'd long since surpassed these humble beginnings, and there was no reason for her to take a giant leap back to relive them.

She and I were temporary. We were the very definition of temporary.

A woman coming to town for a short time and having some fun with the local boy she might have had an unrequited crush on was every woman's fantasy of temporary.

All I could offer her was a chance to live it out.

And I hated what it said about me that I didn't much care what it said about me. I was here for the fantasy.

I'd lick my wounds later, in private, after she'd gone. I'd allow the regrets to creep in over the temporary aspect of all of it. But not now. Now,

I'd soak up every minute we had together and wrap my heart in memories later on.

I was in the middle of kneading dough for the last rise before baking when I heard raised voices coming from the front of the bakery. That was unusual. People didn't get bent out of shape over baked goods.

Julia had gone to the front with a basket of baguettes we'd made earlier. Normally, we did sourdough rounds only, but today we'd branched out. It was part of what I dug about baking with her.

The shared love we had for something as basic as baking bread made me feel like we were kindred spirits. Goofy, wheat-sniffing, kindred spirits.

At first, I thought Julia was arguing with Daniel, but the voice that pierced the air didn't sound like Julia's brother. It had an accent, for one thing. And it didn't sound kind. "Jules, what the actual hell?"

My instinct was to protect her from the angry man, regardless of who he was. I wiped my hands on my apron and hurried out to the front of the store.

Now I could see him—dark hair, styled with some sort of product, aristocratic cheekbones but a weak chin. He ignored me and fixed his dark-eyed stare on Julia.

I didn't recognize him, but from the way she fixed her jaw, Julia did. Everything about her posture was stiff and stressed. I'd barely seen that side of her since she'd been in town. I didn't like it.

"Trevor, what's going on? Why are you here?"

Did that name sound familiar? Had she mentioned him?

I had a strong urge to throat punch him. From the way Julia stiffened and balled her fists, I gathered she felt the same way.

"Everything okay out here?" I asked. Julia flinched when she heard me behind her. She glanced back and nodded before returning to glare at Trevor.

"Seriously, why are you here?" she asked again, and my eyes swept over him while a feral possessive streak made me want to hurt him. Badly.

"Why are you *still* here, Julia? With everything that's happened. You need to come back. It's irresponsible to be away this long." His clipped accent offended me with its bossiness.

"I have business to take care of here. I told you that."

"And I told you you're needed at home." *Home?* Did she live with Trevor?

A surge of bile hit my throat. I felt more stupid than sad, angry at myself for allowing the thoughts to dance in my head about the two of us having more than a temporary fling.

Meanwhile, this Trevor asshat had taken a step toward Julia, putting his hands on his hips, which did nothing to make him look more formidable. Still, I didn't like the threatening implication of his posture. I imagined him as some sort of lawyer or business guy, and he was probably used to intimidating people this way.

I knew my way around an ax and a shotgun, however, so his stance did nothing for me.

Julia took a step forward and stood in front of him, crossing her arms over her chest. Then she shook her head at him, unimpressed. "Stop trying to bully me, Trevor. Why did you fly here?"

He stared at Julia and waited for her to finish. I loved her more by the second for facing him down and refusing to cave to him when it didn't suit her. "Because you're not returning my calls. What else was I supposed to do?" he asked finally.

"Fine. Just tell me what you need from me, and let's get this done. I can't imagine that whatever it is required you flying here on a private jet."

I had no idea how she knew he'd flown on a jet, except that maybe he always flew on private jets. And for the first time, I glimpsed her LA life—this man with his crisp shirt sleeves, his expensive haircut, his obvious money.

Was this a part of who she was? Something she was trying to escape?

Or was all of this—the time here in the country, the lazy days with me—just a getaway from her real world?

If this man embodied the kind of man Julia wanted to be with, she'd quickly tire of me.

But I pushed those thoughts aside while I decided whether or not this dude named Trevor deserved to be sucker punched for his mere existence.

I was pleased to see I had a good six inches of height over him and equally embarrassed at myself for caring.

Dude stuff. Ego. I couldn't pretend to be above making comparisons, especially because I really liked this woman. And damn if I was going to let a man she hadn't seemed to mind leaving behind dictate her future, even if it didn't involve me.

Presenting my hand like a civilized human, I introduced myself. Trevor was about to shake it when he looked down at my smallish hand and recoiled. He tried to cover, gripping my hand limply, but I noticed. Julia noticed.

Her eyes met mine and I shook my head. "Let it go," I silently urged. I'd been doing it my whole life. She could too.

"Well?" Trevor crossed his arms, but it did nothing to improve his weaselly stature.

"Well, what?" Julia asked. "Why did you come here?"

"Obviously, I came to bring you home, Julia. Enough is enough."

Her eyes blazed, and she glared at him so hard I felt certain she could burn a hole in his gabardine trousers. I also felt certain he probably wore silk boxers underneath. Fancy-ass cocksucker.

"Bring me home?" She looked incredulous. "That's not your job to do." Mirroring his stance, Julia put her hands on her hips.

He shook his head. "Who else, then? You're behaving like a diva. This isn't who you are."

Julia huffed a laugh. "I'm touched that you flew all the way out here to tell me that, but I'm free to make my own decisions."

"I don't accept that."

Julia waved a hand in his face, dismissing the idea. "I'm not going to talk about this now. It's not appropriate to just show up here and tell me what to do."

It was then that Julia backed away and reached for my hand, the good hand, interlacing our fingers.

He presented his hands, palms up, and I couldn't help noticing his long fingers. "Well, I'm here now. Can we talk?"

Julia shook her head and took a step away. "Not here. I'm at work."

"Work?" he spat out, incredulously. "Oh, come on. Enough playing small-town baker. Time to get back to the real world." What an ass. I'd rarely dealt with his type, but I knew his type—always looking for an angle, certain he'd get what he wanted.

Once again, I found it hard to imagine Julia finding someone like him appealing based on what I knew about her, and it made me worry I didn't know her as well as I thought.

Trevor seemed willing to leave the bakery as long as Julia promised they'd meet later and talk. He ordered a bag of chocolate chip muffins and went on his way, the sag in the back of his khaki pants daring my foot to make contact with his ass.

Julia watched the door close behind him and turned for the kitchen without a word, grabbing my hand as she passed and pulling me with her. Blithe's eyes followed us as we went, but she didn't say a thing.

Once we were alone in the kitchen, Julia turned to me, visibly upset. Shaking her head and pressing her lips together, she seemed to be fighting back emotions, and for a moment I thought she might cry.

Instead, she practically spat, "I'm so sorry. That was . . . unexpected."

She'd said she wasn't dating anyone when I asked, but we hadn't talked about who she'd dated before coming to town. I couldn't be sure of her reasons why, but part of that had been intentional on my part. I didn't want to know. I didn't want to think about what she might be going back to when she left.

Maybe that was naïve, a piece of my brain living in a fantasyland that included her not leaving. The less I knew about what she'd left behind—especially when it sounded like she wasn't entirely happy with it—the more I could imagine her staying.

But getting a front row seat to what her life must've been like threw me for a loop. And from the look on Julia's face, it threw her too. But for different reasons.

"You don't need to apologize."

"He's unbelievable. But...he's right. I have been gone too long."

"Who is he?"

"Trevor Hobart. My partner."

"Your partner . . . ?"

She waved a hand as if to clarify. "My business partner. Though we did date. Briefly. Years ago. Many years ago."

Digesting this information, I went back to rolling out some dough for pie crusts. The butter had gotten too soft in the few minutes I'd left the dough unattended, however, and it started sticking to the rolling pin. Taking my frustration out on the dough, I threw it aside.

"That's a relevant detail, Jewel."

"Relevant or not, it's long since over. We just work together now." She dusted the bench with flour and spent an overly long time smoothing it out in a thin layer. "I hope you don't think I'm the kind of person who'd keep someone on my payroll because I carry a torch for him."

"I wasn't saying that." I kept my voice even, gentle. I could tell the conversation with Trevor had her rattled, and I didn't want to make things worse. "But it sure seems like he carries a torch for you. Can't say I blame him. If it was a one year relationship or a one hour relationship, it wouldn't matter. I wouldn't be able to get over you."

I hadn't planned on handing her that piece of my heart, but my words came without warning. I guess that's what happens when your feelings decide they're more important than your power to control them—they get bossy.

Eyes wide with surprise, Julia looked up from the floury mess. "Shane . . . "

174

I blinked hard, not wanting to see her face when she told me I'd said too much. By the time I opened my eyes, she'd moved directly in front of me and placed her hands on my chest. "Yeah?" I felt bold enough to ask.

"I've wished for those words since just about forever."

Her hands slid up my chest, leaving a dusting of flour on my shirt as she went. I wiped my own hands on my apron and ran them along the sides of her face as our lips connected.

This kiss felt very different from even the most passion-drenched versions of the past few weeks. My thoughts flew free—as did all those feelings I'd been keeping under lock and key for fear of disrupting our "casual good time" with anything resembling seriousness.

Tasting her lips now felt like a promise of everything I'd ever wanted. Within reach for the first time.

Her quiet sigh as our lips found their perfect complement in each other fueled me to give her everything she ever wanted. If she wished for my words, I'd tell her everything I felt. I'd risk my own sadness for her happiness. I'd content myself with these moments long after she was gone.

She drew back a couple inches and drew her finger across my forehead and down one cheek. "This face. I love this face. Always have."

"Jewel . . . " My voice sounded like the hoarse growl of a tortured animal. I wanted to tell her everything. I wanted to say I loved her. Not just her face. Not just today. But I couldn't. It would be too much, and she didn't need another guy putting pressure on her today.

I wanted to be the good guy, the one who didn't force her to make decisions. I'd always wanted to be that guy, often at the sacrifice of my own happiness. I'd learned to be a little more selfish as I'd gained confidence and discovered my self worth, but all that went out the window with her.

"I'm going to give you time to sort things without me breathing down your neck," I said, hanging my apron on the hook. I felt certain Jenn would understand why I needed to leave work early if she asked.

Julia nodded numbly. Before I got two feet away from her, she reached out and grasped my right hand. Her firm grip fortified what I already believed to be true—I'd sacrifice my happiness for hers.

I knew it the way I'd known the French horn would be my way out of my shy purgatory. I'd do it. I'd love her as much as I possibly could while she was here, and then I'd let her go. I wanted her to have everything, even if only for the time she was here.

So I dove in. I didn't worry about the consequences.

There'd be time for that later.

CHAPTER 24

SHANE

*O*nce I'd chopped through a cord or so of wood, I'd managed to sort through my thoughts.

Okay, that's a lie.

I'd sorted through my thoughts by the time I arrived at Clay's house. They weren't all that complicated.

1. I was jealous that Trevor Hobart had spent years working with Julia when I'd only gotten a month.
2. I was worried he'd somehow convince her to leave immediately for her "real life" and I'd lose her entirely.
3. I couldn't act like A, or I'd ensure that B would come to pass.

After I'd come to terms with the shitstorm swirling in my brain thanks to the arrival of Trevor Hobart III (I felt certain he was the third or fourth or eighth in a long line of douchebag Trevor Hobarts), I came home and took my aggression out on another hunk of fallen tree in Clay's yard.

I was just stacking the logs neatly by the back door and deciding what to tell Clay when Julia's car pulled up. Her long legs emerged first, and I was so transfixed by them, as usual, that I didn't notice whether she had a passenger in the car.

A second later, I focused on that aspect, and it was probably a good thing she hadn't brought Trevor with her because I still had an ax in my hands.

"Shane . . . " Face laced with concern, she walked toward me tentatively. When she stopped a few feet away, I was confused until I saw her staring at the ax on my shoulder. I lowered it to the wood stump and closed the distance between us.

"Hey. Everything okay?" I tried to sound casual, but there was a shake in my voice I was certain she heard. Julia nodded.

I waited. She didn't say more.

"Um, you want to talk about it?"

She nodded again. Now I could see that something was bothering her, and despite my fear that our conversation would conclude with her telling me she was going home with Trevor, I cared for her too much to be an asshole about it.

Bottom line, I wanted her to be happy. She deserved it, even if she found it someplace else. Thinking about that last part made it hard to swallow— hard to breathe, for that matter—but I knew it was true.

It was why I'd turned down a prom date so many years earlier. I had more confidence in myself now, but little else had changed.

Opening my arms to her, I welcomed her in. She clung to me for an extended moment, leaning her cheek against my chest. I breathed her in and felt the knots untwine in my neck and back. When she released me, she said only, "Thank you."

I walked us into the house and made us a pot of coffee. Then I took out some whiskey because I might need that too.

"Talk to me, Jewel. What happened?"

She sat on my comfortable blue couch, and I took the plaid armchair to her right. As much as I wanted to comfort her if she needed that, I also understood that physical contact between us would take us in only one direction, and fast. If she wanted to talk, I needed to create some physical distance.

Julia stirred milk into her coffee and stared into the mug for a long time without speaking. I watched the expression on her face cloud with something I couldn't decipher. Then she seemed to relax. Then she looked confused again.

Finally, I couldn't take it. "You're going back with him?" Might as well rip off the bandage.

Her head jerked up, eyes wide with confusion. "What? No. Not leaving, at least not for a while." She closed her eyes and shook her head.

My relief at hearing that was tempered by how agonized she still looked. I scooted my chair closer to the couch and reached for her hand. "Tell me."

"It's about the business. He handles all the finances, so he was the person who got approached."

"Approached by who?"

"An investor who already bought a big stake in the business and wants to be the majority owner."

I didn't know much about stakeholders and business ownership, but I knew enough. "Aren't you the majority owner?"

Julia nodded. "I own fifty-one percent. So no one can force me to sell. But the people who approached Trevor have a lot of industry clout. They could cut off my supply chain to get me to agree. They want me to sell my stake, or at least a part of it, so they'll have majority control."

For the life of me, I couldn't understand why she even wanted to fight them. She hated what her job had become. She'd admitted it. "Would that be so bad? Maybe it could give you some freedom to do . . . things that make you happier?"

She inhaled a breath so large I was surprised that much air fit in her lungs. When she slowly let it out, I felt some of her fight go with it.

Then her shoulders dropped and she slumped. "I can't. I just . . . can't give up on it. It'll make me just like my parents."

I nodded. They hadn't been in the picture for a long time, and I remembered from back in high school that her Gram was raising her. I just never knew much more than that. "Is that what drives you?"

She shrugged. "Not entirely . . . but, sure, yeah."

"Okay."

Her words exploded from her like they'd been sizzling on a lit burner. "No. It's not okay. It's very not okay. And I've been running from being them for so long, it took over the story."

"Ah. I see." It made some sense, her drive to make something of herself, her relentless pursuit of stability and success.

"When I was a kid, I watched them constantly change their plans. At first, when we were little, they moved from place to place. I barely remember it, and by the time I was in elementary school, my Gram insisted they bring us back here, said it was no good for us to be moving like a band of nomads."

"Is that when you moved in with her?"

Julia leaned her head back against the couch and shook her head. She began running the fringe of my gray throw blanket through her fingers absently.

"No, but every time they'd travel, we stayed with Gram. The trips kept getting longer. Eventually, they didn't come back. Always had to keep moving. Like a shark—like they'd die if they stayed in one place."

"Some people are like that."

"I'm not like that."

"I know you aren't."

She met my eyes then, her expression rueful. "I think I tried a little too hard. I worked my tail off learning about baking, apprenticed and stayed the course in the one thing I was good at, worked my way up, opened the bakeries, built the business."

"You did. You did it all."

"And then I forgot to do all the other things. I forgot to look up. I don't have joy." I'd never seen such sadness on her face—on any person's face.

She had a look of defeat that hit me in the gut. I didn't want it for her, and I'd do anything to help her, but I knew it wasn't enough. It wasn't the solution.

"You need to be who you are. You're you, not because of or in spite of your parents. You can't close yourself to living a full life," I said gently, hoping the words didn't sound like criticism. They weren't. Not at all.

She nodded slowly like she had a hill to climb.

It broke my heart because I loved to hike and run uphill, and I loved her. But this wasn't my battle. She had to do it on her own.

Which meant she had to go back to LA and figure it out.

Leaning back on the couch, Julia draped an arm over her eyes. She spoke without moving it. "I feel like I've been doing what's expected for so long I've forgotten how to do anything else. Maybe that's a good thing. Doing what's expected has gotten me pretty far."

I took a deep breath because I wasn't ready to agree. But when she took her hand away and looked at me, the vulnerability in her eyes told me I needed to offer my support.

"It has. And if you need someone to give you permission to be done, I'm here to offer that. But you have to decide it's what you want."

She nodded. "I know. And I'm not ready. At least not today."

I didn't need to hear her say the words to know they were true. Or maybe hearing them was exactly what I needed.

Sooner or later, I'd have to let her go.

CHAPTER 25

JULIA

*E*ven though I was annoyed with Trevor, his presence drove home the fact that I'd been avoiding reality. Since he'd left, I felt a looming expiration date on my time in Green Valley, but I tried not to let it color the time I spent with Shane. We could still have fun. We would still enjoy every bit of our time together.

At least, that's what I hoped.

But things were already different, even if I pretended they weren't.

"I'm not sure I understand the point of this game." Shane stood with his hands on his hips in protest when I insisted we could have as much fun at his kitchen table as we did on his hike.

I'd spread newspapers all over the table and stood dangling a nondescript brown box from an attached handle. "The point is to guess what's in the box, but since it weighs twenty pounds, I don't want to hold it for much longer."

"You should put it down. Then you should lay down on the table." His eyebrows bounced and he ran his tongue over his bottom lip. It was almost enough to make me forget what I'd been planning. It also made me want to mess with him a little.

"Now I'm thinking we should go to the library instead. We can browse the historical fiction section together and then check out the almanacs."

His expression turned to distrust. "Almanacs?"

"Yeah. I can lay down on your kitchen table anytime, but how often do we get a chance to roam among map books and encyclopedias? Doesn't the idea of bound periodicals get you excited?"

Now he was downright glaring at me. Some people could take a joke when it came to ridiculous ideas for foreplay. Shane, I was quickly learning, was not one of those people.

"No."

"Because you can't see the obvious endpoint where we'll have sex in the stacks?"

"Um, pretty sure that's not allowed at the public library." He stood in front of me with his arms crossed, acting downright pissy. Definitely not thinking creatively. I'd have to nudge him along.

I reached for his hand, unfolding his arms in the process. "Do you trust me?" As usual, my question carried more weight than simply the implications of this particular game on this particular day.

His sour expression softened. "I do. Implicitly."

And as usual, in just a word or two, he had the power to melt my heart. "Well, that's more than anyone could ask for," I said softly. "I promise not to betray that trust."

"Not ever?" He no longer seemed aggravated.

I shook my head and kissed him, another soul-melting kiss that obliterated my will to joke about taking us to the library where we couldn't actually have sex in the stacks.

I was falling hard and fast for the guy, and if I hadn't just gotten an emergency call from my Chief Operating Officer altering me to an unscheduled investor meeting, I'd allow myself to admit I was fully in love with him.

I am fully in love with him.

Despite the lump in my throat that formed at the thought of leaving, even for a little while. I'd been here for a month, which was a month longer than I'd ever left my business in the hands of other people. And according to the COO, that was enough time for everything to implode. He had a flair for dramatics, but still. I'd neglected things for far too long. It was irresponsible not to go back and attend to the crisis in person.

I'd yet to tell Shane I'd bought a ticket to fly back, but I would. Today.

Then I'd tell him I planned to come back.

I hadn't figured out the how or when of that part, but I would. At least, I hoped I'd be able to come back. I couldn't see my way clear to making it happen until I worked things out with my business back home.

Thinking about that gave me the first prickles of anxiety I'd felt in weeks. What if I couldn't come back here? What if I couldn't see Shane again for months?

I pushed those thoughts aside when he kissed me again. His soft lips brushed against mine, and all worries fell away. Time skidded off the road and I sunk into the moment.

When he drew back, his smile reflected the lazy contentment I felt, the kind of bleary hope that things would work out. Somehow.

Flicking the lid off the brown box, Shane looked down at the brick of gray clay and nodded, pressing his lips together.

"I call your bluff on the library, but I'm down for the clay," he said, lifting my palm and kissing it. "A lot can be done with a bucket of wet clay and a good imagination. I'm yours to corrupt, Jewel. Have at it."

"Ha. I like this change of heart."

"Oh, I plan to get creative." His voice dropped an octave and the growl sent shivers over my skin. "What do you want to do with your clay?"

I answered before thinking. "Make you a coffee cup. Something you can use every day. I found a place to get stuff fired in Knoxville." My hands flitted toward the window in the direction of the distant town like a game show host.

His face fell, but then his lips twisted into a smirk. "I'm here with an image of painting your naked body with wet clay, and you're thinking coffee cups."

I blinked back a touch of embarrassment at my workaday interpretation of our art project. "I'm not only thinking coffee cups," I admitted.

"Good," he said, pulling me toward him. He ran a hand up my back and into my hair before dropping a kiss on my lips.

It only took the tender, reverent way he kissed me, looked at me, and treated me to make me want to give up on all the hard work that had gone into launching my business and stay in Green Valley forever.

Even though it was impossible.

Even though Shane had voiced his opinion that we were temporary. Of course we were. My time here had an expiration date, even if I'd pushed the reality away.

I'd be insane to throw away everything I'd worked for to extend a temporary fling.

"Um, I forgot what we were doing," I admitted when Shane's lips left mine and I found my brains utterly scrambled. Anything other than tearing my clothes off seemed irredeemably dumb.

He waggled his eyebrows. "That may have been the idea."

"Should we just forget about this?" I pointed to the brown box that sat on the floor.

His expression sobered. "Forget covering your naked body in clay? No way."

I couldn't help but smile. "Now the whole thing seems unnecessary. I just want to be with you. I don't need to conjure up a project as an excuse to do that," I said. What I didn't say was that with our time together running out, I didn't want to waste time. And anything other than being wrapped in his arms felt like a colossal waste.

"We can do both. Let's just see where the afternoon takes us." His smile made me infinitely agreeable.

I nodded. "Come." I beckoned in the direction of my car, where I had two bags of groceries I'd almost forgotten when I hauled the box of clay into the house. Shane followed, grabbing my hand as we walked outside. I'd never had this kind of comfort and familiarity with anyone, and the irony wasn't lost on me—somehow Shane felt permanent even though we didn't have a future, at least not one I could come up with readily.

The sky was too evenly blue and too pretty to spend too much time worrying. "Look at the day. It's gorgeous." Tennessee's full palette of colors unfolded before us—the myriad green tones that fought for dominance over the grass-covered hills on our right, the deeper greens of the trees snaking through the mountain passes off to our left, the simple uninterrupted aqua of the sky.

After staring at the blue-purple hue, I tried to recall the sky in LA, which I was having a harder and harder time remembering. Maybe because I never took time to examine it the way I did here. Always headed to work or to a meeting or to a restaurant location, I'd never paid much attention to the outdoors.

It was someone else's scenery. Mine was the workplace.

The thought settled in a pit in my stomach, immovable now that I'd allowed it space. The thought of going back sent a low chill of anxiety coursing through me, so different from the effervescent, lovely chill of newness I felt each and every time Shane's skin grazed mine.

The choice between the two seemed simple.

If only life were simple.

"I can see the wheels turning. Care to share?" Shane interrupted the downward spiral of my thoughts by resting his hand on my thigh. I wrapped my fingers around his and gave it a squeeze.

"Just thinking about the rest of our day together," I lied.

"Lotta coffee cups?" he deadpanned.

"I'm thinking a lotta loafing, sex, and food."

That evoked a guttural groan from deep in Shane's chest. "My god, I think I just died. You just killed me."

"Yeah?" I smirked. "Did I just hit on your every fantasy in one afternoon?"

He turned his hand beneath mine and squeezed. "No."

I turned to find his eyes locked on me, serious. "No?"

"No."

"Okay."

"No," he said again, tugging on my hand and bringing it to his chest. He shook his head. "Make no mistake, Jewel." He spoke slowly, his voice low and insistent. "The fantasy is you. Without you, those are just words and ideas. But with you, they're everything."

Swallowing hard, I felt my heart soar and my core light up with an aching need for him. We deposited the grocery bags in the kitchen and Shane lifted me into his arms. Carrying me toward the stairs, he moved swiftly and surely up the path like I weighed eleven pounds. I'd never been so grateful for all the hours he'd spent wielding that ax above his head.

Shane took the stairs two at a time and deposited me gently on his bed. He kneeled over my legs, and the stormy sea in his eyes said he wanted to devour every inch of me.

I made it easy, sitting up and taking his face in my hands. "You're making this too easy. I was planning to seduce you with my cooking." I slipped my fingers through his hair, running the strands between my fingers and pressing my lips against his and feeling my nerve endings fire against his touch.

"You don't have to. It's done. I'm seduced," he said against my lips. Then he kissed the line of my jaw and followed with his tongue. He knew it drove me crazy. His seduction technique was in top form and if this was a contest, we were both playing our A-game.

I slipped out from under him, stood up, and reached for his hand. When he took it, I led him into the bathroom and turned on the steam shower. When I pointed at his shirt, he gamely removed it. Then his pants.

"I can do better," I slid my hand over the ripple of his abs, running my nails over the skin until I heard him suck in a breath.

"You're not exactly playing fair," he groaned, showing no sign of real protest. I lifted my shirt over my head, and his lips were at my breasts, suckling one while he palmed the other.

"Fair is as fair does," I gasped, my head tipping back. I didn't even know what my words meant or if they made sense. I couldn't be bothered to care.

Taking two steps backward, I led us into the shower. Then I got on my knees and looked up at him through wet lashes. His eyes grew wide, and he ran his hands through my wet hair.

"Get ready for more unfairness."

He opened his mouth to respond when I ran my tongue down his length and sucked. Nothing he said after that made a whole lot of sense. And I loved it.

I wanted to take him deep, to let his thrusts hit the back of my throat until he couldn't hold back another second. His growl turned to a string of curses as I tried to make him feel a fraction of what his lips and tongue had done to me over and over.

As he came undone beneath my hands and in my mouth, he braced himself against the shower walls. The cascading water from the rain shower mixed with his release and I felt his knees go soft as he leaned against the shower wall.

Kissing my way up the hard planes of his abs, I held on firmly, knowing how it felt when I went boneless and weak for him. But he didn't seem to need time to recover.

Lifting me to my feet, he covered my mouth with his and spoke wordless volumes that told me I'd succeeded in my seduction, however unfair my rules proved to be.

If I had to leave town in a day or two, I wanted to leave him with a way to remember me. And I wanted to give myself a reason to return.

CHAPTER 26

SHANE

*J*ulia had been quieter than usual. At first that didn't worry me, but when she had nothing to say about an obscure fact I'd dug up on Queen Elizabeth, I knew something was wrong.

Her phone pinged and she glanced at it briefly before shutting it off.

She looked like she had something to say. After spending nearly every free moment I had with her over the past few weeks, I'd learned to read her.

"What?" I demanded, nudging her with my elbow. Julia didn't look up right away, still focused on the lump of clay before her, which only looked slightly more like something than a lump of clay.

I'd lay money on it being a freeform bowl by the time she finished since she'd already pushed out a hole in the middle with her thumbs so that now it resembled a fat gray donut.

"*What* what?" she asked, her eyes roaming to my own lump of clay before she turned them on me.

"You're waiting to tell me something. Or ask me something. So . . . out with it." I grabbed a wet wipe from the dispenser and cleaned my hands, done with the clay molding for the time being if we needed to have a serious talk.

And everything about the crease between her brows pointed to a serious talk.

"Ugh, yes. You're right."

Her phone had been blowing up all afternoon and I had a feeling it had to do with work, which she'd been obvious about avoiding when I gently prodded, asking how things were going back home. Trevor's unexpected visit had tipped me off to more issues with the business than she'd let on, and I didn't want her to keep me in the dark, especially when something was clearly eating at her.

"D'you need to get that?"

She rolled her eyes. "Probably." But she made no move to do it.

"What's up, Jewel?"

"More issues at work. We lost a key vendor, which means we're buying from a hodgepodge of people until we sew up that hole. And that means we're paying more than we should be. Maybe it's related to the attempted buyout, someone trying to pressure me. I can't know until I sort everything out in the office. They're waiting for me to get back."

It didn't sound catastrophic. "So, maybe you should fly back and get everything back on track. Then you can come back here. And hang with me." I smiled at the thought and at the tactic I hoped might convince her not to worry.

But she looked worried. "Yeah, I'd like to do that, but I don't know what that all looks like. I've been gone a month already."

I didn't like where this was headed, but I didn't want to let my fears take over. She'd told me she didn't want to leave, so I had to trust that.

"Take your time, do what you need to do," I told her calmly, smoothing a strand of hair behind her ear and tipping her chin up to face me. Kissing her lips, I reassured her, "I'll be here when you get back. And maybe while you're gone, I can help with the house, fix it up with Daniel so you can put it on the market eventually."

I wanted to remind her she had reasons to return other than me, just in case I wasn't enough.

Her face fell. I felt another admission coming. "We're not going to sell the house."

"What?"

"I think it should stay in the family. Daniel will keep living in it and fix it up when he has time."

So that was it. The house issue was settled, and the bakery needed her in LA. She had no reason to stay.

Desperate for a solution, I let words tumble out of my mouth without editing them. "I could come with you."

Her eyes went huge and round. "You mean a vacation?"

I didn't know what I meant. That was the danger of blurting things out without thinking them through. But when I thought about it, I knew I wanted to be with her, and if it meant dragging my ass to LA, I could do that. "Or longer. If that's where home is for you, I could make that work. At least try."

It sounded reasonable. At least to me.

"You hate big cities." Julia didn't even take time to think it through. So definitively certain, she practically answered before the words had left my mouth.

The room started to spin along with everything in it. The piano was suddenly on its side, and nothing I could do would right it.

"I don't particularly like them, but I'd do it for you."

"That's the wrong reason. I can't let you do that."

I didn't have a rebuttal prepared because, as usual, I'd misread the situation and thought she might be delighted at the idea that things didn't have to end between us.

"You wouldn't be letting me do anything. I'd do it because I want to," I stuttered, trying to make sense of her words. Why wasn't she happy? Had the last month we'd spent together been completely one-sided?

No, it hadn't.

She'd been with me for every gasp, shudder, and whimper while we made love, and after we'd gotten the bare lust out of our systems, that's what it had been—making love, not fucking. Sure, it was fun and wild and satisfying, but there was feeling in every part of it.

Then we'd left the fun and frivolous stuff behind, and I had no doubts about our connection—the late-night confessions, the joy we had together, our intertwined bodies that were two parts of one being.

Neither of us could bluff that. I felt sure of it.

There had to be something I hadn't accounted for, but wracking my brain produced no ideas. If she was pushing me away, it had to be out of some desire to protect herself, and I desperately needed her to understand that I would do the protecting. All her vulnerabilities were safe with me.

"We're right for each other. I've questioned a lot of things in my life, made a lot of decisions that turned out to be U-turns, but I've never had a moment of doubt about you."

"Sure you did. In high school, you did."

"Yeah, when I was young and idiotic and foolish. And I explained that. I told you how much regret I had back then, and I sure as hell don't want to feel that regret now. Which is why I'm not afraid to leave here."

"But this is your home."

"It doesn't have to be."

She shook her head and put some distance between us, scooting her chair back and pulling her hand from mine. She tucked it into her lap, out of reach.

"Shane, no. You can't."

This made no sense. Why was she so certain the conversation was a non-starter? "I can. I'd like to try to make this work between us. Why are you so dead set against it?"

Her expression looked pained. I'd never seen her look at me like that and I hated it.

She swallowed hard and dropped her head into her hands. "Because it's wrong. This isn't what you should be doing with your life, following me back to LA because we're having a good time."

"Jewel . . . that's not what this is. We're . . . we're more than a good time."

Shaking her head, she pressed her eyes closed, a sadness overtaking her features that I hadn't seen before. "No. That's exactly what we are. We're temporary, while I'm in town. We knew it when we started. Isn't that what you said, we'd keep things light? We both agreed." Her eyes grew hard and distant, and I had no defense against her shutting down in front of me.

She stood from the couch and began pacing, still not looking me in the eye. It was unnerving seeing her unravel like this, shedding the closeness we'd shared minutes before and reclaiming her solitary existence like a vice she couldn't quit.

I didn't buy it and I told her so. "Bullshit. That was before."

"Before what?"

Now she met my eyes, challenging. Did she want me to say it? Did she need to hear that I was ass over teakettle in love with her? Did she require something I hadn't given her yet in order to believe that I meant everything I'd said to her?

Fine. I'd give her everything.

"Before I fell in love with you."

"Shane . . . " She blinked hard again, and I swear I saw it—the welling of a tear, the proof I needed that her brain was trying to resist something her heart didn't want.

Well, good. My heart didn't want it either.

"I love you, Jewel. And I want you more than I want to stay in my home-town. I don't want to stay if you're not here."

She took my hands in hers, both of them weighted equally, never any hesitation to treat both hands and all of me like the most cherished, beautiful thing in the world.

Which was crazy. Because the most cherished beautiful thing in the world was standing in front of me holding my hands. For what I could sense were fleeting moments.

"I can't let you leave a place you love—a life you love—to be in a place you'll hate with me. You'll resent me eventually." She shook her head again, more emphatically, as though willing herself to believe it.

The words spilling out of her mouth didn't square with the way I knew she felt. And from the way she couldn't meet my eyes, I doubted she believed them either.

"You told me to find happiness. I need to figure out how to do that, and part of figuring it out is going back and dealing with my responsibilities. I can't let you upend your life while I sort out mine."

"Even if you love me?"

"Especially because I love you." Her voice broke as she said it, but she turned her back before I could see her tears fall. It didn't matter. I had my own to contend with. In a flurry of motion, she whipped around and pressed her lips to mine, burning them with how much it hurt to anticipate her backing away.

It hurt even more when she did it.

Then she ran away from me without looking back. Again.

CHAPTER 27

JULIA

I started crying the minute the door closed behind me. I'd been holding back the tears against a lump in my throat so big and awkward and painful I was surprised I'd gotten the words out at all.

Never in my life had I done anything so difficult and painful. Even though I knew it was the right thing to do, I was miserable.

Every fiber of my being told me to turn around, run as fast as possible back to Shane's front door and pound on it until he opened it. My heart urged me to take him up on his offer, to let him try living in LA and see if we could make something work.

If we were together, he'd be happy.

No, he wouldn't. He told you as much at the top of the hiking trail.

I packed as quickly as I had for the trip out and hugged Daniel goodbye with the promise it wouldn't be another four years. I knew it wouldn't, but with my LA reality crashing back into my world, I couldn't be held to much more than a vague idea.

It didn't help matters that the airplane was only playing sad movies. Even the romantic comedies seemed tinged with melancholy.

Okay, full disclosure: It was me.

I was the sad one. And I was more than tinged.

I was downright painted from head to toe with a blue mood I'd never experienced any of the prior times I'd left Green Valley for the West Coast. In the past, I'd looked forward to newness and adventure.

Go West, young woman. Be brave. The future looks bright.

Now, I couldn't help but look back.

And since I'd taken advantage of the plane's Wi-Fi, my phone started pinging with incoming texts as soon as we were in the air.

Daniel: Did you get on the plane?

Me: Yes

Daniel: Damn

Me: Why, did you bet someone I wouldn't?

Daniel: Yeah, you just lost me twenty bucks. Kidding. I just hoped you'd reconsider.

Me: You know why I couldn't.

Daniel: I do. Make yourself happy, Jules.

Me: I'll try.

Was going back to LA making me happy? Absolutely not.

The thoughts churned in my brain as my head tipped to the side, supported by my blue neck pillow. And before I had too much more time to think, I fell into a dreamless sleep.

* * *

"Order up!"

The unforgiving shouts and commands came from the kitchen at my flagship bakery location where I sat in the restaurant above the bread shop. It had already been a week since I'd returned to town, and the sounds and smells of the kitchen weren't doing much to lift my spirits.

My mood had been undercooked cake batter since the plane touched down, and nothing I did could change it.

Normally, the din of customer chatter, the smell of food, and the complexity of running a huge business took over my thoughts. I'd counted on it, certain that working hard would keep me from being alone with my thoughts. Because all my thoughts were of Shane.

I felt like a stranger in the place that had been my home for a decade. I couldn't remember what had ever felt right about being here. I didn't love it. I didn't have joy. None.

And I couldn't stop thinking about the look on Shane's face when I left. If I lived to be a hundred, I'd never forget the hurt and betrayal in his eyes at my hasty exit.

What kind of person says she loves an incredible man and leaves on the next plane?

194

A crazy one.

Tucked into a bistro chair at a butcher block table for two in a corner of the restaurant, I had a full view of the open kitchen. The chefs and sous chefs spun past each other in an elaborate dance that somehow resulted in dozens of perfect plates of food and very few accidents in a space that didn't look like it could fit a dozen people, all working at different stations.

I'd always loved the design of the space, all materials that would normally be used outside—concrete, brick, exposed wood—and in the large loft space above the bakery, all those materials were warmed by skylights that kept trailing plants and potted trees alive in every corner of the room.

The grays, browns, and greens all faded into the background when the white plates of food appeared on dark wood tables, and the aroma filled the air. I'd pointed and picked out what I liked when I first met with the designer, who did such a great job executing the perfect dining space that we'd won two design awards.

Normally, sitting at the table off to the side filled me with pride in what we'd accomplished, but today my heart wasn't in it. And I had no appetite for the pretty plate of crudites next to a tomato pesto tart. And I always had an appetite for that.

Being here fueled my senses a little bit, but it did nothing to wipe away the dull sadness I'd felt without Shane.

"Hey, you're back!" Sammi, my pastry chef and first official employee slid into the seat across from me. Her wide smile dimmed when her eyes met mine, and she signaled to someone I couldn't see over my shoulder, calling out, "Can you rustle up a couple of options from the gin and tonic bar? Looks like we're not waiting until happy hour."

Checking my watch, I exhaled. "It's always happy hour someplace, right?" I didn't bother telling her I was fine. There was no point in lying to my friend of nine years who'd see through my charade in milliseconds. She already had.

"Yeah, and I know you're not here because it's the best place to go over . . . " She pulled my pile of papers over and eyeballed them, shaking her head. "Heirloom tomato orders? It's not even the right season for that. Oh, girlfriend. What are you trying to drown in paperwork?"

Before I could respond, one of our waiters appeared with a tasting tray of six different kinds of gin, tiny bottles of tonic water, and cut limes. We'd begun offering a gin and tonic tasting with our Sunday brunch and it had caught on like wildfire. "And could you have the kitchen make us some shoestring fries and that special aioli?" Sammi asked.

I'd never been so glad to own a place that could cook up whatever comfort food I felt like, and Sammi didn't have to ask to know that fries were the right call. Neither did Shane, I thought, unable to keep him from infiltrating every thought.

"Oh, Sam, I don't know how this happened. I'm so lost over a guy, and I feel like I made the biggest mistake of my life coming back here."

She began pouring tonic water and mixing drinks. In moments, she handed me a perfect drink and I took a healthy sip before recounting everything that had happened between Shane and me over the past month, with a healthy sprinkling of stories from high school as well.

I didn't stop talking for a good half hour, and when I stopped to slug down the rest of my drink, Sammi stared at me, wide-eyed. "I love this for you," she said, finally.

"What? Didn't you hear me? I'm miserable."

"Yes, but that's only because you're in love with him and you left. Stupid, stupid. Why would you leave?" She asked the question as though it had an easy answer. Or any answer.

"Because I live here. I work here. My entire life is here, as Trevor so kindly reminded me."

She rolled her eyes. "Um, sure, your business is here. And your dumb partner who treats you like he's the one who owns the place."

I didn't want to touch that. I hated the idea that other people saw issues with Trevor that I'd ignored. But if I'd learned one thing during my time in Green Valley, it was that I didn't know anything about anything. All my assumptions about people had been wrong, at least in my personal life.

And maybe in my professional life too. Maybe I'd been wrong about myself.

I'd always believed I had a special knack for choosing the best. Sammi was a case in point. She had a sterling resume—Cordon Bleu pastry school, apprenticed with Sweet Lady Jane—but none of that mattered when we had our first conversation.

I knew I liked her because of her wide smile, her can-do attitude, and her philosophy that sugar should be used as a seasoning rather than a main ingredient. I asked her to spend a day at the bakery when it was just one bread assistant and me, and by the end of an hour, we had music cranked in the kitchen, a greater variety of gorgeous pastries than I'd ever seen in one place, and the room smelled like melted full-fat butter.

But more than that, Sammi worked like a professional, but she talked and listened like a friend. Every person I'd hired after her had possessed some magical combination of being the kind of person I'd want to spend an entire day working with, as well as trusting them to have my back in a pinch.

In the interviews I did with culinary blogs or the occasional magazine spread, I always talked about the human ingredients to a business that couldn't be sourced from a catalog or bought in a store. The people were what made my business successful, more than any recipes or secret bread starters.

"Hello, are you lost in the sauce?" Sammi tapped my glass with her fingernail before unwrapping my fingers from around it and picking it up. She measured the ingredients for another gin and tonic carefully and replaced it in my hand, which still sat in the same position on the table.

"Yeah, a bit." I was a little comatose and I knew Sammi wouldn't want me to apologize for it. But I was wrong about that too.

"You shouldn't be here." She shrugged. When her shoulders fell, there was a finality to her statement that dared me to argue.

"I work here. I'm trying to hold onto the business so nothing changes. Isn't that what everyone here wants?"

"Sure, but you don't have to do it for us. Things change."

I put my drink down and stared at her. No doubt my jaw had become unhinged because it hung open. "Why would you say that?"

"Because it's true. You were gone for a month. Did the doors fall off? No. Did we stop baking and feeding customers? Also, no. Which means you can be gone for longer. Or sell the place entirely. Someone else can own us and pay the bills and we'll keep doing what we do, honoring the traditions you created, baking damn good bread."

Looking around at the bustling restaurant, where every table sat occupied by content customers eating plates of food and day drinking in the middle of a work week, I had to admit Sammi was right. The place was doing gang-buster business.

I'd barely glanced at a spreadsheet or supervised a provisions order while I'd been gone. I didn't need to, because I had a trusted team of people who did it as well or better than I could.

As I sipped my second drink, I came to terms with the fact that my return to LA had very little to do with wanting to be here. It had everything to do with thinking I should.

And Shane had been willing to sacrifice his own happiness to let me do it. If that wasn't a reason to get on the next plane back to Tennessee, I couldn't think of what was.

Still, it felt huge. Too huge.

"He offered to come out here with me, but I couldn't let him do it. He hates the city. He made the right choice for his life. And I made the right one for mine. Right?" As I defended myself and the last conversation I'd had with Shane, I saw my own doubt reflected in Sammi's eyes.

She didn't need to say a thing. And she knew it. After this many years, she understood me well enough to know that I'd come to the right realization myself.

"Sounds like he made a lot of good choices," she observed, squeezing another lime into her drink and taking a sip.

Across the room, a table for six had started singing happy birthday to a bright-eyed brunette who looked delighted as the sparklers on a piece of lemon cheesecake threw off tiny bits of light. She closed her eyes, presumably making a wish.

All around us, waiters bustled about, making people happy by lighting birthday candles, bringing a fruity alcoholic drink if someone wanted it to celebrate on an ordinary afternoon, relieving people of the need to cook and serving them delicious food in a pretty setting.

I'd done well in opening my business and growing it into what it was now. So why did joy feel so elusive? "This is just crazy," I finally admitted to Sammi. "When I left here, I was basically happy."

Her brow lifted almost imperceptibly, but she didn't challenge my truth. "So, what changed?"

"I got some perspective. I saw wide open skies. I remembered who I was before I screamed out of my hometown with my tail on fire because of a boy."

"And is that person so different from the one who's sitting in front of me here?"

I sighed. It would be so easy to slip back into my LA persona, to be the people pleaser I'd learned to be and thrive on making other people happier than I made myself. It used to be enough.

"It probably sounds crazy, but . . . yeah. I think I forgot to fight for myself. In my relationships, in my day to day. I just kind of gave up on trying to find my own joy because I convinced myself I'm not the kind of person who could ever really have it."

Sammi sipped her drink and studied me. Her round eyes flitted over my face as she drew some sort of conclusion I couldn't decipher.

"You're a freaking idiot."

Well, maybe I could decipher that.

"Yeah. In many ways. Let's hear your list of reasons why."

She threw a hand up, then gestured around the room. "Look at what you've built. This place is every chef's dream. Not to mention that it's really hard to start a business and run it and you've kicked serious ass. But none of that means squat if you're alone and miserable."

"I'm not alone."

"No? I don't see that guy you spent a half hour melting over. He's back there. You're here. Ergo, alone."

"Great, now you're hitting me with Latin?"

"Better than hitting you with my fist. You're acting like a moron."

Suddenly, despite my melancholy state, I started to laugh. And I couldn't stop. "Oh my god, Sammi. I love you so much. I am a moron. And I don't want this whole company resting on my shoulders anymore."

Then she started to laugh. "Good. You're a moron, but you're a lovable one who just made the right decision, so that helps."

Signaling one of the servers, she made some motions I couldn't interpret, and with minutes a cheese plate with baguette slices, fig jam, and Marcona almonds was placed on our table by invisible hands.

"How do you do that? Even I can't get them to hop to it when I ask for things."

"Sexual favors," she deadpanned, making me crack up again.

"Oh wow, laughter feels good. I've been so sad since I got on the plane. Gosh, so sad."

Sammi held up a finger while she used the other hand to spread a swipe of brie cheese on a small round of bread. She handed it to me. "Eat this. I know you haven't eaten anything since you got off that plane."

Looking at Sammi, one of my closest friends, I felt sad again, but for a different reason. I'd no longer see her every day at work, not if I did what my heart had been urging me to do from the moment my plane lifted into the air.

"I don't know how I'm going to survive without seeing you every day."

"We'll do video calls. You'll see me. Don't think you can drift off to some adorable Tennessee hamlet and forget all about me. You'll still be in charge, even if the sale goes through. They're insisting on you running things for at least a year. You'll just be doing it remotely."

"You really think it'll work?"

"Um, yeah. All the cool kids are doing it. You can too."

Leaning back in my chair, I scrubbed both hands through my hair and pulled it into a ponytail. Then I twisted it into a bun, tighter and tighter until I felt the pull of it against my temples. And I let it all go.

As the hair fell heavy against my shoulders, I felt a different kind of weight release. Maybe it was the end to my stubbornness in thinking I had all the answers. Maybe it was the realization that the only answer that mattered was where I wanted to be.

And I knew it without question—wherever Shane was, that's where I belonged.

CHAPTER 28

SHANE

I was miserable for a week straight after Julia left.

At first, we tried to text or talk on the phone, but she had a lot of meetings to go to when she got back. Apparently, being gone for a month resulted in a shit-ton of meetings. We kept missing each other, and I started to wonder if she just wasn't answering her phone.

I thought I knew her better than that, but what can you know about a person after only a month?

Answer: a whole lot.

But really, I knew the Green Valley her. I had no idea who she was in LA, running a multimillion-dollar company that spanned the third-largest state in the country. When I thought about it like that, it was a wonder she'd been able to get away for a month.

But . . . she'd been able to get away for a month and she'd seemed happy about it. I had to put faith in that.

I also had to do a bit better when it came to my own happiness after pushing and prodding her to chase after hers. If I was completely honest, I was missing a small chunk of happy. That is, aside from her being gone.

"The truth is, I miss playing," I admitted to Clay one night while we sat by his firepit and put some of the wood I'd chopped to use.

He handed me a cold beer and clinked his bottle against mine. "You play all the time. You played last night."

"I don't mean the jam session."

"Hey, I take offense to that. Are you saying a bunch of local boys aren't as good as a 'horn section?' I'll take a flannel shirt any day over a tux."

"I'm with you there. But yeah, I miss playing with a full orchestra. Not a lot. But a little."

"Then you should find a way to play with a full orchestra a little. Is that a thing? Want to go back to SOOK?"

I shook my head and leaned back in the low beach chair which was almost the same height as the fire pit. "I want something bigger than that. I dunno. Guess I could find out."

"Guess you could find out."

I huffed out a laugh. "Do you enjoy repeating everything I say, or are you drunk already?"

"No idea. I just provide dead trees for you to plunder when you're aggravated."

I wiped a hand over the back of my neck. We really didn't need the fire on a warm summer night, but it was nice to watch the flames.

In the distance, the off-and-on lights of fireflies reminded me of what I'd said about Julia. Everything reminded me of her.

"Should I get out the ax?" Clay regarded me warily.

I slugged down half my beer in one go and wiped my mouth on the back of my hand. "Nah. I'm good."

"You were, anyway."

"What's that mean?"

"It means you need to find a way to make it work with Julia. She's the one for you. If I hadn't graduated high school two years ahead of you, I'd have seen it and told you so back then. Saved everyone a shit-ton of trouble."

"Yeah, it's pretty much your fault she went back to LA too."

"No, man. That's on you. But you gave her the talking to she needed. She'll be back. Just make sure you're sorted when she comes."

I finished my beer and stood up. "You want one more? I'm buying."

"Ha. My house, my beer. But sure. Get us some refills. And spit shine that French horn while you're at it. Something tells me you'll be playing it again real soon."

I went inside for the beer. I could accomplish that task. As for the rest, I'd figure it out tomorrow.

CHAPTER 29

JULIA

One Week Later

Knowing exactly where I'd find Shane on a Friday night, I had my Uber driver take me straight from the airport to the community center. I didn't want to risk Shane leaving before I got a chance to talk to him.

I heard the music as soon as I exited the car, and I ran through the double doors to where the jam session was underway. As expected, I saw a group of a dozen or so musicians, most of them playing guitars, banjoes, and fiddles.

There wasn't a French horn in the mix. I should have been able to tell that from the sounds I heard on my way in, but I scanned the faces in the circle to be sure. Then I scanned the faces in the crowd.

My heart sunk when I realized Shane wasn't here.

I didn't know why I assumed he would be. It wasn't his duty to be where I expected him to be, especially when I hadn't told him I was coming.

But a room full of people, clapping and stomping and happily playing music was not where I wanted to be. Not when I was about to burst into tears.

I did not run from the room. I walked. Calmly.

I fought every instinct that told me to scream out of the parking lot in the next available Uber and scream back out of town on the next plane. I was built for stability and the steady path. This wasn't it. But I didn't run.

Shuffling slowly toward the door, I tried to run through my options. I could stick around, try to track Shane down, and have a conversation like an adult. Novel concept.

Or I could—

"I'd say you're a sight for sore eyes, but my eyes feel just fine." The voice behind me was like a hug.

Cletus. I whirled around, and before I could explain what I was doing here, he offered the information I needed. "He's in Nashville. Tonight's Symphony night. They invited him to play. I encouraged him, told him it was like a jam session for people in suits."

"Nashville?" I needed to make sure I'd heard him right because Nashville was at least two hours away, and I'd need to retrieve Gram's Impala first and gas her up.

"Nashville." He checked his watch. "Y'all better hurry."

* * *

I was late.

So late.

Maniacal driving in Gram's Impala didn't get me to Nashville in time for the symphony performance—not even close. It was a two-hour drive on a good day, but I had Friday evening traffic to contend with.

That meant that I was hard-pressed to get the car parked and find my way to an available seat before the very end of the performance. I missed all but the last few minutes.

Ah, but that was enough.

I knew that if Shane was performing the Mahler's Symphony Number Five, he'd have the obbligato horn part at the end. He'd told me about it, and I was pretty sure I remembered it correctly.

Without a program, I had no way of knowing if it was Mahler or not, but when Shane put his bell up and played, I took in every beautiful note.

The sound of the horn was every bit as soulful and delicate as that first night I heard him play at the jam session in the community center, but this time he was playing as it was meant to be heard. He wore a suit, and even from my faraway balcony seat, I could tell he looked unbelievably handsome. And yet, I still loved him most in a flannel.

For a moment, hearing him play made me sad—sad for the boy who felt like he was less than everyone else because of something he couldn't control, something he was born with, something that made him beautiful to me. I felt sad that he'd felt the need to hide.

But there was nothing sad about the music he played.

It was glorious.

He played the final notes and brought the bell of the horn back down, holding it in his lap and looking up at the conductor. Then, the roar of applause took over the auditorium. It was practically deafening, and I hoped Shane could feel the rumble of the seats and the floor. It was all for him. At least, that's how I saw it.

As abruptly as I'd plowed through the row to my seat, I jumped up and moved in the opposite direction to get out.

I needed to make sure I caught Shane before he left the concert hall, and I had no way of knowing if he had a sneaky secret exit door, but I hoped he'd use the back door behind the stage.

I'd had Daniel do a little recon for me while I drove, and he'd called me back and assured me that the back door would be where the musicians exited. He'd called an old girlfriend to find out, and he considered her reliable.

Armed with information, a hope, and a prayer, I made my way to the back door, which opened into a service alley behind the concert hall. A loading dock and a parked truck were my only company.

I stood there for five minutes. Then ten. The door didn't open.

I waited a bit longer, now going on fifteen minutes, and I started to worry. Was there another stage door? Had Daniel's old girlfriend known her stuff?

Finally, the door opened and a cleaning crew pushed a trash barrel on wheels out the door. One woman held a mop. The other bustled along with a wide broom.

"Excuse me, is this where the musicians' exit?" I asked them. One of them pointed to the other side of the building, and I took off in that direction, cursing the minutes I'd already squandered waiting in the wrong place.

A few stragglers walked out, but when I asked them if Shane was still inside, I was told he'd already left.

So I drove two hours back to Green Valley, knowing I wouldn't sleep until I talked to Shane. The drive reminded me of our road trip, and that recollection fueled my belief that we were meant to be together. I stepped a little harder on the gas pedal, and the Impala gave me all she had.

* * *

If I went home and waited until morning, I wouldn't be able to sleep anyway, I reasoned. And if Shane had driven back to Green Valley as well, he'd have arrived just a little sooner than me.

Therefore, he couldn't possibly have gone to bed.

Therefore, I went straight to his house.

Shane opened the door so quickly, I felt certain he was expecting someone. My heart sank, imagining him waiting for a brand new girlfriend, a pretty musician who didn't run away from him.

Then, for a split second, I worried he'd be disappointed when he realized it was me.

But only for a fraction of a second. Because his warm eyes melted me like a popsicle in the sun and I knew I was home.

I couldn't look away from those eyes—never could. But now, I knew I never would again.

His own gaze locked on mine, patiently waiting for whatever explanation I had. He was always good that way, never rushing things, always letting me draw my conclusions in whatever time frame it took.

Maybe he deeply understood that once I settled on a truth I could believe, it was immovable. Something to trust for life.

"It's funny, you know? On birthdays we make wishes and cast our hopes in the form of luck or chance. At least, that's what I always did. I don't know why it took me over thirty years to realize that I'm in charge of making my own wishes come true."

He nodded.

"Were you expecting someone?" I couldn't help asking.

"Only you."

"How'd you know it was me?'

"I didn't. But every day since you left, I hoped. I held out hope that every footfall outside my door would be yours. Though I tried to tell my heart to stop hoping because it seemed impossible."

"It's not impossible. It's possible. We are very possible."

His hand reached around my shoulder and pulled me to him. I felt his breath heave into his lungs and out again in a rhythm with my own.

"I went to Nashville. I heard you play tonight."

He pulled back, eyes wide. "You did? You just drove here from Nashville?"

Nodding, I pointed at the Impala in the driveway as though it provided proof of a road trip. "She's reliable, just like Cletus said."

"I wish you hadn't driven alone."

I looked at him, aghast. "Is that your biggest concern? I'm fine. It was fine."

His face settled and relaxed as a shy smile fought its way through. "Did you like it, the music?"

I was tempted to lie and tell him I'd seen the entire thing, but I didn't want to start things up with him on a lie, if things were even starting again. Shaking my head, I admitted, "I missed most of it. I came to find you at the jam session, and when I heard you were in Nashville, I went there. I heard the obbligato." He was staring at me, dumbfounded.

"You're telling me you went to the jam session, then you drove to Nashville and back, just now?"

I nodded. "After flying here from LA." It had been a long day, wasn't gonna lie.

"But why?" He still wasn't getting it. I reached for his hands, both of them, and he extended both of his to me.

"I don't know why I kept telling myself I needed to leave here and go home," I told him, my face half-buried in his shirt, which smelled like the forest and the remains of a campfire. "This is home."

"LA is your home."

"No. LA is where I live. Or, technically, it's where I used to live. I'm going forward with the sale. The Bread Winner can chug on without me running it day to day, and hopefully the new owner won't ruin it too badly."

He nodded, but he looked a little dazed, like maybe he didn't fully understand what I was telling him.

"Home is wherever you are, Shane. It's wherever we're together."

"You really think you'll be happy in Green Valley?"

"I don't think you need to ask me that. You already know the answer. You witnessed it every day for a month. And my friend Sammi will explain to you just how miserable I was back in LA without you."

"So this is real? You're staying here?"

"I'm staying here. You told me I should find joy." I tipped my face up and his lips met mine in a gentle kiss. "Being here, with you, is what brings me joy."

EPILOGUE

JULIA

One Year Later

$\mathcal{I}$t was a few weeks before July Fourth, and I was in a cherry pie mood.

That is to say that my life had been coming up cherries every single day since Shane and I had been together.

Every. Single. Day.

I started my day at four in the morning, as usual, even though it was my day off from Donner Bakery. I still wanted to bake.

First, I made a pot of coffee, did my fifteen minutes of yoga stretches in the middle of Gram's kitchen—now my kitchen—and checked on the Royal Family. They were spending the week at Windsor Castle to host the Order of the Garter ceremony. I took a peek at the Royal Family's Twitter feed for photos.

Then I took out the ingredients I'd need to make a peach pie. I didn't normally bake too many pies, but I couldn't resist using the early summer crop of peaches. It was one of Shane's favorites, and it reminded me of the night we'd had dinner before getting two flat tires.

I still looked back on that night fondly because I credited the forced proximity with breaking down our walls and getting us together. Shane swore we'd have found some other way, but I couldn't be sure.

He'd gotten up earlier than me so he could get a few meaningful hours of work in before the heat turned murderous. I knew exactly where I'd find him when I went outside with the pot of coffee and a tray of mugs.

"You finished yet?" I yelled from the back porch, grateful that the nearest neighbor was two acres away and wouldn't be disturbed by my voice at that hour.

Two heads popped up from the workbench over near the big tree out back. "Actually . . . we're close," Shane said, spreading his arms wide. "Come see."

"Really?" My voice might have had a squeak to it because I'd been coming out here nearly every day for a month and they'd always given me the same answer. "Not yet. Be patient. Soon."

Daniel nodded and beckoned me over before wiping the sweat from his brow with the back of his sleeve.

Putting the coffee pot and cups on the picnic table, I walked around behind the sheet the two of them had hung from the tree to prevent me from seeing what they were working on. I had a view of their workbench from the house, but all I could ever see were pieces of wood they were sawing and hammering.

I'd have been a bit worried since Shane mostly chopped wood into pieces rather than using pieces to build new things, but my brother assured me that with his construction experience I had nothing to worry about. But Shane's brother and his friends also came by regularly to help out, so I let them be.

But I was curious as all get-out, so I dashed around to the other side of the sheet, expecting to see a bench or a garden box or something outdoorsy with lots of right angles that could be built easily in a month's time.

It was not a bench or a garden box. Not at all.

My hand flew to my mouth to cover my surprised gasp. "You guys, it's beautiful."

There, in place of the old hammock, was the exact type of hanging bed frame I'd dreamed of when Daniel and I were kids. I'd idly done a few internet searches but had given up when nothing really fit the vision I had in my head.

"Remember what Gram said?" Daniel asked, looking proud of his work. "What's the point of a swing for two if you have no one to share it with?"

The swing hung low from ropes anchored to fat branches of the tree. It really was the perfect specimen to carry a swing.

It had a twin bed mattress for a cushion, which they'd covered with a plaid flannel sheet. "Just a placeholder," Shane promised. "You can pick whatever fabric you like, add pillows. Make it comfy."

"It's amazing, you guys. Better than I even imagined, and I love how deep the seat is." It was so deep I could probably sit on it with my legs straight out in front of me and not have them reach the edge.

"Yes, it's the size of an entire bed, and no, I don't want to think about what you two will do with something at the mere mention of the word bed. TMI, sis. Forever TMI."

Shane laughed at Daniel and handed him a cup of coffee before pouring his own. It filled my heart that these two got along so well. Shane had insisted that Daniel stay in the house as a condition of moving in with me there.

"That's a little twisted, man. I had no idea you had it so bad for me," Daniel had quipped, but I knew he appreciated the gesture. He'd been making noise about finding a smaller place where he could live on his own, but so far, he hadn't done anything about it.

That was fine by me. I liked having him around, and the house was plenty big enough for all of us. I considered it an added bonus that Daniel liked to cook and did it often, sometimes with Shane's help. Sometimes Shane's brother would join us as well.

For someone whose parents had wandered away without her, I felt like Daniel and I had done a good job of building our own family. We were on our way to having the kind of family of friends that Gram had her whole life.

"Well, go on," Daniel urged, stepping away from the area and moving toward the house.

"Go on, what?"

"Have a seat. Try it out."

"Where are you going?"

"Back to bed," he said. "Have fun, you two."

I couldn't imagine that he was telling us to have sex on the bed swing, so I looked at Shane. He gestured toward the seat. "Try it out. See how it suits you."

I put my coffee down so as not to spill it on the gorgeous new swing and sat gingerly on the seat. It swayed under my weight, but the sturdy branch of the tree held it steady. "This is incredible. I—"

My jaw hung open and my early morning eyes weren't certain of what they were seeing, but I could no longer form words because Shane had knelt in front of me and was holding a ring box. "Shane . . . "

"Yeah."

"Yeah?"

He shrugged. "I hope. Yeah."

"Oh, yes. For sure, absolutely, a thousand times, yes."

Then I started laughing because it was perfect. Our shorthand of nothing words and shrugs had served as a proposal and an acceptance.

"I had a whole thing planned. Really nice words about how happy you make me every goddamn day of my life—"

I pressed a finger to his lips. "I know." I nodded because I really did know. I didn't need all the words because they lived in my heart. They had for years. "I love you."

"I'm glad because I love the heck out of you." He straightened and came to sit beside me on the swing. The branch did its job, and we scooted to the very back of the cushion. Sure enough, my feet didn't quite reach the edge.

"I love this swing. Thank you for building it."

"I love this woman," he said, opening the box and slipping a diamond solitaire ring on my finger. "And there's nothing I wouldn't do or build to make you happy. So please, just let me."

I nodded, placing my left hand in his right one. The ring shone brightly in the barest light of early dawn.

I brought his hand up to kiss it. And then I held on tight.

THE END

ACKNOWLEDGMENTS

My grandfather, Sam Weisberg, was the first person I ever knew with symbrachydactyly, and I was always struck by the confidence with which he presented his hand for a shake when he met anyone new. His gregarious personality and wide smile overtook the room, and his smaller hand became a detail. He was in fact a French horn player who went to Julliard in the 1940s. He eventually gave up his career with the New York Philharmonic to work as a furniture salesman and raise a family.

I owe a huge debt of gratitude to Briony May Williams for reading an early draft of this book and making sure I portrayed symbrachydactyly in an accurate, positive light. Her badass baking on the Great British Bake Off inspired me in so many ways, and I was 'chuffed' to have her as an early reader and adviser.

To the tremendous Penny, Fiona, and Brooke at Smartypants Romance—OMG, I can only say that it's been a joy and a privilege to work with you all, and I still have 'pinch me' moments that this book has become a reality with you.

Thank you to Nancy Smay at Evident Ink for the careful edits.

And to my readers, I would not be an author without you, so I will always owe you the biggest hugs and heartfelt thanks.

ABOUT THE AUTHOR

Stacy Travis writes charming, spicy romance about bookish, sassy women and the hot alphas who fall for them.

Writing makes her infinitely happy, but that might be the coffee talking.

She's worked as a journalist, camp counselor, TV writer, SAT tutor, corporate finance researcher, education technology editor, and non-fiction author. When she's not on a deadline, she's in running shoes complaining that all roads seem to go uphill. Or on the couch with a margarita. Or fangirling at a soccer game.

She's never met a dog she didn't want to hug. And if you have no plans for Thanksgiving, she'll probably invite you to dinner.

Stacy lives in Los Angeles with her very tall sons and a poorly-trained rescue dog who hoards socks. And she's serious about the Thanksgiving thing.

Find Stacy Travis online:
Facebook: https://www.facebook.com/stacytravisromance
Facebook Reader Group: https://bit.ly/2B1psS4fbgroup
Instagram: https://www.instagram.com/stacytravisauthor
TikTok: https://www.tiktok.com/@stacytravisauthor

Find Smartypants Romance online:
Website: www.smartypantsromance.com
Facebook: https://www.facebook.com/smartypantsromance
Twitter: @smartypantsrom
Instagram: @smartypantsromance
Newsletter: https://smartypantsromance.com/newsletter/

ALSO BY STACY TRAVIS

The Summer Heat Duet

1. The Summer of Him: A Mistaken Identity Celebrity Romance

2. Forever with Him: An Opposites Attract Contemporary Romance

The Berkeley Hills Series – smalltown romance series of standalone novels

1. In Trouble with Him: A Forbidden Love Contemporary Romance (Finn and Annie's story)

2. Second Chance at Us: A Second Chance Romance (Becca and Blake)

3. Falling for You: A Friends to Lovers Romance (Isla and Owen)

4. The Spark Between Us: A Grumpy-Sunshine, Brother's Best Friend Romance (Sarah and Braden)

5. Playing for You: A Sports Romance (Tatum and Donovan)

6. No Match for Her - an Opposites-Attract Friends-to-Lovers Romance (Cherry and Charlie)

San Francisco Strikers Series – sports series of standalone novels

1. He's a Keeper: A Grumpy-Sunshine Sports Romance (Molly and Holden)

2. He's a Player: A Second Chance Sports Romance (Jordan and Tim)

3. He's a Charmer: A Brother's Best Friend Sports Romance (Linnie and Weston)

ALSO BY SMARTYPANTS ROMANCE

Cipher Office Series

Weight Expectations by M.E. Carter (#1)

Sticking to the Script by Stella Weaver (#2)

Cutie and the Beast by M.E. Carter (#3)

Weights of Wrath by M.E. Carter (#4)

Common Threads Series

Mad About Ewe by Susannah Nix (#1)

Give Love a Chai by Nanxi Wen (#2)

Key Change by Heidi Hutchinson (#3)

Not Since Ewe by Susannah Nix (#4)

Lost Track by Heidi Hutchinson (#5)

Educated Romance
Work For It Series

Street Smart by Aly Stiles (#1)

Heart Smart by Emma Lee Jayne (#2)

Book Smart by Amanda Pennington (#3)

Smart Mouth by Emma Lee Jayne (#4)

Play Smart by Aly Stiles (#5)

Look Smart by Aly Stiles (#6)

Smart Move by Amanda Pennington (#7)

Lessons Learned Series

Under Pressure by Allie Winters (#1)

Not Fooling Anyone by Allie Winters (#2)

Can't Fight It by Allie Winters (#3)

The Vinyl Frontier by Lola West (#4)

Out of this World
London Ladies Embroidery Series

Neanderthal Seeks Duchess by Laney Hatcher (#1)

Well Acquainted by Laney Hatcher (#2)

Made in the USA
Monee, IL
30 May 2023

34966906R00135